* * *

"You'll be engrossed by McBain's fast, lean prose."

—*Chicago Tribune*

*

"He can stop you dead in your tracks with a line of dialogue."

—*Cleveland Plain Dealer*

*

"The reader is drawn in from the start, and the pages seem to turn themselves."

—*Publishers Weekly*

*

"McBain has stood the test of time. He remains one of the very best."

—*San Antonio Express-News*

*

"McBain's characters age, change, and stay interesting."

—*Arizona Daily Star*

*

"McBain has . . . an unfailing ability to create tricky, engaging plots."

—*Roanoke Times & World-News*

*

"McBain's series featuring Florida lawyer Matthew Hope is . . . a winner."

—*Orlando Sentinel*

* * *

Also by Ed McBain

THE MATTHEW HOPE NOVELS

Goldilocks (1978) *Rumpelstiltskin* (1981) *Beauty and the Beast* (1982) *Jack and the Beanstalk* (1984) *Snow White and Rose Red* (1985) *Cinderella* (1986) *Puss in Boots* (1987) *The House That Jack Built* (1988) *Three Blind Mice* (1990)

THE 87TH PRECINCT NOVELS

Cop Hater • *The Mugger* • *The Pusher* (1956) *The Con Man* • *Killer's Choice* (1957) *Killer's Payoff* • *Killer's Wedge* • *Lady Killer* (1958) *'Til Death* • *King's Ransom* (1959) *Give the Boys a Great Big Hand* • *The Heckler* • *See Them Die* (1960) *Lady, Lady, I Did It!* (1961) *The Empty Hours* • *Like Love* (1962) *Ten Plus One* (1963) *Ax* (1964) *He Who Hesitates* • *Doll* (1965) *Eighty Million Eyes* (1966) *Fuzz* (1968) *Shotgun* (1969) *Jigsaw* (1970) *Hail, Hail the Gang's All Here!* (1971) *Sadie When She Died* • *Let's Hear It for the Deaf Man* (1972) *Hail to the Chief* (1973) *Bread* (1974) *Blood Relatives* (1975) *So Long As You Both Shall Live* (1976) *Long Time No See* (1977) *Calypso* (1979) *Ghosts* (1980) *Heat* (1981) *Ice* (1983) *Lightning* (1984) *Eight Black Horses* (1985) *Poison* • *Tricks* (1987) *Lullaby* (1989) *Vespers* (1990) *Widows* (1991) *Kiss* (1992)

OTHER NOVELS

The Sentries (1965) *Where There's Smoke* • *Doors* (1975) *Guns* (1976) *Another Part of the City* (1986) *Downtown* (1991)

ED McBAIN

THREE BLIND MICE

MICE

WARNER BOOKS

A Time Warner Company

The characters and events in this book are fictitious. Any
similarity to real persons, living or dead, is coincidental and
not intended by the author.

This is for Lou and Alice Weiss

WARNER BOOKS EDITION

Copyright © 1990 by Hui Corporation
All rights reserved.

Published by arrangement with Arcade Publishing, a division of
Little, Brown Company (Inc.),
34 Beacon Street, Boston, MA 02108

Cover design by Jackie Merri Meyer & Amy King
Cover illustration by Rich Mahon

Warner Books, Inc.
1271 Avenue of the Americas
New York, NY 10020

Ⓦ A Time Warner Company

Printed in the United States of America

First Warner Books Printing: May, 1991

Reissued: May, 1994

10 9 8 7 6 5

THREE
BLIND
MICE

1

You woke up every morning on sodden sheets, the air heavy with moisture, the bloodred line of the thermometer already standing at seventy-five degrees, and you knew the temperature would climb high into the nineties before the day was done. In August, the heat was relentless.

It rained every afternoon, whether for five minutes or an hour. Torrents of rain spilling from a swollen black sky. The asphalt steamed under the onslaught of the rain. Great clouds of steam rising. But the rain cooled nothing, and the heat persisted.

There was no relief at night either. Even with the sun gone, the humidity was there, a twin to the heat. In August, there wasn't a breath of air to be had anywhere in Florida, day or night. You suffered.

The room smelled of blood.

Blood wasn't supposed to smell, but the aroma was palpable. Or maybe it was only the stink of torn yellow flesh. Outside in the palmettos, the insects chattered. Full moon tonight, a

person could clearly read the dial of a watch in the moonspill. Eleven-twenty. And ticking. Waiting for Ho Dao Bat to get home from The Pagoda. Waiting to bid him good night.

The other two were already dead to the world.

A joke, grant me my little joke.

So solly, sleep tight.

Ho Dao Bat was next.

Dead on a hot, moist night in the middle of August. So solly, plick.

The house was in a section of Calusa known as Little Asia, so-named because of the many Orientals who'd settled here over the past several years. In a city not particularly famous for its hospitality to nonwhites, any Chinese, Japanese, Korean, or Vietnamese who came here invariably drifted to this area between Tango and Langhorn, just west of the Tamiami Trail. At the turn of the century there'd been only a whorehouse and a saloon on these two and a half acres of land. Now there were more than three dozen tiny wooden houses strewn among the palmettos. Brimming with Orientals. Night like tonight, they were all outdoors, vainly hoping for a breeze to remind them of a mountain village halfway across the world.

So solly, no bleeze.

Only knife.

See plitty knife?

The blade of the knife glittered in the moonlight spilling through the open window. The two little men lay dead and bleeding on the floor, one on either side of the bed closest to the door. Three single beds in this ground-floor room, the stink of yellow everywhere, the stink of red, the stink of blood. A calendar on the wall, pretty Chinese girl on it, wearing a kimono and smiling shyly over a fan. The kimono was red, the color of luck, the color of blood, where was Ho Dao Bat? The job would not be done until Ho got his.

Another look at the watch.

Eleven-thirty.

Come on, Ho. Come meet the knife.

Somewhere outside, there was laughter. Drifting on the stillness of the night, floating in through the window and into the room where the two men lay unhearing on the floor. A voice singsonged something unintelligible on the night, and there was more laughter, men and women laughing, foreigners from another world enjoying the steamy Florida night, come meet the knife, Ho, come say hello to the knife.

Waiting.

Time.

The buzz of a fly discovering the blood on the corpses.

Ho would be here soon. Ho Dao Bat, the third little man in the triumvirate. The leader. A follower tonight, in that the other two had already led the way to perdition, the other two were now on the floor waiting sightlessly and mutely for Ho to join them. Come on, Ho, come join the party, see how the other two are enjoying the food?

Another little joke, you must forgive me.

More flies now.

Buzzing in through the open window where a moment earlier there had been the rush of laughter and the babble of voices, a squadron of flies buzzing in and seeking the runway, circling the faces with their bleeding sockets, their bleeding towers, Fly One to Tower, request permission to land. The room buzzed with flies greedily drinking, a veritable fly frenzy, try *that* on your Asian tongue, try *this*, Ho Dao Bat!

And thrust the knife at the air.

This!

Again.

There were sudden footsteps on the gravel path outside.

Someone was approaching the front door.

Detective Morris Bloom stood tall and wrinkled and grizzled in the early-morning sunlight streaming into the room. No time to

shave this morning, not when the seven A.M. call from downtown had reported three dead men in a room that reeked of ritual murder. No time to search in his closet for a freshly dry-cleaned suit. Time only to throw on a clean shirt and the rumpled seersucker draped over the chair near the dresser, time only to quickly knot a tie and then telephone Rawles to pass on the address of the crime scene.

The two detectives stood side by side in the sunlight. Across the room, the Medical Examiner kept trying to shoo the flies away from the corpses. It was a thankless job. Rawles looked bandbox fresh. Tan tropical suit, pale lemon-colored shirt, striped brown and gold tie, dark brown loafers. He resembled a stylish cop on the defunct *Miami Vice*, but this was Calusa, on the opposite coast.

Rawles was bigger and heavier than Bloom. Some six feet four inches tall and weighing in at two forty, he was the kind of mountainous black man people down here crossed the street to avoid. Bloom, at six one and two twenty, with a broken nose and the oversized knuckles of a streetfighter, wasn't the kind of person you'd care to meet in a dark alley, either. Together, they made a formidable pair, except that it was almost impossible for them to play good cop/bad cop since they *both* looked like bad cops. Well, perhaps there was a slight difference. In Bloom's dark and somber eyes, there was always a look of ineffable sadness, an unfortunate failing for a police detective.

"Mighty pretty," Rawles said.

He was not normally given to irony, but the bodies across the room demanded a certain dryness of humor. Either that, or you went outside to throw up. The only time he had thrown up recently was on a rough cruise to romantic Bermuda, which he'd taken with a girl who worked as a legal stenographer at the courthouse. Bloom, on the other hand, had been married for a good long time now and did not take too many cruises to romantic Bermuda. The last time *he'd* thrown up was Saturday

night, when he'd eaten a bad fish at Marina Lou's. This was now Tuesday morning, and he felt like throwing up again.

The three men across the room had had their throats slit. And their eyes gouged out.

And their penises cut off and stuffed into their mouths.

Rawles had seen things like this in the jungles of Vietnam. The Cong had done things like this to the grunts in Vietnam. It was he who'd suggested that maybe these were intra-racial murders. This being an Asian community and all, and the way the bodies had been mutilated. Alex McReady, the sergeant who'd first responded to the radio call from the car patroling Charlie sector, was of the opinion that these were drug-related murders, probably Jamaican in origin. The Jamaican posses that had filtered into some parts of Florida were particularly vicious in their killing techniques. And it was a known fact that in their homelands, Asians smoked dope as a matter of course.

Bloom wondered about the validity of this. To him, this business did not seem drug-related, Jamaican or otherwise. Rawles may have had a point about it being linked to something in the community, but then again you did not have to be Asian to do unspeakable things to a fellow human being, dead *or* alive.

He walked over to where the M.E. was closing his satchel. Flies swarmed up around the M.E.'s head as he got to his feet. Both men shooed them away.

"For the record," the M.E. said, "as if you didn't know, all three had their jugulars severed. The eyes and the rest of it undoubtedly came later."

"Skilled or what?"

"The surgery, you mean?"

"Yes."

"A butcher. By the way, I found all but one of the eyes. They're in a jar there on the windowsill. You might want to send them along with the bodies."

Bloom wanted to throw up all over again.

"Take a look at this," Rawles said, coming over.

He was holding a man's leather billfold in his hand.

The telephone was ringing when Matthew Hope got out of the shower that Thursday morning. He wrapped a towel around his waist, said, "I'm coming, I'm coming," and rushed dripping wet into the bedroom. He picked up the receiver just as the answering machine clicked in.

"Hello, you've reached 349-3777," his voice said. "If you'll . . ."

"Hang on," he said, "I'm here."

". . . leave a message . . ."

"I'm here," he said.

". . . when you hear the beep . . ."

Damn machine, he thought.

". . . I'll get back to you as soon as I can. Thank you for calling."

"I'm still here," he said. "Please hang on."

The machine beeped.

"Hello?" he said.

"Dad?"

He visualized her on the other end of the line. Long and lanky and bursting with adolescent energy, hair a brighter gold after a summer in the sun, eyes as blue as a Caribbean lagoon. His daughter, Joanna. Who wanted to be a brain surgeon and who practiced tying knots inside matchboxes. Joanna. Whom he loved to death.

"Hi, honey," he said, beaming. "I was going to call you later today. How are . . . ?"

"Promises, promises," she said.

An impish grin on her mouth, no doubt, promises, promises. Fourteen years old and already sounding like a stand-up comic.

"I mean it," he said. "I've got a ten o'clock meeting with a potential client, but I planned to . . ."

"Still chasing ambulances, Dad?"

The grin again, he was certain of that.

"I gather you're enjoying your summer," he said.

"I adore it up here," she said. "But there are no boys, Dad."

"I'm sorry to hear that."

"Well, there are *two* of them. One's a nerd and the other is twelve. I met a nice girl, though. Her name is Avery, which I think is sort of neat, and she's on her high-school swimming team in New York. Did you know they had swimming teams in New York? I didn't. She's teaching me a lot of things I didn't know, as for example how to swim in *very* choppy water. Do you know how cold the water is up here? Well, she's in the ocean every day for at least an hour, and it doesn't faze her at all. Waves chopping everywhere around her, she's an actual *shark*, Dad, you should see her. Avery Curtis, remember that name, she's going to win Olympic gold medals one day. Also, she's a Libra, her birthday's the fifteenth of October."

"Birth date of great men," Matthew said, but did not amplify.

"Mom says to tell you hello, she's making pancakes."

"Tell her hello back."

"Would you like to talk to her?"

"Sure," Matthew said, "why not?"

"Just a sec."

Susan Hope, Matthew's former wife. Dark, brooding eyes in an oval face, brown hair cut in a wedge, a full, pouting mouth that gave an impression of a sullen, spoiled, defiant beauty. To their mutual surprise and delight, he had begun dating her again some years after the divorce. But that was in another country, he thought now, and besides the wench is dead. The other country had been right here in old Calusa, Florida, but it

had seemed like shining new terrain, a pristine landscape glistening with promise. And the wench wasn't really dead, merely gone from his life again. For now, at any rate. Matthew was not the sort of man who took bets on the future. Not concerning Susan, anyway. Not after the tempestuous rekindling of their passion years after the divorce.

"Hello?" she said.

Susan Hope.

"Hi," he said. "I hear you're making pancakes."

"Terrific, huh?" she said, and he visualized her pulling a face. Cooking had never been Susan's favorite pastime.

"How's the summer going?" he asked.

"No boys," she said.

"Pity."

"Mmm. Why don't you come up for a weekend? The house is huge."

"Too dangerous," he said.

"Who says?"

"You."

"True."

"We'd fight in front of the child."

"Probably."

"For sure."

"I sometimes miss you," she said.

"Me, too."

"Not often, but sometimes."

"Me, too."

"I think it's sad we can't get along for any reasonable amount of time."

"Yes."

"But I guess it's better this way."

"Yes."

"Don't you think?"

"I do. What's bothering you, Susan?"

"I don't know. But we did have some good times together. And this doesn't seem like a vacation house with just me and Joanna in it."

"Well," he said.

"So if you should find yourself up in old Cape Cod one of these days . . ."

"I don't think I will."

"You could get to see me making pancakes."

"Uh-huh."

"I'm wearing only high heels and an apron."

"Sure," he said.

But the words had their desired effect. He immediately conjured her in high white patent-leather pumps, a short white apron tied at the waist, the bib partially exposing her breasts, the tails of the sash hanging down over her naked buttocks. She also had a spatula in her hand.

"Put Joanna back on," he said.

"Chicken," she said, but he knew she was smiling.

He was smiling, too.

"Did you two get it all out of your systems again?" Joanna asked.

"None of your business."

"I'll never understand either of you."

"Yes, you will," Matthew promised. "When you're sixty years old and we're both dead."

"Don't even *joke* about it!" she said.

"Honey, I have to get dressed, I'll call you this afternoon, okay?"

"No, Avery and I are going to this dumb social in the vain hope some new boys'll show up. I'm beginning to think the twelve-year-old is kind of cute, can you believe it?"

"I'm beginning to think *you're* kind of cute," Matthew said.

"Sweet talker," she said.

Grinning again, he guessed. Like her mother.

"Honey, goodbye," he said. "I'll call whenever."

"Love you, Dad."

"Love you, too," he said, and hung up and looked at the dresser clock.

Frantically, he began dressing.

Matthew had never met a man who looked comfortable in jailhouse threads. Stephen Leeds did not look comfortable in them now. A well-built blond man, six feet four inches tall and weighing some two hundred pounds, he seemed straitjacketed in the undersized denim garments the city had provided. Bail had been denied because of the heinous nature of the crimes. He would be dressed this way for quite some time.

This was the sixteenth day of August, two days after Charlie car had responded to a call from a Chinese dishwasher who had stopped by at 1211 Tango to pick up his three friends so they could all drive to work together.

"Did you kill them?" Matthew asked.

"No," Leeds said.

"At the trial, you threatened to kill them."

"That was at the trial. That was right after the verdict was read. I was angry. People say things when they're angry."

"Dangerous thing to say. That you'd kill them."

"I realize that now."

"But now you say you didn't. Kill them."

"That's right."

"Any idea who *might* have killed them?"

"No."

"You didn't *hire* someone to kill them, did you?"

"No."

"Or ask anyone — out of friendship, or debt, or for whatever possible reason — to kill them for you?"

"No. I had nothing to do with killing them."

"You're sure about that, are you?"

"Positive."

"Tell me where you were on Monday night. The night of the murders."

"At home. With my wife."

"Anyone else there? Besides the two of you?"

"No. Why? Won't her word be good enough?"

"She's your wife," Matthew said simply.

Studying the man. Trying to find innocence or guilt in those blue eyes of his. He would not represent him if he thought he was guilty. As simple as that. In this world, there were enough lawyers willing to represent murderers and thieves. Matthew Hope was not one of them. Nor would he ever be.

"You realize how this looks, don't you?" he said.

"Yes."

"Your wallet is found at the scene of the crime . . ."

"I don't know how it got there."

"But it's unmistakably yours, isn't it?"

"Yes."

"Your driver's license is in it . . ."

"Yes."

"Your credit cards . . ."

"Yes."

"Unmistakably yours. The State Attorney could make a case on that alone. Your wallet found on the floor in a room where three men accused of raping your wife . . ."

"I wasn't anywhere near . . ."

". . . and later acquitted . . ."

"But they did it."

"Not according to the jury."

"The jury was wrong. They raped her."

"Whether they did or not is academic. Last Friday, all three of them were acquitted. And last Friday, you jumped to your

feet and threatened to kill them, in the presence of hundreds of witnesses. And Monday night, they were, in fact, killed. And your wallet was found at the scene."

"Yes."

"So why should I defend you?"

"Because I'm innocent," Leeds said.

Eyes as clear as still water. Sitting on the edge of his narrow cot, looking up into Matthew's face. Matthew standing opposite him, against the white wall of the cell covered with graffiti left by the army of prisoners who'd been here before Leeds. Innocent or guilty? Decide. Because once you agreed to take it on, you were committed to it, you owed.

"Any idea how your wallet got in that room?"

"No."

"Had you missed your wallet at any time Monday?"

"No."

"When's the last time you saw it?"

"I don't remember."

"When's the last time you used money that day? Or a credit card?"

"I guess . . . while I was renting the video."

"When was that?"

"On my way home to the farm. I'm a farmer."

An understatement. Leeds had inherited three thousand acres of rich farmland on Timucuan Point Road from his father, Osgood, who'd died six years ago. He was the grandson of Roger Leeds, who — as one of the first settlers here in southwest Florida — had bought up hundreds of thousands of acres when land was still going for peanuts. The family still owned trailer parks in Tampa and choice sections of real estate in downtown Calusa.

"I was visiting my broker," Leeds said. "He has an office on Lime."

"Small world," Matthew said, and smiled. "So do I."

"I go there every day."

"Yes, so do I."

"For an hour or so," Leeds added.

Explaining the meaning of the word *rich*.

Matthew got back to why he was here.

"What time did you see your broker on Monday?" he asked.

"Around three. Jessie asked me to pick up a movie on the way home . . ."

Jessica Leeds. Who had called Matthew late yesterday, after the grand jury had brought in a true bill and the judge had denied bail. Telling him she'd heard he was the best criminal lawyer in Calusa — a premise Benny Weiss may have hotly contested — and asking if he would defend her husband. Which was why he was here this morning.

"So I stopped by at the video store . . ."

"Which one?"

"Video Town? Video World? They all sound the same to me. It's on the Trail, near Lloyd. Just before the cutoff to the Whisper Key Bridge."

"Which video did you rent?"

"*Casablanca*. Jessie loves those old movies. We watched it together that night. After dinner."

"Did you leave the house at any time that night?"

"No."

"What time did you go to bed that night?"

"Around eight-thirty?"

"Isn't that early?"

"We got into bed to watch the movie."

"You didn't sleep in your clothes, did you?"

"No. My clothes? Of course not. My clothes?"

"You undressed before you went to bed, isn't that right?"

"Yes, of course."

"What'd you do with your wallet?"

"Well, I . . . I suppose I . . ."

Matthew watched him. Sudden uncertainty. A simple act

someone performs every day of the week. Uncertain about it now because his life might depend upon what had happened to that wallet. In the state of Florida, the penalty for first-degree murder was death in the electric chair. Matthew waited.

"I normally put it on the dresser," Leeds said. "With my keys and my change. I guess I did the same thing that night."

"But you're not sure."

"Well, actually, I'm not. Because . . ."

Again, a slight hesitation. Then:

"I was out on the boat that afternoon, and I may have left it there."

"The boat?"

"Yes, I own a thirty-nine-foot Med. I took it out for a spin before dinner that night."

"And you think you may have left the wallet on the boat?"

"Possibly."

"Have you done that before?"

"I sometimes stow it below. So it won't accidentally fall in the water."

"But have you ever left it on the boat before?"

"Only on one other occasion."

"You forgot your wallet on the boat?"

"Yes."

"And you think you may have done that Monday night?"

"Well, yes. And someone probably took it from the boat. Otherwise, how could it have . . . ?"

"When did you discover it was missing?"

"Tuesday morning. When the police showed it to me. When they came to the house."

"What time was that?"

"At about nine. They showed me the wallet and asked me if it was mine, and when I said it was they asked me to come downtown with them."

"Which you did, of course."

"Yes."

"Without any resistance."

"Yes."

"Mr. Leeds, are you familiar with the area of Calusa known as Little Asia?"

"I am."

"Have you ever been there?"

"Yes."

"When?"

"When they were arrested."

"Who?"

"The three men who raped Jessie."

"Do you know where 1211 Tango Avenue is?"

"Yes."

"Is that where you went when these men were arrested?"

"Yes."

"So you're familiar with the address."

"Yes."

"Familiar with the house."

"Yes."

"Have you ever been *inside* that house?"

"No. All I did was drive by. To see where they lived. To see where those animals lived."

"You were not in that house on the night of the murders?"

"I was not."

"Or at any time before the murders?"

"I was not."

"How old are you, Mr. Leeds?"

"Forty-one."

"Were you ever in the armed forces?"

"Yes."

"When?"

"During the Vietnam War."

"Were you in combat?"

"Yes."

"Did you ever witness bodies mutilated the way the bodies of these three victims were mutilated?"

"They got what they deserved."

"But did you ever . . . ?"

"I resent your calling them *victims!* They *raped* my wife! Whoever killed them should get a *medal!*"

Blue eyes shooting laser beams, lips skinned back over even white teeth, fists clenched. Put him on the witness chair, have him say what he just said, and the next chair he'd be sitting in would be wired.

"Mr. Leeds, in combat, did you ever . . . ?"

"Yes, I saw American soldiers in the same condition."

"Eyes gouged out . . ."

"Yes."

"Genitals . . ."

"Yes. Or the trigger finger. The gooks used to cut off trigger fingers, as a warning. And sometimes tongues. We'd find corpses with their tongues cut out." He hesitated and then said, "We did the same thing to them. A guy in my company made a necklace out of gook ears. He used to wear the necklace into combat."

"Did *you* ever do anything like that?"

"Never."

"Are you sure?"

"I never did anything like that. It was bad enough without doing anything like that."

There was a long silence.

In the corridor outside the cell, Matthew could hear two policemen talking. One of them laughed.

"Mr. Leeds," he said.

Looking directly into his eyes again. Searching those eyes. Had the man killed his wife's accused rapists? In order to correct what he'd perceived as a miscarriage of justice? Or had his wallet been planted at the scene of murders that had been com-

mitted for whatever other reason or reasons, by whichever other person or persons?

"Mr. Leeds, tell me again that you didn't kill those three men."

"I didn't."

"Say the whole thing."

"I did not kill those three men."

In Calusa, Florida, during the summer months, a person was lucky to get off with only two showers and two shirt changes a day. On particularly sticky days, three was the rule. One at home in the morning, another at the office after lunch, and a third at home again, at the end of the working day. In the shower that evening, Matthew wondered if he'd made the right decision.

The rain had started, it always came sometime during the afternoon, you could set your calendar by it, if not your watch. A torrential downpour, as always. Florida never did anything half-heartedly. When the wind blew, it blew at hurricane force. When the sun decided to shine, it cooked you to a crisp. And when the rains came, they came — in bucketsful.

Probably shouldn't even be in the shower, he thought. Lightning bolt'll come in through the window and sizzle me on the spot. Benny Weiss would secretly chuckle over the freak accident and then express deep public sorrow. State Attorney Skye Bannister would tell the press that Hope had been a worthy opponent, credit to the community, tremendous loss, a good lawyer and a good man. His former wife, Susan, would weep huge crocodile tears. The several women he'd known since the divorce would come to the funeral wearing black. They would toss tear-stained red roses onto his coffin. Alas, poor Matthew, I knew him well. Struck by lightning in his prime.

Alas, poor Matthew.

Especially if he'd made the wrong decision today.

He turned on the needle spray. Washed away the soap and the grime. Tried to wash away the lingering doubts as well. The man's knowledge of the crime scene, his wallet in the room, his brutalizing experience in Vietnam, his rage over what had happened to his wife, his public expression of that rage in the form of a death threat directed at all three men — put all of that in Skye's hands, and the state would one day have a big electric bill.

He turned off the shower.

Climbed out of the tub, reached for a towel, caught a glimpse of himself in the mirror over the sink, and shook his head in disapproval. He'd gained ten pounds on his recent trip to Italy. It showed, too. Six feet tall, you'd think a few extra pounds might have distributed themselves more evenly over all that length. But no, they'd gathered exclusively around his middle, that's where they were, all ten of them. Why did men and women gain weight in different places? For men, it was always the middle. For women, it was the ass. A phenomenon of nature. His face looked the way it had before he'd made the trip, though, a narrow fox face with dark brown eyes that matched the hair now clinging wetly to his forehead. In a world of spectacularly handsome men, Matthew considered himself only soso. *Ma che posso fare?* he thought, and grinned at his own image in the mirror.

When he'd returned to the office on Monday, he'd said, "Well, I'm back."

His partner, Frank, had said, "Some of us didn't even know you were gone."

That was on Monday.

And yesterday, Jessica Leeds had called.

Welcome home, and once more unto the breach, dear . . .

There was the sound of screeching brakes on the street outside. And then a tremendous bang. Something hitting something. Metal against metal. He grabbed for the white terry robe

hanging on the back of the door, pulled it on, and ran bare-footed out of the bathroom and through the house and into the street. He had left his new Acura Legend at the curb. Instead of pulling it into the garage. Because he knew he'd be going out again tonight, and he didn't want to go to all the trouble of . . .

Brand new.

$30,000 on the hoof.

He'd taken delivery on it two weeks ago, just before he'd left for Venice. A replacement for the Karmann Ghia he'd been driving for God knew how many years. Low and sleek and smoky blue, with leather seats, and a sun roof, and a computer that told you when your gas tank was almost empty. When you hit the pedal on that baby, you zoomed from zero to sixty in eight seconds flat, a rocket to the moon.

"Oh dear," the woman said, getting out of the little red Volkswagen that had smashed into the left rear fender of the brand-new smoky-blue Acura that had cost Matthew thirty grand two weeks ago.

He came thundering down the walk from the front door to the curb, fuming, wanting to strangle her even if she was tall and leggy and blond and beautiful and blue-eyed and standing without an umbrella in the pouring rain. She looked now from the fender of the Acura to the grille of the VW, and then to the skid marks on the wet asphalt. The marks clearly defined the course her little car had taken before wreaking its havoc. She shook her head as if amazed by the wonder of it all. Red silk dress to match the car, red high-heeled shoes, rain spattering the roadway, rain pelting everywhere around her, long blond hair getting wetter and wetter and wetter, Matthew was glad he was wearing a terry robe.

"I'm awfully sorry," she said.

"Sorry, my ass," he said.

"I didn't want to hit the cat," she said.

"What cat?" he said.

And anyway, he thought, *hit* the damn cat! And was im-

mediately sorry. A cat he had loved with all his heart had long ago been hit by a car — and killed. So no, he would not have preferred her hitting the cat instead of his brand-new low, sleek, smoky-blue automobile, but *Jesus!*

"He ran out into the road," she said, still talking about the damn cat. "I hit the brake and . . . I'm sorry. Really. I am."

Brand new, he was thinking.

Thirty thousand dollars.

"I'm an attorney," she said, "I know what we have to . . ."

"So am I," he said.

"Well, good, that should make it simple. Can I please see your driver's license . . . or some . . . your insurance card . . . some identifi . . ."

"Are you okay?" he asked at once.

"Yes, I'm fine. Thank you. A little wet, but fine."

"Would you like to come inside? We can exchange all the . . ."

"No, thank you, I'm due at a party."

"I thought . . . out of the rain . . ."

"Well, I can't get any wetter, can I?" she said.

She was, in fact, thoroughly wet. Dress soaked through to the skin. This was the scene where they're in Africa, he thought, and the gorgeous starlet falls in a pool near a waterfall, and when she gets out of the water you can see her nipples through her wet clothes. Matthew could see her nipples through the wet red dress. He looked away.

"Why don't we . . . uh . . . at least get in the car, okay? Out of the rain. Really. There's no sense standing here in the rain. The papers'll get all wet."

"Yes, you're right," she said. "I hadn't thought of that."

He went around the VW to the door on the driver's side of the Acura, and was starting to open the door when he realized . . .

"It's locked," he said. "My keys are in the house. My wallet, too."

I normally put it on the dresser. With my keys and my change.

"Well, okay," she said, and reached down to take off first one shoe and then the other. "These are totally ruined," she said as she followed him to the house, walking barefooted through the puddles that had gathered on the walk, a shoe in each hand. "Brand new," she said. "Two hundred dollars."

Brand new, he thought.

And took another look at where the VW had its nose buried in the Acura's fender. Shaking his head, he opened the door of the house and stepped aside to let her by.

"Come in," he said. "Please."

And realized by the sound of his voice that he hadn't quite succeeded in quashing his anger.

She caught the tone.

"I really am sorry," she said.

She looked like a drowned rat. Hair hanging straggly and limp on either side of her face, mascara running under her blue eyes, dress hanging on her like a sack. He felt a sudden wave of sympathy.

"It was an accident," he said gently. "Accidents happen."

"Oh *shit!*" she said.

He looked at her, startled.

"My purse is in the car. With my driver's license in it. And my insurance stuff is in the glove compartment."

"I'll go get it," he said.

"No, don't be ridiculous," she said. "I'm soaking wet as it is."

"So am I."

"Well, that's true, but . . ."

"I'll be right back," he said, and went out into the rain again.

He shook his head as he came around the rear fender of the Acura where the VW was still snuggled up against it, brand new, he thought. On the passenger seat he found a beaded red handbag, and in the glove compartment he found a folder con-

taining, among other papers, the car's registration and insurance card. He came out into the rain again, the terry robe soaked through now, his hair plastered to his head, this was truly ridiculous.

She was standing just inside the door to the house when he came in. As if afraid of intruding further on his privacy. He placed a call to the police, reporting the accident, and then they exchanged driver's licenses and insurance cards, which is when he learned that her name was Patricia Demming, and that she was thirty-six years old, and that she lived at 407 Ocean, which was on Fatback Key.

It had stopped raining by the time the police car arrived. One uniformed officer in it; in Calusa the police patrolled solo. They gave him all the details of the accident, and then they ascertained that Patricia Demming's car was still drivable, and Matthew watched her as she backed its nose out of his fender and drove off up the street to her party.

Brand new, he thought again.

2

"I'm the only black man in Calusa with a high-top fade," Warren Chambers said.

Matthew thought he was talking about an automobile. A High-Top Phaed. Some kind of foreign convertible. Automobiles were very much on his mind this Friday morning. He was waiting for a call from his insurance adjustor.

"Next one I'm going to get will be a ramp," Warren said, and ran his hand over the top of his head. It was then that Matthew realized he was talking about his haircut. A high-top fade. Which looked like a flower pot turned upside down and sitting on top of Warren's head, the hair below it shaved very close to the scalp. He did not want to ask what a ramp might possibly be. He figured a man's hair was as sacrosanct as his castle; too many battles had been fought over hair in the sixties. This was the here and now.

"How was your trip?" Warren asked.

"Wonderful."

"So you came back to *this*, huh?" Warren said, and indi-

cated the copy of the *Calusa Herald-Tribune* lying on Matthew's desk. There was another picture of Stephen Leeds on the front page; the paper had been running his picture every day since his arrest. The headline read: WITNESSES SAW LEEDS. The subhead read: *Wife Questioned Again.*

"Who're these witnesses?" Warren asked.

"Bannister hasn't yet sent me his list. I'll be stopping by there later today."

"You think they've really got anyone?"

"I hope not."

"Why do they keep questioning the wife?"

"She's his alibi. But there's also a rumor running around town. To the effect that they were in it together. Leeds *and* the wife."

"Uh-huh," Warren said, and nodded thoughtfully, giving the impression that the idea might be worth consideration.

He was a soft-spoken man in his mid-thirties, his shy, reserved manner and horn-rimmed glasses giving him the look of an accountant (even *with* the high-top fade) rather than what one imagined a private eye should look like. Beanpole tall and thin, a former basketball player for the University of Missouri — which he'd attended for two years before joining the St. Louis P.D. — Warren still moved like an athlete and somehow appeared graceful even when he was sitting, as he was now. He was a meticulous investigator and a dead shot; Matthew had seen him put away a raccoon and a human being with equal aplomb. His eyes were the color of his skin, as dark as loam, pensive and serious now.

"How'd the rumor start?" he asked.

"In yesterday's *Trib.* Some guy wrote a letter."

"A nut?"

"Sure. But you know the *Trib.*"

"And this time around they've got a real ax to grind."

"Oh?"

"Leeds's father once tried a hostile takeover. This was ten years ago, before he died. A big chain in the South won out. But the publisher's still pissed about the old man's move."

"Where'd you learn this?"

"At the *Trib*'s morgue," Warren said, and grinned.

"So you think we may be in for a media trial, huh?"

"Let's say you might start thinking about a change of venue. How'd Leeds explain his wallet at the scene?"

"He said he may have left it on his boat."

"When?"

"The afternoon of the murders."

"Very flimsy," Warren said, shaking his head. "If a person plans to do murder, he doesn't first go to the Leeds boat on the off chance he'll find a *wallet* there."

"Not necessarily a wallet. *Anything* personal."

"Even so."

"Something he could plant at the scene. To link the murders to Leeds. It's easier to get onto a boat than into a house, Warren."

"Granted."

"We've got to find out how that wallet got at the scene. Because if Leeds himself dropped it there . . ."

"Goodbye, Charlie," Warren said.

"Mm," Matthew said, and nodded gravely. "So what I'd like you to do . . ."

"Where does he keep the boat?" Warren asked.

In the city of Calusa, Florida, the State Attorney's office used to be a motel. It still sat across the street from a ballpark that once was used for big-league spring training before the team moved to Sarasota; nowadays, teams sponsored by beer companies played there. The old motel sat behind what used to be the biggest hotel in town. You could still see the twin white towers of the hotel — now an office building — from a courtyard

surrounded by what used to be motel units but were now offices for the State Attorney's staff.

The sun at eleven A.M. that Friday morning beat down unmercifully into the courtyard. The motel-now-office units served to form a sort of wall around the courtyard, preventing any circulation of air, boxing in the area, giving it the feel of a small, suffocatingly hot prison cheerfully planted with palm trees, bougainvillea, and hibiscus the color of blood. The sign outside read:

OFFICE OF THE STATE ATTORNEY
TWELFTH JUDICIAL CIRCUIT
Skye Bannister
807 Magnolia Boulevard
Office Hours Monday–Friday
8:30 A.M.–5:00 P.M.

Matthew was relieved to discover that the air-conditioning system in Skye Bannister's office was working; in Calusa's government offices, bureaucratic red tape often made a mockery of maintenance. Bannister's receptionist, a dark-haired girl in her early twenties, asked him if this was about the witness list and statements. Matthew told her it was. The receptionist said the case had been turned over to an Assistant State Attorney and added that Matthew could go next door to see her if he liked, her office was in room 17.

The Assistant S.A. was Patricia Demming.

"Oh dear," she said.

She looked a lot less wet this morning than she had last night. Long blond hair pulled back into a neat ponytail fastened with a ribbon that matched her blouse, her tailored suit, and her startling blue eyes. She was wearing as well high-heeled blue leather pumps, blue pantyhose (he guessed), and silver earrings with turquoise stones. No mascara or eye shadow here at work, only lipstick. She looked cool and efficient and very State Attorney–ish, albeit enormously surprised to discover that

Matthew was defending the man she'd been assigned to prosecute. Matthew was thinking that Skye Bannister had been confident enough of his case to turn it over to an assistant. A *new* assistant, at that; Matthew came in and out of the State Attorney's offices on an almost-daily basis, and he'd never seen her here before.

"How's your car?" she asked, and smiled.

"I'm supposed to hear from the adjustor today," Matthew said.

"I barely made it home from the party last night. They think I'll need a new engine."

"I'm sorry to hear that. How was the party?"

"Very nice. Do you know the Berringers?"

"End of the street. Yes."

"Nice people."

"Yes. A doctor, isn't he?"

"A dentist," she said, and smiled again. "You're here about the witness list, I'll bet. And the statements."

"Yes," he said, and took off the gloves. "Miss Demming," he said, "I have to tell you that I don't like to be surprised by newspaper stories."

"I'm awfully sorry about that, really, but . . ."

"Because, you know, Miss Demming, it's a little disconcerting to learn that documents are being released to the press . . ."

"No one released any documents to the . . ."

". . . even before the man's *attorney* has seen . . ."

"Mr. Bannister merely answered some questions put to him by . . ."

"Is Mr. Bannister prosecuting this case, or are you?"

"I am. As of this morning. But yesterday . . ."

"But yesterday Mr. Bannister was handing out press releases, right?"

"Wrong. A reporter called to ask if there'd been any witnesses to the . . ."

"So the State Attorney felt it was okay to release this infor-

mation before *I* had the witness list, before *I* had the witness statements."

"I admit that may have been premature. Are you looking for a fight, Mr. Hope?"

"I'm looking to protect my client," Matthew said.

"I was only assigned the case this morning. I didn't even know you were the defense attorney till you walked in here. In any event, I planned to *send* the . . ."

"I'm here now. May I have them please?"

"I'll ask my secretary to get them," she said.

"Thank you."

She picked up the phone receiver, pressed a button in its base, and asked someone named Shirley to bring in the Leeds witness list and statements. Putting the receiver back on its cradle, she looked up at Matthew and said, "It doesn't have to start this way, you know."

"Okay," he said.

"Really. If you like, I'll ask Mr. Bannister to let *me* handle any further contact with the press."

"I'd appreciate that."

"Done."

"Tell me something."

"Sure."

"Why'd he turn the case over to you?"

"Why not? I'm a very good lawyer."

"I'm sure," Matthew said, and smiled.

"Besides, it's a sure thing."

"All the more reason for Mr. Ambitious to try it himself."

"Maybe he's got bigger fish to fry," she said, and then, immediately, "Oh dear, forgive me. That was unintentional."

"What can be bigger than a pillar of the community killing three little Vietnamese immigrants?"

"Watch the newpapers," she said, and smiled secretively.

The door opened.

A redhead came in carrying a sheaf of papers. She put

them on the desk, asked if there was anything else before she went to lunch, and then smiled at Matthew and went out again. Matthew looked at the cover sheet on the top batch. The witness list. He glanced at the other stapled papers. Witness statements. Two of them. Asian names on both.

"What nationality are they?" he asked.

"Vietnamese."

"Do they speak English?"

"No, you'll need an interpreter. Also, one of them's out of town just now, visiting his son in Orlando."

"When will he be back?"

"I'm sorry, I don't know. Would you care for some coffee?"

"Thank you, Miss Demming, but I have an early lunch date."

"Patricia," she said.

He looked at her.

"The other stuff is for the movies. We can be antagonists without being enemies, can't we?"

"I'm sure we can," he said. "Patricia."

"Good. What do people call *you*? Matthew? Matt?"

"Matthew, usually."

"Is that what you prefer?"

"Actually, yes."

"May *I* call you Matthew?"

"Please," he said.

"Matthew," she said, "I'm going to put your man in the electric chair."

From a pay phone on the sidewalk outside, Matthew called his office and asked the firm's receptionist, Cynthia Huellen, to put him through to Andrew, please. Andrew was Andrew Holmes, twenty-five years old, a recent law-school graduate who had taken his Florida bar exams last month and was now waiting to learn whether he'd passed them or not. Andrew had his Juris

Doctor degree from the University of Michigan and was currently earning forty thousand dollars a year as a so-called legal assistant at Summerville and Hope, with the promise that they'd jump him to fifty the moment he was accepted to the bar — a foregone conclusion in that Andrew had been editor of the *Law Review* at U Mich and had graduated from the school with honors.

He came onto the phone sounding breathless.

"Sorry, I was down the hall," he said.

"Andrew, I need everything you can get me on Patricia Demming, she's the A.S.A. who's been handed the Leeds case. I want to know where she went to law school, where she practiced before she came to Calusa, whether she's ever handled a murder case, what her track record is, her courtroom style, and so on."

"Demming, did you say?"

"Demming. Double m, i-n-g."

"How old is she, would you say?"

"Thirty-six."

"When do you need this?"

"I'll be back in the office by two."

"Mmm," Andrew said.

"Also, line up a Vietnamese interpreter for me, I'm going to need one when I talk to these witnesses."

"Vietnamese interpreter, right. Easy to come by in old Calusa."

"Do I detect a touch of sarcasm, Andrew?"

"No, no, Vietnamese interpreter, right."

"Switch me over to Frank, will you?"

"Hold on."

There was clicking on the line, and then Cynthia's voice saying, "Hello?" and Andrew asking her to transfer the call to Mr. Summerville's office, and then Cynthia saying, "Just a sec," and then Frank's voice saying, "Matthew, where are you?"

"I just came out of the S.A.'s office. Bannister's assigned the case to someone named Patricia Demming. Ring a bell?"

"Never heard of her."

"I've got Andrew running her down. I had to pry loose the witness list and statements . . ."

"I saw the *Trib* this morning."

"Two witnesses, Frank. Both Vietnamese."

"We'll be fighting the goddamn war all over again."

"Did the mail come in yet?"

"Hours ago."

"Anything on my demand for discovery?"

"Little early for that, Matthew."

"I just don't want to read all about it in the paper again."

"Want me to call Skye?"

"No, I'll take care of that."

"Where are you headed now?"

"To the farm," Matthew said.

The farms out on Timucuan Point Road were rapidly succumbing to the developers' bulldozers. Where once fruit and vegetables had grown in abundance, there were now artificial lakes surrounded by houses with their own swimming pools and tennis courts. Country estates, they were called. Once upon a time, you could drive three miles east out of Calusa and you'd be in real country. Now you had to drive out at least twenty miles toward Ananburg before you began seeing the ranches and the citrus groves and the farms.

Jessica Leeds had invited Matthew to a twelve o'clock lunch.

He got to the farm at ten minutes before the hour — in August, the roads in and around town were virtually deserted — drove through the wooden posts on either side of the main gate, and then parked his rented Ford alongside a red Maserati.

The customized license plate on the car read JESSIE 1. He assumed there was a JESSIE 2, but it was nowhere in sight. Out on the fields, a tractor moved slowly against a vast blue sky. Not a cloud in sight. Not yet.

The farmhouse was a vast and sprawling one-story building, the sort of structure that had been added onto over the years, room by room, with connecting links and passageways that jigged and jogged this way and that to create an architectural labyrinth. There were several doors here and there on the rambling facade, but the front door was clearly identifiable, painted a bright red that announced itself as the entrance. Matthew went to it and pressed the bell button. Chimes sounded within. He waited in the noonday heat, hoping the closed door signaled air conditioning inside, hoping too that Jessica Leeds would ask him to take off his jacket and loosen his — the door opened.

She was a woman in her late thirties, he supposed, several years younger than her husband, tall and slender and tanned by the sun, casually dressed in sandals, skirt, and a white blouse that revealed one bare shoulder.

"Mr. Hope?" she said, and extended her hand. "Please come in."

Wedge-cut auburn hair, green eyes, high cheekbones, a wide mouth, her grip firm and dry. They shook hands briefly, and she led him into the house, her sandals slapping on a cool lemon-colored tile floor. He had expected a wooden floor. Pegged. This was the country, this was a farmhouse. But now there was modern furniture, all leather and stainless steel, another surprise. And what looked like a genuine Miró was hanging on the living room wall over a leather sofa the color of milk chocolate.

"Something to drink?" she asked.

"No, thank you."

"Lemonade?"

"Well, yes."

"Allie?" she called, and a young woman came from what Matthew supposed was the kitchen. She was wearing jeans and a white blouse with red embroidery decorating its scalloped scoop neck. In her early twenties, Matthew guessed. "Could you bring in the lemonade, please?" Jessica said, and the girl smiled and said, "Yes, ma'am," and went out into the kitchen again.

"You don't know how happy you've made me," Jessica said.

"Oh?"

"Taking on the case. Sit down, please. Take off your jacket, won't you?"

"Thank you," Matthew said, and took off the jacket and folded it and draped it over one of the leather easy chairs. Jessica sat at one end of the sofa, tucking her long legs under her. Matthew sat opposite her, in the other easy chair. The sliding glass doors behind her showed acres and acres of fields rolling away toward the horizon. He could no longer see the tractor. A sprinkling system watered rows and rows of plants growing in the sun. Allie came back with a tray bearing a pitcher of lemonade and two tall glasses brimming with ice. She set the tray down, said, "Lunch is ready when you are, ma'am," and went back into the kitchen. Jessica poured. She handed the glass to him. He waited for her to pour her own glass full, and then they both drank.

"Good," he said.

"We have more sugar, if you'd . . ."

"No, no, perfect this way."

"I should have asked her to bring in the bowl. And some spoons."

"Really, it's fine."

"We'll eat whenever you like," she said. "It's a cold lunch, just some cucumber soup and chicken and our own tomatoes, of course."

"Sounds lovely."

"Whenever you like," she said.

It occurred to him that she was extremely nervous.

"This *is* a tomato farm, you know," she said.

"No, I didn't know that."

"Yes," she said. "Well, we also plant squash and cucumbers, but tomatoes are our real crop. Fresh market tomatoes. We've got three thousand acres . . ."

"That I *did* know."

". . . of arable land, with thirty-six full-time people on salary. Including the migrant workers who do our picking, we employ some three to four thousand people a year. That's a big operation."

"Sounds like it," Matthew said.

"Yes," she said.

Behind her, way off in the distance, the tractor came into sight again, plodding its way across the fields. And now, far out on the horizon, Matthew could see the first faint beginning of the rain that would come later in the day, the sky darkening to the north.

"We've got twenty-three of those tractors," she said, nodding toward the fields, "and almost as many trucks, including four ten-wheelers. There are bigger farms, of course, but not many out here on Timucuan Point. And not many of them have their own greenhouses and packing house, the way we do, out near Ananburg. That's where our sales office is, too, Ananburg. We grow good tomatoes — prune them, stake them, and tie them, same as they do in Arkansas. We don't let them ripen on the vine the way they do up there, we harvest them green. But ours are better, if you ask me. Well, maybe I'm biased. We do a sixty-million-dollar annual gross, though, and we net something like thirty million, so those have got to be pretty good tomatoes, wouldn't you say?"

"I would guess so."

"Not many people in Calusa like us making so much money — well, nobody *really* likes rich people, do they? Espe-

cially if the wealth was inherited. That's why the newspaper's after us," she said, and fell silent.

They sipped at their lemonades.

The horizon seemed suddenly darker, the storm moving in more swiftly than Matthew had anticipated.

"Have you *seen* today's paper?" she asked.

"Yes."

"They say they have witnesses."

"I know. I already have their names."

"Oh?" she said, surprised.

"They have to supply them," Matthew said. "Anyone they plan to call. We have to do the same."

"Who are they?"

"Two Vietnamese men. One of them saw your husband going in, the other saw him coming out."

"They *say*."

"Yes, of course. And, of course, we'll contest anything they say. Meanwhile, they have him going in at eleven . . ."

"That's absurd. He was lying asleep beside me at that time."

"And coming out at a little after midnight."

"Stephen didn't leave the house all night long. We had dinner, watched the movie he'd brought home . . ."

"Which movie was that?" Matthew asked.

"*Casablanca*," she said.

Exactly what her husband had told him.

"He fell asleep watching it, in fact. He was asleep by nine-thirty, ten o'clock."

"What time did he go out on the boat?" Matthew asked.

"Around five," she said.

"And came back when?"

"Well, we had dinner at six-thirty, seven. So he was home before then."

"Just took the boat out for a spin, he told me."

"Yes, that's right."

"He also said he may have left his wallet aboard."

"That's a possibility, I suppose."

"He thinks someone may have found it on the boat."

"Well . . . that seems farfetched, doesn't it?"

"How do *you* think it got at the scene?"

"I don't know. I've been going over that same question again and again in my mind. I have no answer. Stephen was here with me. But they found his wallet in that house with those three . . ."

She bit off the word before it left her mouth. But her flashing green eyes said the word. The curl of her lip said the word.

"Mrs. Leeds," Matthew said, "the prosecution is going to make a big deal about you being your husband's only alibi. Now that they've got these witnesses . . ."

"Who are they? What are their names?"

"I'm sorry, they're difficult names to remember. I'll phone you when I get back to the office, if you . . ."

"No, I was merely wondering if they're relatives or anything. Half the Vietnamese in Calusa are related. If these two . . ."

"That's a good point."

"Because they couldn't possibly have seen Stephen going in or out of that house. That's flatly impossible. They have to be lying."

"Or merely mistaken."

"Then they should have kept their mouths shut! If they weren't sure! Because I hope you know . . . I hope you realize that those . . . those three bastards . . ."

She shook her head.

Kept shaking it.

"Forgive me," she said. "I'm sorry."

He said nothing. He kept watching her. Her head was bent now. She was staring at her hands. Behind her, the clouds were

rolling in swiftly. The tractor was heading back in this direction. The rain would soon be here.

"They're saying I was with him, aren't they?" she said at last.

Her head was still bent. She kept twisting her fingers, one hand in the other, long fingers with bloodred nails.

"There's a rumor to that effect," Matthew said.

"What do the witnesses say? Did they see *two* of us?"

"No. Only your husband."

"Does that make me innocent?"

"A man writing a letter to a newspaper . . ."

"Well, I'm guilty," she said. "In my heart, I'm guilty."

She lifted her head. Her eyes met his.

"In my heart, I would have done the same thing," she said. "Slit their throats, put out their eyes, cut off their . . ."

She turned away sharply.

A flash of lightning sundered the summer sky. A man in a straw hat and bib overalls was running toward the house, the abandoned tractor behind him. There was thunder on the left.

"Shall we have lunch now?" she asked.

The rain came in over the water in blinding sheets. Warren stood in the small marina office and waited for Charlie Stubbs to come back in from where he was pumping gas into a twenty-five-foot Boston Whaler. Warren liked this about Florida. The drama of it. There'd been drama in St. Louis, too, by way of tornadoes, but down here the action was more varied. And sudden. One minute you had sunshine that could scorch your eyeballs, and the next it was pouring down raindrops the size of quarters. Pelting the wooden dock outside the office, banging on the tin roof, sliding down the louvered glass windows, lashing into the canvas on sailboats caught unawares. This was one hell of a frog strangler.

Stubbs was wearing an orange poncho, one of those plastic

things that weren't worth a damn in a true storm. The poncho kept whipping around his knees, the wind trying its best to rip it clear off him. Stubbs knelt there unperturbed, a dead cigar between his lips, the hose in his hands, the nozzle stuck into the open mouth of the Walkaround's tank. Warren was happy to be inside.

The owner of the boat was wearing grey walking shorts, a white T-shirt, and brown Top-Siders. He was soaked through to the skin. He kept talking to Stubbs as he filled the tank, the words lost to Warren, Stubbs nodding every now and then to let the man know he was listening. Finally, Stubbs got up, hung the hose back on the pump, put the cap back on the boat's tank, gave it a tightening twist with his key, and then came walking back swiftly toward the marina office, his poncho flying all orange and angry around him, the boater following him drenched.

Stubbs was talking as they came in.

". . . wait it out the ten minutes or so, I was you," he was saying.

"Looks to me like it's gonna be longer'n that," the other man said. "You take American Express?"

"Just Visa or MasterCard," Stubbs said.

"I'll have to give you cash then," the man said, and glanced at Warren, and then took out his billfold and said, "What's it come to?"

"Eleven-sixty," Stubbs said.

"Can you break a twenty?" the man asked, and turned to look at Warren again. "Somethin' interestin' you here?" he said.

"You talking to me?" Warren said.

"Ain't but three of us here in this room and I'm lookin' straight at you, now ain't I?"

"I suppose you are," Warren said.

"This money transaction interestin' you?"

"Oh, yes," Warren said. "What I plan to do is hit you upside the head and steal your big twenty-dollar bill."

Stubbs burst out laughing.

"What's so funny?" the man asked.

"Nothin'," Stubbs said, still laughing.

"Man's standin' there watchin' me take out my money . . ."

"Come on now, come on," Stubbs said soothingly.

"How's a person to know *whut's* goin' on inside his head?"

He handed the bill to Stubbs and stood there glowering while Stubbs rang up the sale and made change from the register. He seemed to be debating whether he wanted to start up with Warren or not. He was still debating it when Stubbs brought back his change. He counted it, gave Warren a dirty look, and went out into the rain. His transom hit one of the pilings while he was backing the boat out. Good, Warren thought.

"You get a lot of that?" Stubbs asked.

"Enough," Warren said.

"I thought that was history."

"Sure. Where?"

"I just thought it was. That kind of bullshit."

"Well," Warren said, and let it go. "You were telling me about Leeds taking the boat out . . ."

"Right."

"This was Monday afternoon, correct? Sometime Monday afternoon."

"Around a quarter to five. Was when he drove in. Time he untied the boat and went off, it was maybe ten minutes later."

"What time did he come back in?"

"Around six? Thereabouts?"

"Tied up here at the dock?"

"Same as usual. His usual slip. Number twelve."

"What time did you leave the marina that night?"

"I *don't* leave it. Not *any* night. My house is right there past the storage sheds. I'm here all the time."

"Would you have seen anyone going onto Mr. Leeds's boat after he'd brought it in that night?"

"Except him, do you mean?"

"Yes, I mean *after* he brought it in."

"I know, but . . ."

"Anyone *else* is what I mean."

"I know. But what I'm saying is I was asleep after he tied up the second time."

Warren looked at him.

"He took the boat out *twice*," Stubbs said.

"What do you mean?"

"Once in the afternoon, and again later that night."

"*When* later that night?"

"Well, he called me around nine o'clock . . ."

"Leeds?"

"That's right, Mr. Leeds. Told me he'd be taking the boat out again for a little moonlight spin, said I wasn't to be alarmed if I heard him out there on the dock."

"And *did* you hear him on the dock?"

"I did."

"At what time?"

"He drove in sometime between ten and ten-thirty. Like he said he would."

"You saw him drive in?"

"I saw his car."

"Did you see him getting *out* of the car?"

"Yes, I did. Moonlit night, it was Mr. Leeds, all right. Locked the car and went straight to the boat."

"What time did he bring the boat back in?"

"I don't know. I was asleep by midnight, it had to've been after that. Boat was here in the morning when I woke up, tied up as usual."

"What kind of a car was Mr. Leeds driving?"

"A red Maserati," Stubbs said.

3

Tall and blond, with an engaging smile and an even year-round tan, Christopher Howell was old enough at forty-one to appear beatable to the male players at Calusa Bath and Racquet. He was also young enough at that age to appear attractive to the female members of the club. The fact was that he could, and did, beat the best players the club had to offer. But he seemed aware of the fact that no one liked a tennis pro who came on with the married ladies, and so his manner with the thirtysomething young mothers who flocked to take lessons from him was entirely businesslike and circumspect. As a result, the men did not feel threatened — except by his devastating serve and his ferocious backhand — and the women respected his courteous professionalism. Born and bred in Boston, Kit — as he preferred calling himself — had moved to Calusa almost a year ago, and his speech still carried the regional inflections of his native city, giving him a courtly sound that was entirely becoming. Matthew liked him a lot, even if he normally felt inadequate in his presence.

This Saturday morning, he felt particularly inferior.

Perhaps because he'd overslept and hadn't had enough time to shave. A man needing a shave looked, and felt, particularly unkempt in tennis whites. The club's idiotic rule was whites only. Kit looked magnificent in his spanking-clean whites and his glorious tan. He was also clean-shaven. Perhaps because, being blond, Kit didn't *need* to shave as often as Matthew did. Altogether he looked like some kind of Viking ready to smite an inept foe with his battle-ax. The fact that he was three years older than Matthew did nothing to change the uneven equation.

According to Matthew's partner, Frank, a man's life ran in twenty-year cycles. Twenty years old was young. Forty was middle-aged. Sixty was old. And eighty was dead. *Finito.* With women, it was slightly different. *Their* lives ran in *fifteen*-year cycles. Fifteen years old was young. Thirty was grown up. Forty-five was experienced. Sixty was middle-aged. Seventy-five was old. And ninety was still alive and kicking and hanging in there.

Maybe Frank was right.

Matthew knew that if he himself had his preference, men and women would remain respectively and eternally thirty-seven and twenty-nine. He was now thirty-eight. Over the hill, he guessed.

". . . against a left-handed player," Kit was saying.

Showing off, of course. He was a natural right-hander, but he could play with either hand at will. There were some players, in fact, who said his left-handed serve was even more powerful than his normal serve. Today, he was going to teach Matthew how to play against a left-hander. Matthew could hardly wait. The inside waist button on his tennis shorts had popped while he was putting them on, and they were now fastened only with the outside button. Matthew felt certain they would fall down the moment he tried to return one of Kit's aces. Kit's teaching technique was simple. No mercy. Take no prisoners. He played

against you as if you were facing each other across some disputed battlefield. It worked. Matthew's game had improved a hundredfold since he'd begun taking lessons last October.

"There are a lot of things you have to remember about playing a left-hander," Kit said, "but we'll cover only the two most important ones today, okay?"

"Sure," Matthew said.

He was wondering how many others there were. Two seemed like more than enough.

"The first thing is that he *is* left-handed," Kit said. "You've put on a little weight, haven't you?"

"Yes," Matthew said, and sucked in his gut.

"I thought so," Kit said.

Which made Matthew feel even more terrific.

"Most of the people you play against are right-handed," Kit said, "so you know exactly where to put your serve, you know exactly where the backhand is because you're in the habit of hitting the ball to it, of avoiding the forehand. So you've got to set your mind immediately to the fact that this guy *is* left-handed, and he's going to *remain* left-handed for the rest of the game, that isn't going to change one damn bit."

Unless you're Christopher Howell, Matthew thought. Who is ambidextrous and can change handedness midstream.

"A lefty is a lefty is a lefty," Kit said, smiling, "and if you have to hesitate for even a single second to *remember* that, then he's got an edge on you. So the thing you have to do from minute one is drum that into your head, he's left-handed, he's left-handed, and never for a minute forget it. That's the first thing."

Matthew could hardly wait to hear what the second thing might be.

"The second thing," Kit said, "is that a lefty has a natural curve on his forehand shot. You can see that ball curving in over the net like a baseball curving in over the plate. If you don't set yourself for it, you're going to be a little off on all your

returns. So for now just keep those two things in mind, okay? He's left-handed, he's left-handed — which means you've got to figure out where his backhand is from minute one — and he has a natural forehand curve. Want to start?"

He was merciless.

He drilled his fierce left-handed serves into Matthew's backhand each and every time, the ball hitting the surface and sending up a little spurt of grey dust, and then bouncing up high and almost out of reach. It took almost a full set before Matthew could return any of Kit's serves, and then only to have them pounded back at him in that "natural forehand curve" he'd been talking about, or in a backhand that was, if anything, more powerful than the forehand. Matthew kept telling himself that his opponent was left-handed, left-handed, left-handed, but the more he repeated this in his mind and signaled it to his arm, the more confused he became over where Kit's damn backhand was. *Whaaaap*, and the ball would come back at him, looping over the net in a low, wide curve that didn't seem at all natural to Matthew, that seemed in fact pretty damn *un*natural if you asked him, and then it would bounce and spin away out of reach, leaving him standing there flatfooted.

And when Matthew *did* remember where Kit's damn backhand was, served his hardest serve to that backhand, watched it zipping over the net at what had to be three thousand miles an hour, low and hard and to the right-hand corner for the deuce court or the midline for the ad court, a serve worthy of the men's singles at Wimbledon, Kit just stood there cool and tall and tanned and blond in his still-immaculate whites, bouncing, and setting himself, and bringing back his racket in that fierce one-handed grip, and *whaaaaap*, those zinging strings collided with that yellow ball and it came roaring back over the net like an express train racing down the middle of the track, making Matthew want to get out of its way before it tore his head off, trying to walk around it so he could lay his forehand on it, getting caught in the middle instead, pulling his racket in close

against his chest and watching the ball go past to Milwaukee, Wisconsin, where it sent up another small triumphant puff of grey dust just inside the baseline.

By the end of the hour, Matthew was exhausted. His shirt was drenched with sweat, his hair was wet and plastered to his forehead, his face was red, his tennis shoes were grey, and he felt as if he'd lost five of the ten pounds he'd gained in Italy. He was shaking hands with Kit over the net when he spotted a woman who looked very much like Jessica Leeds approaching the fenced-in teaching court, and then blinked when he realized it *was* Jessica, and suddenly felt even sweatier and smellier and stubblier and shoddier and shabbier and more showerless than he'd felt a moment earlier. As his client's beautiful redheaded wife approached the court in a pleated skirt that showed her long legs to splendid advantage, crisp white cotton shirt with a Head logo just over the left breast, smiling and waving to another woman as she came closer, Matthew wished a spaceship would swoop down and carry him off to Mars.

And then he wondered what the hell she was doing out here on the Saturday after her husband had been charged with murder, wondered about the propriety of her playing tennis while he languished in jail, wondered if anyone from the *Calusa Herald-Tribune* was out here today, wondered if mention of her appearance would be printed in tomorrow's morning edition, wondered if her being here could possibly hurt his case, such as it was, wondered why she hadn't first discussed with him the advisability of this, wondered too damn many things in the several moments it took her to reach the gate in the fence and unlatch it and open it. "Hello, Mr. Hope," she said, and smiled. "Looks like Kit gave you a workout."

"Yes," Matthew said.

"He played a good game," Kit said.

Praise from the Thunder God.

"I'm sorry I'm late," Jessica said.

"No problem," Kit said.

"Nice seeing you, Mrs. Leeds," Matthew said, and then to Kit, "Thanks, Kit, see you next week."

"Look forward to it, Mr. Hope."

Matthew put his racket into its cover, zipped it up, draped his towel around his neck, and started off toward the men's locker room. Behind him, he could hear the steady cadences of Kit and Jessica warming up, the solid *thwack* of racket against ball, the softer *thud* of the ball bouncing on the court's synthetic surface. He wondered again if it was wise of her to have come here. But here she was, for better or for worse, and there was nothing to be done about it now.

He headed for the showers.

"It sounds like you've picked yourself another winner, doesn't it?" Frank said sourly.

They were in his office at Summerville and Hope, a corner office befitting his position as senior partner of the firm, although he was only two years older than Matthew. Frank did not like having to work on a Saturday. Neither did he like what Warren Chambers had just told them. Apparently, a man named Charlie Stubbs — who owned a marina called Riverview on Willowbee Creek — had seen Stephen Leeds driving up in a red Maserati at ten-thirty on the night of the murders.

"Unless he was mistaken," Matthew said.

"It is not likely that anyone could mistakenly identify a red Maserati or a red *anything*," Frank said, and rose from behind his desk, and came around it, and walked toward where Matthew was sitting, and pointed his forefinger at him like a prosecutor about to badger a hostile witness. "Certainly not on a clear moonlit night," he said. "Which means that your man was out of the house at ten-thirty and not home asleep as he *claims* he was."

"My partner's playing devil's advocate," Matthew explained to Warren.

"I'm doing nothing of the sort," Frank said. "I'm advising you to drop the case right this instant. Your man is as guilty as homemade sin."

Frank Summerville often got his Southern expressions wrong; this one should have been as *ugly* as homemade sin. But he was a transplanted New Yorker who still had trouble with local dialect and custom and who spoke constantly about going back one day to the only *real* city in the entire world. London, Paris, Rome, Tokyo, all were penny-ante burgs to Frank Summerville's New York frame of mind. Calusa? Don't even ask. A fly speck on a pile of elephant dung was Calusa, Florida. A city with cultural pretensions, a lousy climate for most of the year, and a population composed of eighty percent rednecks and nineteen point ninety-nine percent immigrants from the Midwest. He hated Calusa. Hated, too, what it did to people. Thinned the blood and addled the brain.

"How's his eyesight?" Matthew asked.

"He wasn't wearing glasses, if that's what you mean," Warren said. "And he was able to read what was on that license plate."

"Which was?"

"JESSIE 1."

"Worse and worse," Frank said, shaking his head. "His wife's name. Worse and worse."

There were people who said that Matthew and his partner looked alike. It was true that they both had dark hair and brown eyes, but aside from that —

Matthew was thirty-eight, Frank had just turned forty. Matthew was an even six feet tall and weighed a hundred and eighty-seven with his new Italian pounds; his partner was five-nine and a half and weighed a hundred and sixty. Matthew's face was long and narrow, what Frank called a "fox face," in contrast to his own full, round "pig face." Moreover, Matthew was originally from Chicago — which Frank would not even admit was the *Second* City. To him, there *were* no second

cities; there was only New York and then every other city in the world.

"Why would he have driven his wife's car over there?" Matthew asked.

"Because he was out doing murder is why," Frank said.

"If he was out on his boat," Matthew said, "then he wasn't out doing murder in Little Asia."

"Unless he *parked* the boat, and got *off* the boat, and *then* went to do murder," Frank said, jabbing his finger at the air again.

"Why?" Warren said.

"Why? Because they raped his wife, why do you *think* why?"

"*Why*," Warren repeated, "would he go clear around his ass to scratch his elbow?"

"Meaning why didn't he drive straight to Little Asia?" Matthew said. "Why all the hugger-mugger with the boat?"

"He was going out to *kill* three people," Frank said. "Did you want him to leave a trail even a Boy Scout could follow?"

"He did that anyway," Matthew said. "A red Maserati with his wife's name on the plate? That's leaving a trail, Frank. That's leaving a highly visible trail."

"No, that's leaving an *alibi*," Frank said. "You said it yourself, not a minute ago. If he was out on that boat, then he couldn't have been over in Little Asia committing murder."

The room went silent.

"You shouldn't have taken this case," Frank said. "I know I've said that about other cases you've . . ."

"Oh? Have you?" Matthew asked, and opened his eyes wide in mock surprise.

"Yes, smartass, I have," Frank said. "But this time you seem to have gone out of your way to . . ."

"No, this is much better than the last one," Matthew said. "Don't you think so, Warren?"

"Oh, definitely," Warren said. "The last one, the man's

fingerprints were all over the murder weapon. This one, there's only his wallet at the scene."

"Yes, wonderful, make light of it," Frank said. "Ha, ha, wonderful. But for someone who's made a *credo* . . ."

"Credo, get that, Warren."

"Credo, yes, of defending only people you think are innocent . . ."

"I *do* think he's innocent, Frank."

"Why, of *course* he's innocent," Frank said, his voice dripping sarcasm. "Any *fool* can see he's innocent. His wallet is laying on the floor . . ."

"Lying on the floor, Frank."

". . . alongside three guys whose throats are grinning from ear to ear . . ."

"Please, Frank, don't be gross."

". . . whose *eyeballs*, for Christ's sake, are rolling around on the floor like *marbles* . . ."

"Really," Matthew said, "that *is* gross, Frank."

"You want gross? How about an enraged husband cutting off their dicks and stuffing them in their mouths?"

"I hope he at least got the right mouths," Warren said, and he and Matthew burst out laughing.

"Laugh, go ahead. Ha, ha, very funny, laugh," Frank said. "But wait and see what the State Attorney does with those three dicks."

"That's a sexist remark, Frank. The State Attorney happens to be a very beautiful young woman."

"Even better. Can you imagine a beautiful young woman telling a jury about three blind guys sucking their own *cocks*, for Christ's sake!"

"Disgusting," Matthew said, and began laughing again.

"Ha, ha, go ahead, laugh. Laugh, clown, laugh," he said, dramatically. "But don't come crying to me later."

"Frank?" Matthew said.

"Yes, *what?*"

"Why would he need the boat for an alibi?"

"What?"

"He already *had* an alibi. He was home with his wife all night long. So why the boat?"

"Because he's a goddamn liar," Frank said, and nodded his head emphatically. "And a murderer, too," he said, and nodded again. "And you're a fool for defending him."

His tan hadn't yet faded, but he'd been here in jail only since Tuesday. Give him another week or so, and the pallor would begin to set in. And the look would accompany it. The caged look that claimed a person's eyes the first time he got locked up. A look just this side of panic. A trapped and helpless look. Leeds wasn't wearing that look yet. It would come later. With the pallor.

The mark of an habitual offender was that he wore his pallor with something close to arrogant pride and never wore a caged look after the first time he was arrested. A murderer was something else again. Most murderers were one-shot offenders. They acquired the pallor and the look and either lost both when they were acquitted or kept both for a long, long time. In Florida, a convicted murderer kept them only until he was executed.

"I want you to tell me everyplace you went and everything you did last Monday," Matthew said. "From the moment you left your broker's office till the moment you went to sleep that night."

"Why?" Leeds asked.

"I'd like to know, please," Matthew said.

Leeds sighed heavily, as if being asked to tell his attorney where he'd been and what he'd done on the day of the murders was certainly burdensome and probably unnecessary.

"It was raining," he said. "This was around three o'clock.

When I left Bernie. Bernie Scott, my broker. Coming down in sheets . . ."

. . . drenching the sidewalks and the streets, running into sewers and drains, flooding the roads. Leeds has always felt uncomfortable driving his wife's Maserati, it is too jazzy a vehicle for him, it promises a playboy when only a farmer is behind the wheel. The car is called a Spyder, with a y, and it lists for $48,000, though Jessie bargained the dealer down to $44,500. Zero to sixty in six seconds, black leather convertible top, wood facings on the doors, dashboard, and console, wood handles on the hand brake and gearshift. Tan leather and suede on the seats, rich black carpeting on the floor, all too rich for Leeds's blood.

He feels even less comfortable driving it in the rain, but his own car has been in the shop for the past week, and they have only the two cars, his and Jessie's, and they've temporarily been sharing the more expensive one. His own car is a ten-year-old Cadillac Seville, in the shop for a new transmission at a cost of twenty-one hundred dollars, but he loves that car, the look of it, the luxurious feel of it, he would trade ten Maseratis for his steady old Cadillac.

He stops at the video store on the South Tamiami Trail, just off Lloyd, between Lloyd and Lewis, he remembers the name now, it's called VideoTime. The man who owns the store has only one eye, he wears a black patch over the other one, his name is Roger Carson. Just running from the car to the front door soaks Leeds to the skin. The shop is almost empty at three-fifteen, which is when he gets there. A woman with a baby strapped to her back is shopping the racks of tapes. Carson himself is behind the counter, staring glumly out at the rain. Leeds remembers wondering whether rain is good or bad for the video business.

He tells Carson what he's looking for — he has come here specifically for *Casablanca*, this is the movie Jessie wants to watch

tonight — and Carson comes out from behind the counter and leads him over to a section called Classics, or Movie Classics, or something similar. He locates the tape at once and then asks Leeds if he's ever seen the movie, and Leeds says he saw it a few times on television, and Carson asks him does he know what the best line in the movie is? Leeds immediately says, "Round up all the usual suspects!" and both men burst out laughing. The rain slithers down the windows. The lady with the baby browses.

The rain is beginning to taper at three-thirty as he drives south on the Trail to Timucuan and then turns the car eastward, toward the farm. The clouds are breaking off in tatters, blue is beginning to show in patches here and there. The road is wet and black ahead, the low red car hugging it, engine humming, tires hissing on the asphalt. He could get to like this car, he supposes, if he could ever bring himself to be unfaithful to the Caddy. He is beginning to think he might take the boat out. If it clears up. Drive over to the marina, dry off the seats, take her out for a little spin. Maybe run her up to Calusa Bay and back. Half-hour each way. If the weather clears.

By four o'clock, you'd never know it had rained at all. It is that way down here in Calusa during the month of August. It happens, and then it is gone, and the heat is still with you even though the fields lay emerald green and sparkling under a late-afternoon sun and the sky has been swept clean. He asks Jessie if she'd like to come out with him on the boat, but she tells him no . . .

"She's not a boat person," he tells Matthew now. "Never got the hang of running it, never enjoyed being on it . . ."

. . . so he drives all the way back into Calusa again. It takes about twenty minutes, this time of year, door to door from the farm to the marina. In the wintertime, when the snowbirds are down and the roads are packed, it'll take a half hour, sometimes forty minutes. Those are the times he wishes he had a little house on a deep-water canal, keep the boat right there at the dock, take it out whenever he wanted to. Come and go as he

pleased. Free. But the farm is his business, of course, his liveli-
hood. He's a farmer. The farm is what his father left him. His
sister in Tampa got the trailer parks, and his brother in Jacksonville got the downtown real estate. The farm is a big money-
maker, Leeds has never regretted his inheritance.

The marina is off Henley Street, just past the big Toys "Я"
Us warehouse. You go down the Trail heading south, and you
make a right on Henley and follow it around past Twin Tree
Estates, and then you take the little dirt cutoff leading down to
the creek. Charlie Stubbs calls his marina Riverview, but it's
really on a little creek, is all it is, leading out to the Intercoastal.
Willowbee Creek, it's called. Sometimes the water's so shallow
you can't get anything but a raft up it. Got to check the tides,
give Charlie a call, ask him how it looks, can you move a boat up
the creek? No such problem now when it's just quit raining, and
the tide's coming in, and the draft on his boat is only three feet
four inches.

The boat is a thirty-nine-foot Mainship Mediterranean.
Powered with a pair of freshwater-cooled Crusader inboards,
the Med is capable of doing almost thirty miles an hour, but
Leeds has never pushed it that far. He loves this boat almost as
much as he loves the Caddy. To him, the boat spells luxury.
Well, it *should* spell luxury, it cost him close to $145,000. The
Caddy is a comfortable old shoe, but the boat is a diamond-
studded glass slipper.

It is one of those afternoons.

Matthew knows just what Leeds is talking about; he himself has been out on a boat on a day like the one Leeds is now
describing, the sky a soft powder blue, the water still and
smooth and golden green, a bird crying somewhere off to the
right, shattering the silence, the cry echoing, drifting, and at
last fading entirely. And all is still again. There is only the sound
of the boat's idling engines.

Mangroves line the shore on either side of the creek,
reflecting in the water. Beyond these, receding into the land-

scape, there are palmettos, a scattering of sabal palms, a hummock of oaks trailing moss. The boat glides. A great blue heron stalks the edges of the shore, delicately lifting one spindly leg after the other. There are signs on slanted wooden posts in the water. NO WAKE. Gliding. Gliding. IDLE SPEED ONLY. The Burma-Shave signs of boaters everywhere in America.

Leeds stands at the helm, a grin on his face. He is wearing jeans and a T-shirt, Top-Siders and a nylon mesh cap that was part of a giveaway two, maybe three years ago, when the Brechtmann Beer people down here were making a big push for their new Golden Girl Light. The cap is yellow, with a pair of interlocking red *B*'s — for Brechtmann Brewing — back to back in a circle above the peak. The cap is perfect for boating, Leeds wears it every time he goes out. If it's a chilly day, he also wears a yellow windbreaker he bought at Sears. It is not a chilly day today. It is a normal day for August, insufferably hot and humid. But out here on the water, it is also heartachingly beautiful.

He hates to take the boat back in.

He cruises all the way up to Calusa Bay, moves slowly under the big bridge there, and makes a wide arcing turn on virtually deserted water. He feels utterly alone in the world. Alone with God. Who is being exceedingly good to him. And he forgets, for a little while at least, that there is anything in the world but peace and solitude.

He gets back to the marina at twenty past six and then drives the Maserati out to the farm again. He arrives there at a quarter to seven, somewhere around that time. Pete is just coming in from the fields, he waves hello from the tractor and Leeds waves hello back. Pete Reagan — no relation to the former president, whom Leeds *hates*, by the way — is his foreman, one of the thirty-six regulars employed by Leeds and his wife, an indispensable part of what has become a vast and very profitable operation since the death of Osmond Leeds six years ago.

For dinner that night, Jessie has asked their housekeeper/

cook, Allie — who is Pete's wife — to prepare steamed lobster, corn on the cob, and a mixed salad. The corn comes right from their own farm, as does the lettuce in the salad, but none of these is a cash crop like the tomatoes that are also in the salad. They sit down to dinner on the screened patio overlooking the pool. It is still stiflingly hot, but the water promises relief if the heat and humidity become unbearable, and the icy-cold beer in tall, frosted steins does much to dissuade thoughts of the weather. Besides, Leeds feels — and Jessie agrees with him on this point — that lobsters demand to be eaten outdoors at a long wooden table.

It is still a good day for Stephen Leeds.

God is still being good to him.

"When did you go out on the boat again?" Matthew asked.

"The boat? What do you mean?"

"What time that night did you go out on the boat again?"

"I didn't."

"You didn't drive over to Riverview . . ."

"No."

". . . in your wife's car . . ."

"No, I didn't."

"Didn't you call Charlie Stubbs . . . ?"

"Charlie? No. Why would I call him?"

"To tell him you'd be taking the boat out for a moonlight spin . . ."

"A moonlight *spin?*"

"A moonlight spin, yes. That's what Charlie Stubbs says you . . ."

"He's mistaken."

"You *didn't* call him?"

"I did not call him."

"You didn't ask him not to worry if he heard someone starting the boat . . ."

"I just told you I didn't call him."

"He says you called around nine."

"No, I was already in bed by then."

"He says you arrived at the marina around ten-thirty . . ."

"I told you, he's mistaken. Or lying, either one. Jessie and I had an after-dinner drink, and then we got into bed and turned on the video. I must've fallen asleep watching it because the next thing I knew . . ."

There is a loud knocking at the door. And the bell is ringing. The knocking and the ringing overlap. Leeds struggles up out of sleep, opens his eyes to see Jessie putting on a robe. Sunlight is streaming through the bedroom window. The ringing and the knocking suddenly stop. As Jessie rushes out of the room, he hears voices from below. And then Allie calling up the steps, "Missus? It's the police."

Two of them, one bigger than the other.

A black cop and a white cop.

Is this your wallet? Is this your wallet? Is this your wallet? Is this your wallet?

It is his wallet.

It is indeed his wallet.

God has stopped being good to Stephen Leeds.

The detective's name was Frank Bannion, and he'd been working out of the State Attorney's office for the past three years now. Prior to that he'd worked for the Calusa P.D., and before that he'd been a uniformed cop and then a detective-sergeant in Detroit. He told all the other detectives on the S.A.'s squad that he had once done research for Elmore Leonard back in Detroit. What happened, actually, was that Leonard was hanging around the station house asking questions, soaking up atmosphere for one of his books, and he asked Bannion a few questions, and Bannion gave him a few answers. So now Bannion walked around as if he'd co-authored the damn thing with his good old buddy Dutch.

Bannion was also proud of the fact that he still had his own

teeth and his own hair. He told anyone who would listen that all the men in his family — his father, his brothers, his cousins on his father's side — had lost their hair and their teeth by the time they were forty. Bannion was forty-two years old and he still had his own teeth and his own hair. He attributed this to the fact that he had once bit a burglar on the ass. The burglar was going out the window when Bannion grabbed him and bit him. He had pictures of his teeth marks on the burglar's ass as proof because the defense attorney had tried to get the case kicked out by showing Bannion had used unnecessary force.

Bannion was telling Patricia Demming what he had learned out at the Riverview Marina. Patricia had sent him there because Stephen Leeds had suggested to arresting detectives Bloom and Rawles that perhaps he'd left his wallet on the boat when he'd taken it out on the afternoon of the murders. Patricia wanted to find out if Leeds had truly been out on the boat. Because (A) if he hadn't, then he couldn't possibly have dropped his wallet there, and (B) if he hadn't, then he was lying, and if he was lying about one thing then he could be lying about everything. Or so she would try to convince a jury.

She was now hearing that he had taken the boat out *twice* that day.

"This is what Stubbs told me," Bannion said. "Charlie Stubbs, he owns the marina, sixty-two years old, a grizzled guy looks like Jonah and the whale."

"Told you Leeds took the boat out *twice*?"

"Twice," Bannion said. "First time in the afternoon, around four-thirty, tide was still good, second time at night around ten-thirty, tide coming back in, Leeds could've got the boat in and out easy."

"Did Stubbs see him both times?"

"Saw him both times," Bannion said. "Talked to him the first time, but not the time at night."

"Does he seem like a reliable witness?"

"Is my mother reliable?"

"I'm sure she is," Patricia said, "but how about Stubbs?"

"Very, you ask me. Sober, sharp, a very good witness, you want my opinion."

"What'd they talk about?"

"They talked *twice* actually."

"I thought you said . . ."

"Three times, in fact."

Patricia looked at him.

"He drives over in the afternoon, he parks the car, stops by the marina office to tell Stubbs he's taking the boat out, they chat about how hot it's been, Leeds takes off. Stubbs watches him go up the creek into the Intercoastal, he hangs a right, which means he's heading north toward Calusa Bay. He comes back in around six, talks to Stubbs again, tells him how beautiful it was out there on the water with God, and so on. That was the second time."

"And when was the third time?"

"Nine o'clock that night. Stubbs is still in the marina office, catching up on his paperwork, the phone rings, it's Leeds on the other end. He tells Stubbs it's such a beautiful night, he's thinking of taking the boat out for a moonlight spin, doesn't want . . ."

"Were those his exact words?"

"Exact. There *was* a moon the night of the murders, by the way."

"Okay."

"Tells Stubbs he doesn't want him to be alarmed if he hears the boat going out . . ."

"Was that the word Leeds used? Alarmed?"

"Yeah," Bannion said, and looked at her, puzzled. "Why is that important?"

"I like to know exactly what people say," Patricia said.

"That's exactly what he said. Alarmed. Or at least that's exactly what Stubbs *said* he said."

"Okay."

"True to his word, Leeds shows up around ten-thirty. Stubbs is home by then, he lives in this little house behind the sheds where they've got boats up on trailers for storage. He sees the car pulling in . . ."

"What kind of car?"

"A Maserati. Stubbs told me it's the wife's car. It's got her name on the license plate. A red Maserati."

"What does the plate say exactly?"

"Her name, Jessie, and then the number one."

"Spelled out? The number?"

"I didn't ask him."

"Ask him. And then check the plate with Motor Vehicles."

"Okay. So Leeds gets out of the car and goes straight to where his boat is tied up . . ."

"What's the name of the boat?"

"*Felicity.*"

"What a pissy name," Patricia said.

"Yeah."

"Was it backed into the slip?"

"No. Not when I was there."

"Then Stubbs couldn't have seen the name on the transom, right?"

"From his house, do you mean? I don't think so. He was in the kitchen getting himself a bottle of beer when Leeds backed out. The kitchen windows face the dock area, but I don't think he could've seen the name."

"What I'm looking for . . ."

"I'm with you. You want to know did Stubbs see Leeds get on a boat named *Felicity* instead of some *other* guy getting on a boat named *Lucky Lady* or *Serendipity.*"

"You've got it."

"I'll go back later, check out the sight lines, talk to him again."

"Also, if Stubbs didn't *speak* to Leeds . . ."

"Yeah, how did he know it was Leeds and not some other dude?"

"Did he say?"

"He said it was Leeds."

"But how did he *know* it was Leeds?"

"The hat. And the jacket."

"What hat? What jacket?"

"A hat Leeds always wears on the boat. This yellow billed cap some beer company was giving out a few years back. He wears it all the time."

"And the jacket?"

"A yellow windbreaker. One of these with snaps up the front and at the cuffs. Leeds was wearing it the night of the murder."

"Get a search warrant this afternoon . . ."

"Can't do that till Monday when the courts . . ."

"No, do it today. Find yourself a circuit court judge . . ."

"They don't like being disturbed on Saturday, Miss Demming."

"And I don't like evidence being destroyed on Saturday."

"I understand where you're coming from, but . . ."

"Someone has to be covering at the courthouse . . ."

"Well, I'll try, but . . ."

"Don't *try*, Bannion. *Do* it."

"Yes, ma'am."

"And then go out to the farm and get that jacket and hat for me."

"Yes, ma'am."

"Unless the wife's already burned them," she said.

"Patricia Lowell Demming," Andrew said, "thirty-six years old . . ."

"She looks younger, though," Matthew said.

"Born in New Haven, Connecticut, where her grandfather was a superior court judge. Lowell Turner Demming. Ring a bell?"

"No. Is that where she got the middle name?"

"Presumably," Andrew said. "On the other hand, Lowell means 'beloved' in the Anglo-Saxon, so perhaps her parents named her adoringly."

"Perhaps."

"Knew she wanted to be a lawyer when she was seven years old and saw Gregory Peck in *To Kill a . . .*"

"Where'd you get *that*?"

"In an interview she gave to the *Herald-Tribune* when she joined the State Attorney's office."

"Which was when?"

Andrew lifted his glasses onto his forehead and consulted his notes. Wearing the glasses, he looked scholarly, almost judicial. With the glasses on his forehead, he looked like an eager cub reporter. Dark curly hair, brown eyes, an aquiline nose, a somewhat androgynous mouth with a thin upper lip and a pouting lower one. Cynthia Huellen once told Matthew that Andrew reminded her of Mick Jagger. Matthew said he could not see a resemblance. *Sex*wise, Cynthia said, and went back to her typing.

"Joined the staff just before Christmas," Andrew said.

"Where was she before that?"

"I've got this in chronological order," Andrew said. "It'd be easier if I . . ."

"Okay, fine."

"She was graduated from high school at the age of sixteen . . ."

"Smart."

"Very. Attended Yale University for two years and was kicked out one fine spring semester for smoking dope in class."

"Dumb."

"Very. She went from there to *Brown*, no less, where she graduated Phi Bete. There was only one incident there . . ."

"Dope again?"

"No, no. A fist fight. With a football player who called her Pat."

"Where'd you get *that*?"

"Brown faxed me an article from the school paper. The incident made her a celebrity. Apparently this *oaf* . . . her word, *oaf* . . ."

"Nice word, *oaf*."

"Very. This *oaf* came up to her and said, 'Hi, Pat, my name's . . .' and she popped off and hit him. She later told the paper that *pat* was what you did to the head of a child or a dog, or *Pat* was a drunk sitting at the bar with his pal Mike, but Pat was *not* what you called someone you didn't know when her name was Patricia,' which, by the way, means 'of the nobility' in Latin."

"Did she say that?"

"Not the nobility stuff, that's mine. But, yes, she said the rest, I'm quoting directly from the *Brown Daily Herald*. She also said that even the nickname Trish offended her."

"Touchy."

"Very. Went to law school at NYU in New York . . ."

"*Law Review*, of course," Matthew said, and rolled his eyes.

"Surprisingly, no. But top ten percent of the class. Passed the California bar three years later and was hired immediately by a firm called Dolman, Ruggiero, Peters and Dern. Ring a bell?"

"No."

"Stayed there for two years, earned the nickname Wicked Witch of the West, a sobriquet apparently premised on her courtroom manners. She moved from there to New York, the firm of Carter, Rifkin . . ."

". . . Lieber and Loeb. Bombers."

"Apparently. That's where she made her rep."

"As what?"

"*Really* ruthless defense attorney. Strictly criminal law. She's successfully defended crooked oil company execs, Mafia bosses, Colombian drug dealers, tax fraud specialists . . ."

"How about murderers?"

"Three. Tough cases, too. One was a woman charged with strangling her six-month-old baby in his crib."

"What'd she cop to?"

"She didn't. She went for an acquittal . . . and *got* it."

Matthew looked at him.

"Tough lady," Andrew said, and nodded.

"What's her courtroom style like?"

"Flamboyant, seductive, aggressive, unrelenting, and unforgiving. You make one slip and she goes straight for the jugular."

"When did she cross over?"

"Left Carter, Rifkin for the New York D.A.'s office, worked there for three years before moving here to Florida. Apparently she wasn't getting where she wanted to go fast enough."

"Where does she want to go?"

"Washington is my guess. Eventually. With Florida politics as the stepping stone."

"Like her boss."

"Yes, sir."

"Who handed her this one because he's got even *bigger* fish to fry. You haven't seen anything in the paper about that, have you?"

"No, sir. What am I supposed to be looking for?"

"God knows. Have you found me a translator?"

"Yes, sir."

"Good. Check on the running time of *Casablanca* for me."

"*Casablanca*, yes, sir."

"And find out what time the tides came in and went out on the day of the murders."

"Yes, sir, the tides."

"What's the translator's name?"

Mai Chim Lee had been airlifted out of Saigon in April of 1975, when she was fifteen years old and all was chaos and confusion. She remembered her father rushing her to the embassy through thronged and deafening streets, her sweaty hand clutched in his firm grip, remembered him hoisting her up into the arms of a black American sergeant, the helicopter lifting off, people clinging to the landing skids, clawing for purchase.

She had not seen her father since that day. He had worked for the United States government as a translator; the Vietcong executed him the moment they occupied Saigon. She did not know where her mother was now. Perhaps they had killed her, too. She did not know. Three years later, when Mai Chim was eighteen, her mother stopped answering her letters. A letter from a neighbor, a woman she had called Auntie Tan, said only that her mother had gone away, she did not know where. Mai Chim could only imagine the worst.

She remembered her mother as a woman who smiled a great deal. Out of happiness, she supposed. She remembered her father as a stern disciplinarian who would smash teapots to the floor if his hot tea wasn't ready and waiting whenever he wanted it. But he'd managed to get her on that helicopter. Mai Chim herself now worked as a sometime translator, although her main occupation was bookkeeping.

She told all this to Matthew as they drove in his rented car to Little Asia late that Saturday afternoon.

She also told him that her true name was Le Mai Chim, the family name Le — one of the three most common in her native land — having descended proudly from the dynasty that had

begun in the fifteenth century, the middle name Mai meaning "tomorrow," and the personal name Chim meaning "bird." Her two older brothers, Hue and Nhac, had been soldiers in the Army of the Republic of South Vietnam. Both were killed in the Tet Offensive in 1968.

Mai Chim Lee — they called her "Mary" at the office where she worked, but she preferred her own name — had been in America for five years, in the hands of one governmental agency or another, before she struck out on her own. At the age of twenty she left Los Angeles, traveling cross-country by bus to settle at last in Florida — first in Jacksonville, next in Tampa, and finally here in Calusa.

She was now thirty-one years old, and although she spoke English fluently, there was still a trace of singsong in her speech, and occasionally she misused idiom or slang. A stranger in a strange city, virtually alone in the world, she dressed like an American — high heels today, and a linen suit the color of wheat, to complement her shining black hair and dark eyes — but she moved as if she were gracefully and delicately padding on sandals over the stones of an ancient village, and in her eyes there was a look of lingering sorrow.

She herself did not live in Little Asia.

She rented a condominium out on Sabal Key.

The people who lived here in the development, she explained, were mostly newcomers, most of them working in restaurants as either dishwashers, busboys, or waitresses. Many, too, worked in light-industry factories, where they performed unskilled labor for minimum wages — or less, if the owners could get away with it. Ten or twelve people often shared these one-family wooden shacks that had been thrown up in the early twenties, when there was still an important fish cannery in Calusa and housing was needed for the cheap black labor imported from Georgia and Mississippi.

The shacks sprawled across the scruffy land in fading, flak-

ing Christmas colors, some green, some red, all up on stilts because flooding was common in Calusa even this far from the Gulf. An automobile was essential here; public transportation existed, but buses were infrequent and unpredictable. One of the first things these immigrants bought was a car, usually chipping in for one they could share on their way to and from work, a wreck as faded as the shacks in which they lived. Mai Chim wondered why so many poor people drove faded blue automobiles. Always faded. Always blue. A phenomenon. On her lips, the word sounded Oriental. *Phenomenon.* She smiled when she said it. A phenomenon. The smile illuminated her entire face and set her brown eyes to dancing. Matthew could imagine her mother beaming this same smile in a safer, more innocent time.

Tran Sum Linh, one of the men who'd claimed he'd seen Stephen Leeds on the night of the murders, lived in one of these shacks with his wife, his six-year-old son, and three cousins — two of them male, one of them female and a cousin only by marriage — who had recently moved cross-country from Houston, Texas. He was thirty-seven years old, a former lieutenant in the ARVN, who had escaped Vietnam by boat to Manila shortly after the fall of Saigon. He was certain that if ever he went back to his country, he would be arrested and executed. He was trying to make a life here. He worked in a supermarket at the South Dixie Mall, stacking and sprinkling fruit and vegetables in the produce department, for which he earned four dollars and twenty-five cents an hour. He did not like getting involved in this business that had happened, this murder of his three countrymen, but he knew it was his obligation to tell the truth. He said all this to Mai Chim in his native tongue; he spoke only several words of English.

They were sitting outside Tran's shack, he on the low steps that led up to the front door, Mai Chim and Matthew on folding chairs he had carried out of the house. Tran was wearing thong

sandals, grey shorts, and a white Disneyworld T-shirt emblazoned with a picture of the minarets of Fantasyland. Matthew was wearing a suit and a tie; he felt like a jackass in this heat.

"This was at eleven o'clock, or perhaps a little past eleven," Mai Chim said. "It was quite hot, do you know, that night . . ."

. . . translating simultaneously and apparently literally, judging from her stilted and somewhat formal phrasing . . .

". . . almost identical to that of my own country during the summer monsoon, the rainy season, do you know? The rain . . ."

. . . is heaviest between June and November when typhoons blow in off the South China Sea. But there are monsoons winter and summer, and there is no true "dry" season, except relatively. *All* of Vietnam lies entirely below the Tropic of Cancer, and the climate is therefore hot and humid all of the time, some eighty degrees Fahrenheit every month of the year, heavy rainfall all year round except during April and May.

"Vietnam is tropical, do you know? So we have mosquitoes and ticks and leeches, same as the Malay Peninsula. And we have, too, crocodiles and pythons and cobras and tigers and leopards and wild dogs . . ."

In the Mekong Delta, where Tran grew up as a boy and fought as a teenager and a man, the land was — and still is — extremely fertile and well cultivated. Tran's father was a farmer, as was his father before him and Tran after him. Rice was their crop. Their little village — situated on a levee close by the Song Vam Co River — consisted of bamboo houses with thatched roofs, narrow streets laid out in a grid pattern, a bamboo fence around the entire site. During the summer monsoon, when the land was flooded, the only dry ground was on the levees and the dikes. Whenever there was a break in the rain, the family would sit outside the farmhouse with its small vegetable garden. Often on a hot, steamy night, Tran would look out over the flooded rice paddies to the mountains beyond Saigon

and dream of wisdom beyond years, wealth beyond imagination. On just such a night, in the city of Calusa, Florida . . .

He has been sitting outside with the others in his family for, oh, it must have been almost two hours, do you know? His wife — two years older than he, but this is considered auspicious according to the horoscope — has already put their son to bed and then gone to bed herself because she must be at the factory at eight tomorrow morning. Tran sits outside with his three cousins. The men are smoking. The woman, who is quite homely, is dozing. In a little while, she and her husband, Tran's older cousin, also go inside to bed.

Tran and the other man talk softly.

Smoke from their cigarettes swirls up on the air.

On U.S. 41, not two blocks away from the development, there is the hum of traffic, trailer trucks heading south to pick up Alligator Alley for the east coast, passenger cars driving down to nearby Venice or farther south to Naples or Fort Meyers.

The night is gentle.

Soft.

Tomorrow there will be deadly dull toil for subsistence wages, but for now there is the soft, gentle night.

At last, Tran's younger cousin rises and yawns and goes into the house. The screen door slams shut behind him. Tran sits alone on the steps with his thoughts and the hot, still moistness of the night. The moon is full. He remembers nights like this on the delta, the rice fields stretching away to the horizon under an orange moon floating above.

He smokes.

He drifts.

He sees the man first from the corner of his eye.

A flicker of bright color, almost as if a sliver of moon has broken off and fallen to earth, glowing for an instant and then gone.

The house Tran and his family are renting is situated one row east and one house south of the one shared by the three men who were first accused and later cleared of raping that farmer's wife. In his native Vietnam, before the Communists took over, murder and aggravated assault were among the most serious crimes, punishable by from five years in prison to death by guillotine, a means of execution inherited from the French occupiers. Tran further knows that rape in his country was considered aggravated assault, and he assumes that the crime is equally serious here in his adopted land.

He does not know how the Communists deal with such matters now, and he cannot possibly know that sexual battery — as rape is politely known in the Bible Belt state of Florida — is punishable by anywhere from fifteen years to death in the electric chair, depending upon the age of the victim and the amount of force threatened or applied. But it is his strong belief that crimes committed by any member of an ethnic or racial group reflect upon *all* members of that group, and therefore he is pleased that his countrymen have been exonerated of the crime. He knows them only slightly, but he thinks of them as decent, hardworking men, which — he freely admits to Matthew through Mai Chim — may be a biased opinion.

There is another burst of color on the night.

Sudden.

Catching the eye.

And then disappearing again.

It is very definitely a man, tall and broad-shouldered, very definitely an *American* man. Tran himself is slender and slight, his physique not uncommon in a nation where the average height for a grown man is a bit more than five feet and his weight some fifty-five kilos. The man running toward the house where the three men live is easily six feet tall . . .

Matthew's heart begins sinking . . .

And he weighs at least ninety kilos . . .

Which Matthew calculates at two point two pounds per kilo for a total of two hundred pounds . . .

And he is wearing a yellow hat and a yellow jacket . . .

And Matthew's heart sinks entirely.

". . . going into the house," Mai Chim translates, "where the three men were found murdered the next morning, do you know?"

Matthew knew.

4

Monday morning, the twentieth day of August, dawned hot and humid and hazy. Matthew awoke with the sun at ten minutes past seven and was in his pool swimming laps when the telephone rang. He swam over to the steps, picked up the modular phone, hit the TALK button, and said, "Hello?" It could not have been later than a quarter to eight.

"Mr. Hope? It's me. Andrew. I have that information you wanted."

"Yes, Andrew, go ahead."

"Running time of *Casablanca* is a hundred and three minutes. That's an hour and forty-three minutes, sir."

"Yes, Andrew."

Leeds had told him they'd started watching the tape after dinner. He wondered now if Jessica had watched it all the way through. Or had she, like her husband, fallen asleep somewhere along the way?

"High tide was at one-thirty that Monday afternoon," Andrew said, "low at seven fifty-four that evening."

Which meant Leeds still would have had good water when he took the boat out that afternoon, and he'd have beat the outgoing tide when he came back in at six, six-thirty. His story checked out.

But Charlie Stubbs had claimed . . .

"High again at one forty-two on Tuesday morning," Andrew said.

There it was.

The boat *could* have gone out again at ten-thirty, as Stubbs had claimed, when the tide was midway between high and low and the water still good enough for passage. And if the boat had come back in early on Tuesday morning, it would have caught the tide almost at full again, Matthew had no defense based on the navigability of Willowbee Creek.

"Thank you, Andrew," he said, "that was very helpful."

An addendum to the State Attorney's response to Matthew's demand for discovery was waiting on his desk when he got to the office at nine that morning.

Where Matthew had asked for the names and addresses of persons with information relevant to the offense, Patricia Demming was now adding Charles N. Stubbs to her former list of witnesses. She undoubtedly planned to have him testify that he had seen Leeds taking the boat out at ten-thirty on the night of the murder. Exactly what Matthew himself would have done in her position. No surprises thus far. Matthew hated surprises.

Where Matthew had asked for any written or taped verbatim witness statements made to the police, Patricia now included a written copy of Stubbs's statement taken by one Detective Frank Bannion of the State Attorney's office on Saturday, August 18, two days ago.

Where Matthew had asked for a list of any tangible paper or objects to be used at the hearing and trial, Patricia now listed:

One billed yellow nylon mesh cap with interlocking BB monogram in red and one yellow windbreaker with nylon shell and insulated lining.

This *was* a surpirse.

Matthew picked up the phone and asked Cynthia to get Jessica Leeds for him. She buzzed a moment later to say that Mrs. Leeds was on the line.

"Good morning," Matthew said.

"Good morning, I was just about to call you."

"When were they there?" Matthew asked.

"Do you mean the police?"

"Yes."

"Late last night."

"Did they have a search warrant?"

"Yes."

"Who was it? Rawles and Bloom again?"

"No. A detective from the State Attorney's office."

"Did you get his name?"

"Frank Bannion."

"Was he looking *specifically* for the jacket and hat?"

"The search warrant called them 'evidence or fruits of the crime.'"

"But did it say something like 'Affiant specifically requests warrant to search for,' something like that?"

"Yes. The jacket and hat. The warrant described them in detail."

"Did it also describe the farm as the location for the search?"

"Yes. The exact location of the farm."

"Did Bannion sign as affiant?"

"I think so."

"Who granted the warrant?"

"Someone named Amores?"

"Amor*os*. With an *o*. Manuel Amoros, he's a Circuit Court judge."

"Yes, that sounds right."

"Okay, so now she's got the jacket and hat."

"She?"

"Patricia Demming. The Assistant S.A. who'll be trying the case. Tell me again, Mrs. Leeds. Are you sure your husband didn't leave the house at any time on the night of the murders?"

"I'm positive."

"Were *you* at home all night long?"

"Yes. All night long."

"You didn't go out for a walk or anything, during which time your husband might have . . ."

"No, I was home. We were home together. Stephen fell asleep watching the movie, but I watched it all the way through, and then I watched television for a while before going to sleep."

"And slept the night through. Both of you."

"Yes."

"Until you were awakened by the police at nine the next morning."

"Yes."

"Can you remember the last time you saw that jacket and hat?"

"Stephen was wearing the hat when he came in off the boat that evening. Before dinner."

"And the jacket? Was he wearing the jacket, too?"

"No. It was a very hot day."

"Where does he normally keep the jacket?"

"In the hall closet."

"And the hat?"

"The same closet. On the shelf there."

"Is that where he put the hat when he came in that evening?"

"I suppose so. I really don't remember. He was wearing it, but I don't remember whether he put it in the closet or not. I didn't know the hat was going to be important. Why is it suddenly so damn important? Why did they come for it?"

"Because they claim he was wearing it when he committed the murders."

"He *didn't* commit the murders. He was here with me all night long."

"You're sure of that."

"How many times do I . . . ?"

"Are you a very deep sleeper, Mrs. Leeds?"

"Yes."

"Did you wake up at any time that night?"

"No."

"You slept soundly the whole night through?"

"Yes."

"Can you say for certain that your husband didn't get *out* of bed at any time that night?"

"Well, I . . ."

"Because that's what the State Attorney's going to ask you, Mrs. Leeds."

"I can't say that for certain, no."

"Then he *might* have got out of bed . . ."

"I suppose that's possible . . ."

". . . and gone downstairs to put on that yellow jacket and hat . . ."

"Yes, but . . ."

". . . and driven your Maserati . . ."

"No."

"Why not?"

"I didn't hear the car starting. I would have . . ."

"But you were sound asleep."

"Well . . . yes."

"So you *wouldn't* have heard the car starting."

"I guess not."

"So you really *can't* say for sure that your husband was home with you all night long."

"Whose side are you on?" Jessie snapped.

"Yours, Mrs. Leeds. Your husband's."

"I was beginning to wonder."

"No, don't ever wonder about that. I'm only asking you what the S.A.'s going to ask. You're his only alibi. If she can cast doubt on your . . ."

"My husband did *not* kill those men!" Jessie said sharply. "I may have been asleep, yes, I may not have heard everything happening in this goddamn house, but I know he did *not* go out to kill those men!"

"How can you know that?" Matthew asked.

"I just *know* it!"

"How?"

"Because he . . ."

She cut herself off.

There was a silence on the line.

Matthew waited.

"Yes?" he said at last.

"He . . ."

And another silence.

"Yes, he *what*?"

"He rejected the idea," Jessie said.

"What idea?"

"Of having them killed."

"What do you mean?"

"I wanted them killed."

Oh, no, please, Matthew thought.

"I wanted to find someone who'd kill them."

No, you didn't, he thought. Please.

"Have you mentioned this to anyone else?" he said.

"Of *course* not."

"But you *did* mention it to your husband?"

Say no, he thought. Tell me you didn't suggest it to your . . .

"Yes. I told him I wanted to . . . to start asking around . . . discreetly. Find out if there was someone . . . anyone . . . who

would kill those animals for me. Rid the earth of them. There are such people, aren't there? Who do these things for money?"

"Yes, there are such people," Matthew said.

"But Stephen said no. He said the men who raped me would have to live with their consciences for the rest of their lives. That was God's punishment, he said. And God's punishment was enough."

Try selling *that* to a jury, Matthew thought.

"Mrs. Leeds," he said, "at the trial, your husband didn't sound quite that magnanimous. He . . ."

"Yes, his outburst, I know. But that was in anger, and this was much later."

"How much later?"

"We heard the verdict on Friday. This was on Sunday."

"The day before the murders."

"Yes."

"Yes," Matthew said.

There was another silence on the line.

He was thinking, Please don't let Demming get her hands on this.

"My husband didn't kill those men," Jessie said. "Believe me, I *know* he didn't. He couldn't have."

But Matthew was thinking he *could* have.

The name of the place was Kickers.

Until just two months ago, it had been a seafood restaurant called The Shoreline Inn, and six months before that it had been a steak house called Jason's Place, and three months before that it had been known as The Purple Seahorse, which served Continental food as precious as its name in an interior all done up in violet and lavender.

Kickers had opened at the beginning of June, not an auspicious month in that the tourists usually left shortly before

Easter and the native trade down here could not in itself support a restaurant. If you hoped to get through the dog days of summer, you raked in your chips from November through April, and then either closed for part of the off-season or contented yourself with eking out a bare existence till the snowbirds flew down again. Opening at such a lousy time, Kickers should have followed the sad tradition of all the hard-luck joints that had come and gone on this spot, the exterior of the building remaining while the name and the interior decor changed every few months or so.

But against all odds, it seemed to be surviving, possibly because Salty Pete's — a rowdy saloon favored by year-round residents of Whisper Key — had considerably burned to the ground shortly after Kickers threw open its doors. There were those who voiced suspicions that Michael Grundy, the owner of Kickers, had himself engineered the unfortunate blaze at Salty Pete's, but neither the police nor the fire department had found the slightest proof of arson.

Smack on the Intercoastal, Kickers inhabited a big old white clapboard building with a huge outdoor deck overlooking the water and a dock that could accommodate some ten to twelve boats, depending on their size. It was the site, of course, that had encouraged all those previous entrepreneurs to rush right in where angels might have feared to tread. And with a splendid view like this one — the waterway at one of its widest bends, the bridge to Whisper in the near distance, lazy boat traffic constantly drifting by in a no-wake zone — the mystery was why all those other places had failed.

Grundy had opted for the casual air of a honky-tonk saloon, wisely recognizing Salty Pete's (before it burned down) as his only competition for the key's steady drinking crowd. He hired a flock of fresh-faced young barmaids — six of them altogether, four behind the long bar in the main dining room, two behind the circular bar on the deck — and dressed them in white blouses low enough and black skirts short enough to de-

light men while not offending women. And for balance he hired a horde of handsome young waiters and a piano player with a Gene Kelly grin, and he dressed *them* in black trousers and open-throated white shirts with puffy sleeves and red garters. And then he made damn sure he was serving generous drinks, choice cuts of meat, and the freshest fish he could buy, all at reasonable prices. And before you could shout eureka, he had himself a place that looked like a saloon but behaved like a restaurant, attracting customers day and night by land and by sea. A Calusa success story. Of which there were not too many these days.

When Frank Bannion arrived at noon that Monday, the place was already beginning to fill up for lunch, and many of the customers looked like banking people who had driven over from the mainland, a sure harbinger of longevity. He parked his car — prominently marked with the State Attorney's seal on both front doors — alongside a silver Lincoln Continental that looked like a beached shark, and then he followed the sound of a whorehouse piano into an interior bright with sunshine but nonetheless managing to convey the look and feel of a friendly, bustling, happy, cozy joint that had been here for the past hundred years and would be here as long as good food and drink were being served anywhere in the state of Florida. No small accomplishment for this jinxed location.

Bannion nodded his head in appreciation and walked through the main dining room and out onto the deck, where round white tables shaded by huge brown umbrellas overlooked the water. A boat under sail was gliding past on the wind. Boats made you want to be on them, Bannion thought, until you actually *got* on them. He sat at the bar and began chatting up the redhead who took his order for a gin and tonic. He was here to talk about the night of the murders. He had a choice of coming right out and saying he was a detective working for the State Attorney, or else he could just pretend to be somebody curious about what had happened. Sometimes

if you came on like the Law, they froze. On the other hand, if you came on like a snoop, they sometimes told you to fuck off. Six of one, half a dozen of the other. He decided to show his shield.

The girl was impressed.

"Wow," she said.

Twenty-three years old, twenty-four maybe, with an amazing suntan for somebody with red hair. Bannion figured the hair color had been poured out of a bottle. Brown eyes. Little button nose. Her name was Rosie Aldrich, she told him.

"I hate the name Rosie, don't you?" she said.

She'd come down from Brooklyn for a few weeks last winter, decided to stay awhile. She loved working here at Kickers, she told him. What she did, she alternated days and nights, which gave her a chance to spend time on the beach. She loved the beach. Loved the sun. Also, with a job like this, she got to meet a lot of interesting people. Like detectives from the State Attorney's office, wow.

Bannion told her he had once bit a burglar on the backside.

Out of deference to her youth, he didn't say ass.

He showed her the photograph of the burglar's behind to prove it. His teethmarks on the burglar's behind.

The girl shook her head in awe and admiration.

Bannion asked her if she'd been working here on Monday night, August thirteenth.

"Why, what happened then?" she asked.

Brown eyes saucer-wide.

"Routine investigation," Bannion said. "Would that have been one of the nights you were working?"

"What night would that have been, the thirteenth?" she asked.

"A Monday," Bannion said.

He was beginning to get the feeling she was kind of stupid. A sort of airheaded look in those brown eyes. Or maybe she was

on something. A lot of kids these days, you figured them for dimwits, they were in fact stoned.

"Yeah, but *which* Monday?" she said.

Today was Monday, the twentieth of August. One of those flip-up calendars behind the bar displayed the date in big white numbers on a black background. So what Monday *could* the thirteenth have been if not *last* Monday?

"Last Monday," he said.

"Oh," she said.

He waited.

"When was that?" she said.

"Last Monday," he explained. "The thirteenth. Last Monday night."

He was thinking that even if she *had* seen anything, Demming would never put a dope like her on the stand.

"Were you working that night?" he asked.

"Gee, no," she said. "I don't think so."

"That's too bad," he said, relieved.

"Yeah," she said.

"Do you know who *would've* been working that night? Out here on the deck?"

"Why out here on the deck?" she asked.

"Would you know?" he asked, and smiled pleasantly and patiently.

"I'll ask Sherry," she said.

Sherry turned out to be the dark-haired girl serving drinks at the other end of the bar. She was very tall, five ten or eleven, Bannion guessed, giving the long-legged, high-heeled impression that her skirt was even shorter than it actually was. She listened intently to what Rosie was telling her, glanced down to where Bannion was sitting and nursing his gin and tonic, nodded, and then came over to him.

"How are you?" she asked.

"Fine," he said. "I'm from the State Att —"

"Yeah, Rosie told me. What's this about?"

Intelligence flashing in her dark eyes, thank God; he hated stupid people. Sharp nose that gave her the look of a fox on the scent of a hare. Wide mouth, full lips. Actually, quite attractive, he thought. Twenty-seven, twenty-eight years old, in there. He wondered if she knew his teeth and his hair were still his own.

"I'm investigating a murder," he said.

Impress her flat out.

"Uh-huh," she said.

"Were you working out here on the deck last Monday night, the thirteenth?"

"Uh-huh," she said.

Watching him. Gauging him. Was he for real or was this some kind of pitch? Bannion was sure she got guys in here pretending to be all sorts of things they weren't. He figured he'd better show her his shield.

"Okay," she said, and nodded.

"Okay?" he said, and smiled.

He felt he had a very nice smile because all of his teeth were his own.

"I said okay, didn't I?" she said, and returned the smile.

She had a nice smile, too.

"So what's this murder?" she asked.

This morning, Bannion and the S.A. had studied a nautical chart together and had decided that the closest landing to Willowbee Creek was right here at Kickers, just off marker 63. Good dock space, even on a crowded night, and a Monday night wouldn't have been that crowded. Pull the boat in, tie her up, get into a car, and then drive over to Little Asia, not fifteen minutes away. Leeds *had* to have pulled in here. Stubbs had seen him turning left out of the creek, heading south. The next place for docking a boat would've been The Captain's Wheel, off marker 38, too far south to have made it back by car to the scene of the murders within the time estimated in the coroner's postmortem interval. No, Leeds *had* to've got off his boat right here at Kickers.

"Were you here around ten-thirty, eleven o'clock that night?" he asked.

"Yeah?" she said.

"Working the bar here?"

"Yeah?"

"You can see the dock from the bar here, can't you?"

"Yeah?"

"I'm looking for a boat that would've come in around ten-thirty, eleven o'clock. Would've been coming down the Intercoastal from Willowbee Creek."

"Marker 72," she said, and nodded.

"Are you a boater?"

"I've been on a few boats," she said, raising her eyebrows slightly and somehow conveying the impression that she had done some very interesting things on boats in waters hither and yon. There eyes met. Bannion suddenly felt he had a shot at bedding this woman.

"I know the Willowbee Creek marker," she said.

"This boat would've been a thirty-nine-foot Mainstream Mediterranean, coming down the waterway south from Willowbee. White boat with black trim, the name *Felicity* painted on the transom. Guy at the helm would've been wearing a yellow jacket and hat."

"Sure," Sherry said. "What about him?"

Emma Hailey had worked in what the Calusa County Courthouse called its Records Division since 1947, when the town was relatively unknown as a resort. Now in her late sixties, Emma wondered how it had *ever* become popular. The weather here was iffish at best in the wintertime and swelteringly hot in the summer, which melted directly into the hurricane season. There was none of the lushness one associated with tropical climates, nor for that matter any of the riotous show of color you got in Atlanta when the magnolias were blooming, or Bir-

mingham or Tulsa when the azaleas popped, or anywhere in summertime Connecticut when the daylilies bloomed orange and red and yellow along every country lane. Even the springtime blooming of Calusa's jacaranda trees was pale by comparison to the exuberant purple explosion on virtually every Los Angeles street at that time of the year.

Here, there were listless bougainvillea and limp hibiscus, tame by Caribbean standards. The cluster of gold trees that bloomed in the spring on U.S. 41, down near Marina Lou's and the bridge to Sabal Key, were admittedly impressive, but their glorious show of color was short-lived. Most of the year — and especially during the summer — Calusa's foliage looked faded or scorched, and no one seemed to give a damn. Easier to go fishing than to water a garden. Why prune a bush when you could hop on a boat and sail out into the Gulf? The lack of concern showed. Calusa looked like an elegantly dressed woman whose soiled and tattered slip was showing.

Emma thought of it as drab.

Matthew's partner thought of it as tacky.

Matthew wondered if they'd ever exchanged views.

"The trial went on for three weeks," Emma was telling him. "We've got 1,260 pages of transcript here, are you sure you want to read them all?"

"If it's no trouble," Matthew said.

"Long as you carry 'em over to the desk, it makes no difference to me," she said.

Emma was a stout woman with grey hair and a faint limp. She'd had the limp ever since Matthew had known her. He supposed it was from a childhood injury. Or perhaps undetected polio; he remembered with something like surprise that polio had once been the scourge of the earth. He followed her between rows and rows of filing cabinets marked in a system only Emma herself could fathom. The cabinets were of the old oaken style, heavy, sturdy-looking; he remembered with addi-

tional mild surprise that once upon a time many things had been fashioned of wood rather than metal or plastic. It goes by too fast, he thought. Where was the kid with hair in his eyes who played sandlot baseball in Chicago, Illinois? Where were the sandlots anymore?

"Transcript'd be in the People Versus section," Emma said. "Have you got the names of them three? They were tried together, weren't they?"

"Yes," Matthew said.

The defense team, of course, had tried to obtain separate trials, sever each defendant out, present each individually as a confused young man in ill-fitting clothes, a poor put-upon immigrant, sitting at the defense table with his eyes wide in bewilderment. Ladies and gentlemen of the jury, I *ask* you, could this shy, unassuming creature *possibly* have committed rape? Skye Bannister had prevailed. The three had been tried together. But the state had lost the case anyway.

"Ngo Long Khai," Matthew said, reading from the slip of paper in his hand. "Dang Van . . ."

"Hold it, hold it," Emma said. "Let me see that, willya, please?"

He handed her the slip of paper. She studied it in consternation, shaking her head all the while, and then limped down the aisle between the rows of cabinets. "Let's try the Ho one," she said. "I have a feeling I filed it under the Ho."

Matthew could only imagine why.

But sure enough, she found the transcript filed under *Ho Dao Bat, People vs.* and flagged for reference to Ngo Long Khai and Dang Van Con, co-defendants.

"Can't even lift it," she said.

An exaggeration, even if it was a thick file — or rather *files*, in that the 1,200 some-odd pages of transcript had been separated into four more easily handlable bundles, each packaged between pale blue, stiff board binders secured with brass paper

fasteners. Matthew took the binders out of the drawer one at a time, stacking them on top of the cabinet, and then closed the drawer and hoisted the stack off into his hands and his arms.

"Thank you, Emma," he said.

"Call me when you're done, okay?" Emma said. "I've got to sign 'em back in."

He followed her down the aisle. She snapped out the fluorescent lights behind them. The old oaken cabinets vanished in a wink, as if dismissed again to a remote and silent past. Ahead was a room with long windows and a high, beamed ceiling, another throwback to the turn of the century, when the courthouse was built. A long oaken table stood on stout, round legs. A furled American flag was in one corner of the room. A framed picture of George Washington was on the wall beside it. Early-afternoon sunlight streamed through the windows, burnishing the tabletop's golden finish. Dust motes lazily climbed the slanting shafts of sunlight. The room was utterly still. Matthew suddenly remembered why he'd become a lawyer.

Alone, he sat at the table and opened the first of the binders.

It is four days before Christmas.

The weather here in Calusa, Florida, is wonderful for this time of year. No one can complain about temperatures that hover in the mid-seventies during the daytime and then drop to a good bedtime low of fifty-two or -three. No need for air conditioning, you simply throw open the windows and let the prevailing winds blow right on through. During the day, the sun smiles down beneficently, and Calusa's miles and miles of white sand beaches are littered with the bodies of toasting tourists, the waters of the Gulf sprinkled with bobbing heads. Not a single native is in the water; to Floridians, this is the winter and only madmen go swimming in December.

The downtown streets, the parking lots of the malls, are all

hung with Christmas decorations that seem out of place here in this climate. What is Santa Claus doing on a sleigh down here where there has never been snow? Why are there antlered reindeer in a climate better suited to alligators? Why doesn't Frosty the Snowman melt?

But the neo-Floridians who have migrated from distant places north perhaps still remember the bite of a clear December day with a hint of snow in the air, and those who were born and bred here have heard tall tales of fabulous Christmas blizzards, the family snowed in while the turkey roasts and the fire crackles on the grate, and suddenly at the door, arriving with his arms laden with gifts . . . "Son! We knew you'd make it! Merry Christmas!"

And so there is the same frantic shopping mania here in the subtropical Southland as there is away up north in frigid Eagle Lake, Maine. So what if the Christmas trees are sprayed white? So what if the shoppers are wearing shorts and T-shirts? In only four days, it will be Christmas morning. And peace on earth will come to men of good will.

Women, too.

Maybe.

There will be no peace on earth for Jessica Leeds tonight.

Tonight, Jessica Leeds will be raped.

"The mall closed at ten o'clock. I . . ."

A transcript consists of cold type, the words of questioner and witness reduced to something less than conversation, a dialogue lacking inflection or nuance. Matthew can only guess at the fury underlining Jessica Leeds's testimony, the anger she is controlling.

She describes a Chinese restaurant adjacent to the mall.

Cold type.

The restaurant is still open at ten . . . a little after ten, actually, by the time she reaches the car. She has parked it behind the restaurant, which is shaped like a pagoda, and which in fact is *named* The Pagoda. The car is an expensive one, and

this is four days before Christmas. With all the traffic in the mall's lot a dented fender is a distinct possibility, and so she has chosen this deserted spot behind The Pagoda, alongside a low fence beyond which is undeveloped scrub land. As she walks toward the restaurant, the mall's parking lot is rapidly emptying of automobiles, except for those parked row after row outside the movie-theater complex at the far end. It is ten minutes past ten, she supposes, when she places in the trunk of her Maserati the several Christmas gifts she's bought.

There are lights here behind the Chinese restaurant. It is not what anyone would call *brightly* lighted, but there is illumination enough to provide a sense of security. And besides, there's a moon. Not quite full, just on the wane. Anyway, it is only a little after ten, this is not the dead of night, this is not a town where a woman alone needs to be afraid of unlocking the door of her automobile in an adequately lighted parking space behind a brilliantly lighted restaurant on a moonlit Thursday night four days before Christmas. Besides, there are three men standing behind the restaurant, smoking. All of them in shirtsleeves. Wearing long white aprons. Restaurant help. She unlocks the door of the car, closes and locks it behind her, turns on the lights, starts the engine, and is backing away from the low fence when she realizes she has a flat tire.

She tells this to the State Attorney, and she repeatedly tells it to the defense attorneys who come at her one after the other, trying to shake her story. In the transcript, each attorney is initially indentified as he begins his cross, and then the form reverts to a simple Q and A, so that it is not necessary each time, over and over again, to indicate MR. AIELLO for Tran's attorney or MR. SILBERKLEIT for Ho's, or MRS. LEEDS for Jessica herself, it is Q and A, Q and A, Q and . . .

A: I got out of the car to change it. I didn't realize I was going to be raped.

Q: Objection, Your Honor. We are here precisely to *determine* whether . . .

A: Yes, yes, sustained, Mr. Aiello. The jury will please ignore the witness's answer.

The "A" this time is from the Circuit Court judge hearing the case, a man named Sterling Dooley, who has a reputation as a hanging judge. The team of defense attorneys — there are eight of them sitting at the defense table — would have preferred a different judge. They did, in fact, ask for a change of venue because of the publicity the rape (or *alleged* rape, as they would have it) generated in the media, but their request was denied. So they are stuck with Dooley, who now asks the clerk to please read Aiello's question again —

"What did you do when you discovered the flat tire?"

— and the Q and A continues.

A: I got out of the car to change it.

Q: Yourself?

A: Yes, myself. I was alone.

Q: I mean . . . don't you belong to any club offering emergency road service?

A: No, I don't.

Q: Couldn't you have called a garage?

A: I know how to change a tire.

Q: But the way you were dressed . . .

A: The way I was dressed has nothing to do with changing a tire.

Q: I merely thought . . . high heels . . . a short skirt . . .

A: Objection, Your Honor.

This from the State Attorney. Skye Bannister himself. In person. Hair as golden as wheat, eyes the color of his given name. Tall and rangy and enormously good-looking. Undoubtedly leaping to his feet in high dudgeon.

A: Sustained. Leave off that line of questioning, please, Mr. Aiello.

Q: Couldn't you have called your husband to help you?

A: I didn't want to get him out of bed.

Q: You knew he was in bed, did you?

A: He had a cold. He was in bed when I left the house that night.

Q: And this was now what time?

A: A quarter after ten.

Q: So naturally, you didn't want to get him out of bed. Was it a quarter after ten exactly?

A: I can't say exactly. I'm assuming it took me ten minutes or so to walk to the car and put my packages in the trunk.

Q: And you say there were three men standing outside the back door to the restaurant when you . . .

A: Yes. The defendants. The three men sitting right . . .

Q: I haven't asked you to identify anyone, Mrs. Leeds.

A: Well, that's who they were.

Q: Your Honor . . .

A: Yes, strike all that. Witness will please not offer testimony unless it is asked for.

Q: Did you speak to these men?

A: No.

Q: Had you seen these men prior to this time — a quarter after ten, you say it was?

A: Around a quarter after ten. No, I hadn't seen them before then.

Q: That was the very first time you saw them.

A: Yes.

Q: But you're not sure it was a quarter after ten *exactly*.

A: Not exactly. But certainly around then.

Q: Could it have been *half* past ten?

A: I don't think so. It wouldn't have taken me that long to walk back to the car.

Q: How about twenty to eleven? Could it have been twenty to eleven?

A: No.

Q: Or ten to eleven? Could it have been ten to eleven?

A: No. I told you, it was . . .

Q: Or a quarter after . . .

A: No, it was . . .

Q: Let me finish the question, please.

A: I thought you *were* finished.

Q: Could it have been a quarter after eleven? Rather than a quarter after ten?

A: No, it was a quarter after ten.

Q: Mrs. Leeds, what time did you arrive at the mall that night?

A: Around eight o'clock.

Q: To do your shopping.

A: Yes.

Q: Was it dark when you arrived?

A: Yes.

Q: And did you park your car behind The Pagoda at that time?

A: Yes.

Q: Were there lights behind the restaurant?

A: Yes.

Q: Was there anyone standing out back at that time?

A: I didn't see anyone.

Q: Didn't you see three men standing there, smoking cigarettes? Under the light over the back door?

A: No, I didn't see anyone.

Q: Didn't you see the three men you later . . .

A: No.

Q: Your Honor, may I please be allowed to complete my question?

A: Mrs. Leeds, please listen to the entire question, won't you, before you answer? Go ahead, Mr. Aiello.

Q: At eight o'clock that night, when you parked your car behind the restaurant, didn't you see the three men you later claim . . .

A: Objection, Your Honor.

Skye Bannister again.

"Mrs. Leeds has already stated that she did not see anyone standing behind the restaurant. Mr. Aiello is merely asking the same question in a different guise. And it has already been answered."

"Mr. Aiello?"

"Your Honor, we have heard a previous witness testifying to the fact that a conversation took place between Mrs. Leeds and the three defendants shortly after she parked her car that night. We have heard from the defendants themselves what the content of that conversation was. I am merely trying to refresh Mrs. Leeds's memory of the exchange."

"I'll allow the question."

Q: Mrs. Leeds, isn't it true that as you were getting out of your car, you turned to the three defendants and said, 'Good evening, boys'?

A: No.

Q: You didn't see them, so naturally you couldn't have said anything like that to them.

A: I wouldn't have said anything to them in *any* case.

Q: Well, 'Good evening' is only a form of greeting, isn't it? Nothing provocative about that. Nothing seductive. Why *couldn't* you have said, 'Good evening, boys'?

A: Because I'm not in the habit of talking to strange men.

Q: Especially when they're invisible, isn't that so?

A: I don't understand your question.

Q: Well, you said they weren't there, didn't you? That means they were invisible.

A: No, that means they weren't there.

Q: You only saw them later.

A: Yes.

Q: These same three men.

A: Yes. *No.* I didn't see *anyone* at eight o'clock, I only saw these men when I came back to the car.

Q: At a quarter after ten . . .

A: Yes.

Q: . . . or a quarter after eleven, whenever it was.

A: It was a quarter after ten. I've already told you . . .

A: Really, Mr. Aiello.

Q: I'm sorry, Your Honor, but if you'll allow me . . .

A: Where are you going?

Q: I am trying to show, Your Honor, that the witness's account of what happened at what time, or what was said at what time, is confusing at best. And if she's confused about the basic *facts* of the . . .

A: I'm not confused about *anything* that happened that night. *You're* the one who's trying to confuse the facts!

Q: Your Honor, may I please proceed?

A: Let's hear where you're going, Mr. Aiello.

Q: Thank you. Mrs. Leeds, you say these three men were standing outside the back door of the restaurant, smoking under the light back there, when you returned to your car at a quarter after ten.

A: Yes.

Q: You heard them testify earlier, did you not, that they were in the *kitchen* at that time, washing dishes?

A: I heard them, yes.

Q: One of you must be mistaken, don't you think?

A: Not me.

Q: You heard them testify, did you not, that the only time they saw you was at eight, when you parked the car?

A: I heard them.

Q: Are they mistaken about that, too?

A: Or lying.

Q: And were they lying when they said you showed a great deal of leg while you were getting out of the car . . .

A: No one was *there* when I got out of the car!

Q: And that you said, 'Good evening, boys.' Was that a lie? The testimony of all three men to that effect?

A: It was a lie.

Q: Did you hear the testimony of the chef, Mr. Kee Lu, to the effect that these three men were in the kitchen washing dishes at a quarter past ten and could not possibly have been outside smoking at that time?

A: I heard him.

Q: But he must be mistaken, too. Or lying. Or both.

A: If he says they weren't outside, then he's lying.

Q: You alone are telling the truth.

A: About that, yes.

Q: But not about anything else?

A: I'm telling the truth about everything.

Q: As, of course, you've sworn to do. But you say these others are lying.

A: If they claim . . .

Q: Everyone's lying but you, is that it, Mrs. Leeds? But isn't it possible that you're confusing what happened at *eight* o'clock with what happened at a quarter past ten?

A: I wasn't *raped* at eight o'clock!

Q: Nor has anyone said you were. But, tell me . . . were you worried about getting raped when you parked the car?

A: No.

Q: While you were parking the car, you weren't concerned about the possibility of rape?

A: No, I didn't even consider that possibility.

Q: Because if you had, you might have parked the car elsewhere, isn't that so?

A: There weren't very many spaces left when I got to the mall. Anyway, it's an expensive car, I was worried it

might get damaged. So I parked it away from the other cars.

Q: But if you'd considered the possibility of rape, you might have parked elsewhere, isn't that so?

A: No, it was only a short walk to the mall.

Q: You weren't worried about getting raped on your short walk from the car to the mall, were you?

A: No.

Q: Or on your walk *back* to the car after the mall closed, were you?

A: No.

Q: So, really, Mrs. Leeds, you weren't worried at *all* about getting raped there where you'd parked the car, were you?

A: No, I did not expect to be raped.

Q: When you came back to the car, did you expect to be raped then?

A: No.

Q: Even though there were three men standing there behind the restaurant?

A: I knew they worked there.

Q: How did you know that?

A: They looked like kitchen help.

Q: Isn't it possible that you weren't afraid of getting raped at a quarter past ten because there was no one there to rape you at that time?

A: Oh, they were there, all right.

Q: But not when you *say* they were there.

A: Objection!

A: Was that a question, Mr. Aiello?

Q: I'll rephrase it, Your Honor. What time was it when you claim to have seen these three men?

A: A quarter past *ten!* How many times do I . . . ?

Q: While they were washing dishes in the restaurant kitchen!

A: No! While they were raping me on the hood of the goddamn . . .

Q: Objection!

A: Sustained. Please answer the question, Mrs. Leeds.

A: That's the only time I ever saw them. The only place I ever saw them. While I was being . . .

Q: No further questions.

But of course there *were* further questions.

5

She was sitting out by the pool when Matthew arrived at three that afternoon. Green maillot swimsuit to match her eyes, reddish-brown wedge-cut hair catching the late-afternoon sunshine, a green terry band across her forehead, a faint sheen of perspiration on the sloping tops of her breasts above the suit's bodice. She asked if he'd care for a lemonade. Or something stronger. She herself was having a gin and tonic. He said that sounded good, and she went inside to prepare it for him.

He sat watching the fields and the distant yellow-grey sky. The rain had not yet come today; someone must have forgotten to set the alarm. Jessica was back not five minutes later. She had wrapped a short filmy green scarf around herself, knotted it above her breasts. She handed him the drink, and then sat in the chair opposite his. The drink tasted cold and tart and sparkly. Especially after hours of reading transcripts in a room streaming sunlight.

"I'm sorry to bother you this way," he said, "but I have some questions."

"No bother at all," she said. "With Stephen in jail . . ."

She let the sentence hang.

"I was reading the trial transcript this afternoon," he said.

"Something, wasn't it?"

"You know why they were acquitted, don't you?"

"Sure. Guilt."

He looked at her.

"Not *theirs*," she said, "*ours*. Our massive American guilt. For the horrors we committed in Vietnam. This was compensation for that."

"Well, maybe so," Matthew said. "But I think there was a more practical reason."

"And what was that?"

"Time," he said.

"Time?"

"The jury couldn't reconcile the contradictions of time."

"The three of them were lying," she said. "About everything. *Including* time."

"How about the chef? Was he lying, too?"

"He was a friend of theirs. Yes, he was lying."

"And the police?"

"I don't know what you mean."

"The police dispatcher who testified at the trial said that he took your call at twelve-forty A.M. . . ."

"Yes, that's right."

"And that the responding police car — that would have been David car — reached you some five minutes later . . ."

"Those seem to be the correct times, yes."

"But, Mrs. Leeds . . . the mall closed at *ten*."

"Yes?"

"And you yourself testified that you began changing that flat tire at a quarter past."

"Yes?"

"Don't you see what confused the jury?"

"No, I'm sorry, I don't."

"You called the police two hours and twenty-five minutes after the attack started. And during that time . . ."

"During that time, I was being *raped!*"

"That's what the jury couldn't accept. The duration of the rape."

"That's how long it lasted."

"Mrs. Leeds, the movie broke at eleven o'clock . . ."

"I don't give a . . ."

". . . people would have been walking back to . . ."

". . . *damn* about . . ."

". . . their cars, they'd have seen . . ."

". . . the goddamn *movie!*"

They both stopped talking at the same moment. Jessica's eyes were blazing. She picked up her drink and took a long swallow. Matthew watched her.

"I'm sorry," he said.

"No, you're not," she said. "*You* don't accept the contradictions of time, either. Isn't that true?"

"I'm only trying to understand what happened."

"No, you're trying to find out who was lying, me or those men. I'm telling you I was consecutively and repeatedly raped for more than two hours, yes!" She shook her head angrily and then took another swallow of the drink. "But what difference does it make?" she said. "They were tried and acquitted, so what difference does it make if I was raped or not?"

"No one for a moment ever questioned the fact that you were raped."

"No, they only questioned whether or not those three *bastards* could have done it. Okay, they reached their verdict. Not guilty. So who cares anymore?"

"Patricia Demming does."

"Who's Pa — oh, the State Attorney."

"Yes. I feel certain she'll be calling you as a witness."

"To *what?*"

"To your own rape."

"Why?"

"Because she has to show that your husband killed those men in a blind rage. And the best way to do that is to have you describe the rape all over again."

"Can she do that?"

"Sure. To demonstrate motive. Moreover, she'll try to show that the verdict was a just one. She'll say those three innocent little boys did *not* in fact rape you, could not *possibly* have raped you at the time you say they did."

"But they did!"

"She'll say you saw them at eight o'clock, while you were parking the car . . ."

"There was no one there when I . . ."

"Exchanged a few words with them . . ."

"No, no, no . . ."

". . . and remembered them incorrectly as the men who later raped you. She'll play that rape trial for all it's worth, believe me. If she can convince the jury that those men were indeed innocent as found, then she can also convince them that your husband's crime was doubly heinous. Not only did he commit foul and bloody murder, he committed it in error. Do you understand what I'm saying?"

"Yes."

"I want you to tell me everything that happened that night."

"You read the transcript, you know what . . ."

"Can you tell me again what happened?"

"I told it all."

"Please tell it again, can you?"

She shook her head.

"Can you?"

She kept shaking her head.

"You'll have to tell it again in court, Mrs. Leeds. She'll make sure of that. I want to be ready for her."

Jessica sighed.

He waited.

She turned her head away, avoiding his eyes.

"I got out of the mall at ten o'clock," she said, "and walked over to the restaurant. It was still open at ten . . . a little after ten, actually, by the time I reached the car . . ."

She has parked it behind the restaurant, which is shaped like a pagoda, and which in fact is *named* The Pagoda. The car is an expensive one, and this is four days before Christmas. With all the traffic in the mall's lot a dented fender is a distinct possibility, and so she has chosen this deserted spot behind The Pagoda, alongside a low fence beyond which is undeveloped scrub land. As she walks toward the restaurant, the mall's parking lot is rapidly emptying of automobiles, except for those parked row after row outside the movie-theater complex at the far end. It is ten minutes past ten, she supposes, when she places in the trunk of her Maserati the several Christmas gifts she's bought.

There are lights here behind the Chinese restaurant. It is not what anyone would call *brightly* lighted, but there is illumination enough to provide a sense of security. And besides, there's a moon. Not quite full, just on the wane. Anyway, it is only a little after ten, this is not the dead of night, this is not a town where a woman alone needs to be afraid of unlocking the door of her automobile in an adequately lighted parking space behind a brilliantly lighted restaurant on a moonlit Thursday night four days before Christmas. Besides, there are three men standing behind the restaurant, smoking. All of them in shirtsleeves. Wearing long white aprons. Restaurant help. She unlocks the door of the car, closes and locks it behind her, turns on the lights, starts the engine, and is backing away from the low fence when she realizes she has a flat tire.

"That was when the nightmare began," she tells Matthew now. "I got out of the car. I was wearing . . . well, you read the

transcript, you know what I was wearing, the defense made me describe everything I . . ."

> Q: Is it true that you were wearing black bikini panties that
> night?
> A: Yes.
> Q: Lace-edged?
> A: Yes.
> Q: And a garter belt?
> A: Yes.
> Q: Was this garter belt black?

"Your Honor, I *must* object!"

Skye Bannister, on his feet. At last.

"Yes, where are you going with this, Mr. Silberkleit?"

"It will become clear, Your Honor."

"It had better. Witness may answer the question. Read it back, please."

> Q: Was this garter belt black?
> A: It was black, yes.
> Q: And were you wearing seamed nylon stockings?
> A: Yes.
> Q: Black, too, weren't they?
> A: Yes.
> Q: And a short black skirt?
> A: Yes.
> Q: A *tight* black skirt, wasn't it?
> A: Not exceptionally tight, no.
> Q: Well, it wasn't a pleated skirt, was it?
> A: No.
> Q: Or a flared skirt?
> A: No.
> Q: It was a sort of tube skirt, wouldn't you call it?
> A: I suppose so.

Q: In any event, it was short enough and tight enough to reveal . . .

A: Objection.

A: Sustained. Get to it, Mr. Silberkleit.

Q: Were you also wearing black patent-leather high-heeled pumps?

A: Yes.

Q: What color was your blouse, Mrs. Leeds?

A: White.

Q: Sleeveless, wasn't it?

A: Yes.

Q: Silk?

A: Yes.

Q: With little pearl buttons down the front, isn't that so?

A: Yes.

Q: Were you wearing a brassiere under this sleeveless silk blouse?

A: Objection, Your Honor!

A: Witness may respond.

Q: Were you wearing a brassiere, Mrs. Leeds?

A: No.

Q: Tell me, Mrs. Leeds, is this the way you normally dress when you're going out to . . .

A: Objection!

Q: . . . do your Christmas shopping?

A: Your Honor, I object!

A: You may answer the question, Mrs. Leeds.

A: That's what I was wearing, yes.

Q: Thank you, we *know* what you were wearing, don't we? But that was not my question.

A: What was your question?

Q: Is this the way you normally dress when you're going out to do your Christmas shopping?

A: It's the way I normally dress, yes.

Q: When you're going out to a mall, is that right?

A: Yes.

Q: You wear a short, tight black skirt with black seamed stockings and high-heeled patent-leather shoes . . . by the way, how high *were* the heels on those shoes?

A: I don't know.

Q: Well, I have here a list of the clothing you were wearing that night, and the shoes are described as having three-inch heels. Would you yourself describe them that way?

A: Yes.

Q: Shoes with three-inch heels.

A: Yes.

Q: For walking around a mall doing shopping.

A: I feel perfectly comfortable in high-heeled shoes.

Q: And no doubt you also feel comfortable in black, lace-edged bikini panties, and a black garter belt, and black seamed stockings . . .

A: Yes, I do.

Q: And a white silk blouse with no bra under it . . .

A: Yes!

Q: In other words, you feel comfortable in clothes that can be found in the pages of *Penthouse!*

A: No! Clothes that can be found in the pages of *Vogue!*

Q: Thank you for the distinction, Mrs. Leeds. Clothes, in any event, that any man might find provocative and seduct —

A: Objection!

A: Sustained.

Q: Mrs. Leeds, didn't you specifically go to the mall that night in search of . . . ?

A: No.

Q: Let me finish the question, please. Didn't you go there in search of adventure?

A: No!

Q: And didn't you attempt to find this adventure by blatantly flirting with three young boys . . .

A: Objection!

Q: . . . who turned down your advances . . .

A: Objection!

Q: And whom you later accused of having *raped* you!

A: Objection! Objection! Objection!

She knows how to change a flat tire, she has changed many of them in her lifetime, she is not one of these helpless little women who eat bonbons on a chaise longue while reading romance novels. She takes the jack out of the trunk, lifts out the spare, lays it flat on the ground behind the rear bumper, and then kneels beside the right rear tire to loosen the lug nuts on the wheel. She has removed one of them and placed it in the inverted hubcap, when . . .

From the very first instant, there is no mistaking the intent.

Someone seizes her from behind, yanking her over backward, away from the wheel. She drops the wrench on the ground. An arm is around her neck, choking her, stifling the scream that comes bubbling up onto her lips. Someone else twists her arm. The pain rockets clear up into her skull. There is no mistaking the intent, this is rape, she is about to be raped. She is falling backward, backward. The man behind her steps away, releases her as she falls. The back of her head hits the asphalt pavement. She almost blacks out, but danger shrills its warning to her brain, and she regains control of her senses at once.

There are three of them.

The three who were standing behind the restaurant.

One on each side of her, holding her arms. The third one behind her, crouching now, one hand over her mouth, the other twisted in her hair. She hears their voices, unintelligible, urgent, everything is happening so quickly, they are speaking

what she believes to be Chinese, and somehow — she does not know why — this knowledge triggers the vain hope that she is wrong, this is not a rape, all they want is her money.

She starts to tell them they can take anything in her handbag, but everything is happening so quickly, one of them — he has a straggly new mustache over his upper lip, he is the leader — stuffs a soiled handkerchief into her mouth and then slaps her lightly as a warning against trying to spit it out. Slaps her on the left cheek, using his right hand, he is right-handed, she must remember this, the slap stinging but not bruising . . .

> Q: Isn't it true, Mrs. Leeds, that when you were removed by ambulance from the police station to the hospital, the examining physician could find no bruises anywhere on your body?
>
> A: No, that's *not* true.
>
> Q: It's not? Well, I have here the medical report . . .
>
> A: There were bruises on my . . .
>
> Q: Yes?
>
> A: Breasts.
>
> Q: Ah?
>
> A: And thighs.
>
> Q: I see. But you didn't suffer a broken nose, for example, did you?
>
> A: No, but there was a . . .
>
> Q: Or even a bloody nose? Was your nose bleeding when you got to the police station?
>
> A: No.
>
> Q: Had any of your teeth been knocked out?
>
> A: No. But there was a bump at the back of my head, from where I hit it on the . . .
>
> Q: Were your eyes blackened?
>
> A: No.
>
> Q: Any black-and-blue marks anywhere else on your body?
>
> A: I told you. My breasts and my thighs were . . .

Q: You're not saying, are you, that those bruises on your breasts and thighs were the result of being *punched*?

A: No, but . . .

Q: Or *kicked*?

A: They didn't kick me, no.

Q: Did they, in fact, harm you physically in any way whatsoever?

A: Yes! They raped me!

Q: Mrs. Leeds, did these men, who happened to be in the kitchen at the time you say you were . . .

A: Objection!

A: Strike it.

Q: Were you beaten up by these men who allegedly raped you?

A: No, but they . . .

Q: Yes, if you can tell us what they *did* do, without repeating over and over again that they raped you, I'm sure we'd all love to hear it.

A: They held me down.

Q: I see.

A: And they put a gag in my mouth.

Q: What sort of gag?

A: A handkerchief.

Q: I see. Do you watch a lot of movies, Mrs. Leeds?

A: Objection.

A: Sustained.

Q: What else did they do to you?

A: They . . . threatened me.

Q: Oh? In what language?

A: At the time, I didn't *know* what language. I only knew . . .

Q: Oh? You mean you don't speak Vietnamese fluently?

A: I knew what they *meant*!

Q: How could you possibly have known what . . . ?

A: I *knew*.

She knows that the one with the new mustache is giving them orders, whispering urgent directions to the other two. Tear off her panties, he must be telling them, because on either side of her they grasp the legholes and rip upward toward her crotch, leaving her open to their hands. Another command and she is suddenly being lifted off the ground and onto the hood of the automobile. She tries to say something around the filthy handkerchief in her mouth, tries to say I'm a respectable married woman, please don't do this to me, please, but the leader, the one with the mustache, slaps her sharply across the cheek again, and then whispers something to the other two.

"This was Ho. The one giving the orders was Ho. I memorized his face, I could see it clearly in the moonlight, he was the leader."

They rip open her blouse, the little pearl buttons flying upward on the night, catching little glints of moonlight as they explode and fall onto the hood of the car, rattling there, rolling off. Two of them grasp her thighs and yank her legs apart. Ho, the leader, steps between her open legs, she hears the whisper of his zipper in the dark. The other two whisper encouragement. One of them laughs softly, almost a girlish giggle. The other leans into her and kisses her on the breast. Something gleams on his face, she realizes all at once that he has a glass eye, the eye is catching moonlight, reflecting it . . .

"This was Ngo. The one with the glass eye. He was the one who . . . who . . . hurt me the most. Later. When they . . . they . . ."

One after the other, they violate her.

The Maserati, her cherished luxury automobile, becomes a bed of torture for her, she will hate this car for the rest of her life. The hood is a convenient height for these men. Whichever one is between her legs forces her open as he pumps furiously into her, his fingers digging into her thighs until she screams silently in pain around the handkerchief in her mouth. The

other two hold her wrists pinned to the hood of the car on either side of her. With their free hands, they brutally knead her breasts; she will later show the emergency-room doctor the angry bruises their fingers have left, especially around the nipples. Her black panties hang in tatters, both stockings are torn now, one of them undone from its garters and falling to her knee.

When the last of them is finished with her . . .

"Dang Van Con, the youngest one. Eighteen, I learned later, when he was arrested, when they caught him and the other two. He was the one who . . . who went last when I was . . . when I was on my back and they were hold . . . they were holding my legs open. And then, when they . . . when they were finished with me that way . . . they . . . they . . ."

Ho is giving orders again.

The other two roll her over, face downward, on the hood of the car.

She screams No.

But they will not stop, they will not stop.

"For more than two hours, they . . . they did what they wanted to me," she said, her face still turned away from Matthew. "At the trial, they tried to show that I was out looking for trouble and finally found it — but not with those three. I was mistaken, the rapists were three others. Those three were in the kitchen. They couldn't have been outside raping me, I was mistaken."

She turned to him at last.

There were tears in her eyes.

"But no," she said, "I was not mistaken. They were there. And they raped me."

She had repeated those words endlessly at the trial, they raped me, they raped me, they raped me — to no avail. Those words seemed to echo accusingly on the air now, they raped me . . . they raped me . . . they raped me. The pool made a steady,

soothing trickling sound, and in the distant clouds there was the low hum of an unseen airplane. But the words hung on the air, seeming to smother all other sound, they raped me, they raped me, they raped me.

"I still have nightmares about what happened," she said. "For months afterward, I'd take two sleeping pills before I went to bed each night. But they only made me sleep, they didn't stop the nightmares."

She turned to look out over the pool again, beyond the pool, over the fields stretching to the horizon and the yellow-grey sky. Her face in profile was magnificent, the classic nose and jaw, the russet hair swept back from her burnished forehead and cheeks.

"I wonder if the nightmares will ever go away," she said. "Now that they're dead, will the nightmares go away?"

"Mrs. Leeds," Matthew said, "did you take any sleeping pills on the night of the murders?"

She turned to him.

"Did you?"

"No," she said.

"But there *are* sleeping pills in the house."

"Yes."

"Prescription pills?"

"Yes."

"Who prescribed them?"

"My doctor. Dr. Weinberger. Marvin Weinberger."

"Here in Calusa?"

"Yes."

"Is the prescription in your name?"

"Yes."

"Refillable?"

"Yes."

"When's the last time you refilled it?"

"I don't remember."

"Would you know how many pills are left in the bottle?"

"I really don't know. I haven't taken them in a while."

"Would you say it was half full? Three-quar —"

"Half, I guess."

"And you're sure you didn't take any on the night of the murders?"

"Positive."

Can you say for certain that your husband didn't get out of bed at any time that night?

Well, I . . .

Because that's what the State Attorney's going to ask you, Mrs. Leeds.

I can't say that for certain, no.

"Mrs. Leeds . . . did your husband know there were sleeping pills in the house?"

"I . . . guess so. Why?"

"He told me you'd both had an after-dinner drink before you settled down to watch the movie. Do you remember what you were drinking?"

"I had a cognac. I don't know what he had."

"And after that, you watched the movie."

"Yes."

"And he fell asleep."

"Yes."

"And you went to sleep sometime later."

"Yes."

"And slept soundly through the night."

"Yes."

I didn't hear the car starting. I would have . . .

But you were sound asleep.

Well . . . yes.

So you wouldn't have heard the car starting.

I guess not.

So you really can't say for sure that your husband was home with you all night long.

Matthew was wondering if Bloom and Rawles had seen

that half-full bottle of sleeping pills anywhere in the bedroom on the morning they'd arrested Leeds. He was wondering, too, if Patricia Demming knew that a Dr. Marvin Weinberger somewhere here in Calusa, Florida, had prescribed sleeping pills for Jessica Leeds, and that those pills were still floating around the house somewhere. He hoped she didn't know, and he hoped she never found out.

Because then she might start thinking that the reason nightmare-prone Jessica Leeds had slept the whole night through after downing an after-dinner drink was that her husband, Stephen Leeds —

But Matthew himself did not want to start thinking that way.

The body-repair shop was called Croswell Auto, and it was in one of those industrial parks that blighted the Calusa landscape east of U.S. 41. Straddling the major east-west arteries that connected the city to its suburbs, these conclaves of commerce consisted more often than not of World War II Quonset huts sitting cheek by jowl with long, low, peaked, tin-roofed buildings that gave each busy complex a further resemblance to a military staging area.

In each of these greenless "parks" — Matthew found the very label onerous — one could find little unadorned spaces specializing in picture framing, or television repair, or appliance sales, or pet boarding, or pool cleaning, or plumbing supplies, or pest control, or marine engines, or roofing and siding, or any one of a thousand little enterprises eking out small existences where the rents were low and the maintenance minimal.

The owner of Croswell Auto was a man named Larry Croswell who had come down from Pittsburgh, Pennsylvania, long before it was ranked the number-one city in America by Rand

McNally's *Places Rated Almanac*. He did not regret the move. Florida in general, and Calusa in particular, suited his lifestyle right down to the ground. Croswell was a fat man with a sun-burned bald pate, bright blue eyes, white sideburns, fringes of white hair curling around his ears, and a white beard stubble on his Pillsbury Doughboy cheeks and chin. He was wearing either a grey tanktop undershirt or else a very dirty *white* tanktop undershirt. He was also wearing blue shorts and white socks and high-topped workman's shoes, and he was holding a can of Coors beer in the stubby fingers of his right hand. He was telling Matthew and the insurance adjustor just how much it would cost to repair the Acura. The adjustor's name was Peter Kahn. He was a thin, grey-haired man who moved among the debris of wrecked autos like a wading bird who'd mistakenly landed in a metallic marsh. As Croswell spoke, Kahn jotted notes onto a pad attached to a clipboard.

"What we got here," Croswell said, "we got a whole new quarter, plus an inner . . ."

"What's a quarter?" Matthew asked.

"The quarter panel back here," Kahn explained. "Where the other car hit you." He even moved his head like a bird, Matthew noticed, bobbing whenever he spoke.

"Plus the inner panel," Croswell said, and took a sip at his beer. "Plus we got to repair the unibody where it's bent, and you're gonna need a new taillight and bumper, and a new wheel — the wheel alone's gonna cost you three hundred bucks — plus new molding. She done a nice job on you, this lady."

Matthew nodded sourly.

"So what's your estimate?" Kahn asked.

"You're lucky there wasn't no damage to the trunk," Croswell said.

"How much?" Kahn asked.

"I've got to figure three thousand, including the frame repair."

"Let's make it two thousand," Kahn said.

"There's other body shops," Croswell said.

"Don't shlep me all over town, Larry. Twenty-two five and we've got a deal."

"Twenty-five hundred sounds okay," Croswell said.

"You've got it," Kahn said.

"When will I have my car back?" Matthew asked.

"Two weeks," Croswell said.

"Why so long?"

"Lots of labor involved. Also, we're backed up."

"Who pays for the rental?" Matthew asked Kahn.

"We do. Just send us the receipts."

"Let me see if I've got all the keys I need," Croswell said, and began moving toward the office.

"There's only one key," Matthew said. "Do you pay me or him?" he asked Kahn.

"We'll pay him directly, if that's okay with you."

"Fine."

The office was the size of a walk-in bedroom closet. There was a desk behind which sat an attractive woman in her early forties, brown hair piled on top of her head, pencil stuck in it, one long earring dangling from her right ear. She was sitting behind an Apple computer. The wall behind her contained a hand-fashioned calendar with huge squares for each date. Into each square a name was lettered, followed by the name of a car in parentheses. Hanging on the wall alongside the calendar was a wooden board with cup hooks screwed into it. Car keys dangled from the hooks, each key labeled with a small white tag. Croswell went to the board, found a key tagged HOPE, nodded, and then said, "You sure this one key opens the trunk, too?"

"Positive," Matthew said.

"'Cause we may have to get in there."

"The ignition key opens the trunk and also the glove compartment."

"Okay, if you say so," Croswell said. "'Cause I hate having to call anybody about keys. I get people in here, they have two cars, they'll leave the keys to the wrong car. Or else, they'll call me to say they left the house key on the ring, they can't get in their own house, would I please stay open till they got here? You be surprised the shit I have to go through with keys. When did I say?"

"Two weeks," Kahn said.

"Mark that, willya, Marie? Hope, the Acura Legend, two weeks from today. That's when?"

Marie rose from behind the desk and behind the computer. She was a compact woman with a tight, well-formed body. Kahn's eyes went to her backside. So did Matthew's. Croswell was spoiled; he sipped at his beer. Marie ran her hand down the calendar, her finger stopping on the Monday two weeks from today. The third of September.

"You figuring on Labor Day?" she asked.

"What?" Croswell said.

"That's Labor Day, that Monday," Marie said. "September third. We'll be closed, won't we?"

"So make it the Tuesday," Croswell said.

"What time?" Matthew asked.

"End of the day," Croswell said. "Four, five o'clock?"

"Which?"

"Five'd be good," Croswell said.

"Who's driving the rental?" a voice behind them said.

Matthew turned to the door. A man in paint-spattered coveralls was standing just outside the office, one hand on the doorframe, leaning into it.

"The Ford?" Matthew asked.

"That's the one," the man said. "Could you please move it, I gotta get a car out."

"Sure," Matthew said. "Are we finished here?" he asked Kahn.

"If you'll just sign this release," Kahn said.

Matthew read the paper swiftly. It granted boilerplate approval of the repair work to be done on the car, and permission to make direct payment to Croswell Auto. The man in the coveralls waited patiently in the doorframe while Matthew signed and dated the form, shook hands with Kahn, and then told Croswell he'd see him on the fourth.

"Five o'clock," Marie said, without looking up from her keyboard.

"Five o'clock," Matthew said, and followed the man out to where he'd parked the rented car. A Mazda with a bashed-in trunk was parked behind him. Matthew got into the Ford, started it, moved it forward until he had room for a turn, and then drove out of the driveway and out of the park. As he stopped for the traffic light on U.S. 41, some seven blocks away, he realized that he'd be driving this damn car longer than he'd hoped. Nothing wrong with that, he supposed, except that it was a rental. *Who's driving the rental?* And a rental wasn't a $30,000 smoky-blue Acura Legend coupe with genuine leather seats and a sun roof and a zero-to-sixty-in-eight-seconds capability. He had planned on getting away for the Labor Day weekend, maybe drive down to Lake Okeechobee. Now he'd have to make the trip — *if* he made it — in a rented Ford. And probably alone. He did not want to go on another vacation alone. He'd been to Italy alone. Alone was lonely.

The light changed.

He made his left turn and headed home.

He was in bed when the telephone rang at eleven that night. He recognized the voice at once; the only Vietnamese woman he knew was Mai Chim Lee.

"Mr. Hope," she said, "I'm sorry to bother you so late at night . . ."

"Not at all," he said.

"Thank you," she said. "I know you are anxious, however,

to talk to Trinh Mang Duc, and . . ."

"Is he back?"

"Yes, this is why I am calling. A woman I know in the community . . ."

He realized she was referring to Little Asia.

". . . telephoned just now to say he is home from Orlando. Shall I try to arrange an interview for sometime tomorrow?"

"Please," Matthew said.

"All right, then, I will. And excuse me, again, for calling so late. I hope I didn't wake you up."

"No, no."

"Well, good then, I'll talk to you tomorrow. Good night," she said, and hung up.

6

"This was a little past midnight," Trinh Mang Duc said. "I could not sleep because I was so worried about my son in Orlando, why he had not sent for me as he'd promised."

He was speaking in the tongue of his Vietnamese village, a local dialect that had given Mai Chim difficulty at first, but which she had finally got the hang of. This was eleven o'clock on Tuesday morning and Trinh was packing all of his worldly possessions for the final move to Orlando, where his son and daughter-in-law were opening a takee-outee Vietnamese restaurant. He would not be moving till later this week, but he was taking no chances on being left behind; he would be packed and ready whenever the car was. The same nephew who had driven him up there and back would be driving him up there again.

Trinh looked like any one of the old men you saw on television while the Vietnam War was raging, squatting outside a thatched hut, pained eyes squinting into the camera, except that he wasn't wearing the typical black cotton shorts and shirt

and the conical straw hat. He was, instead, wearing a striped short-sleeved sports shirt, khaki trousers, and sandals. But he had the same narrow weather-lined face with the high cheekbones and brownish skin, the same dark eyes with the Mongolian single fold of eyelid, the same straggly white beard. Bustling about from cardboard carton to cardboard carton, putting into each his clothing and the few precious possessions he had carried halfway across the world, he talked about what had happened on the night of the murders.

Last Monday night.

The thirteenth of August.

He had not been able to sleep because his son and daughter-in-law had left for Orlando the week before, to find suitable lodgings for the entire family, and they had promised to send for him immediately, but he had not yet heard from them, and he was worried that they had abandoned him.

Trinh was sixty-eight years old.

In Vietnamese tradition, this was a time of life to be spent with one's own family; a time of peace, introspection, and preparation; a time to be passed in visiting or receiving friends; a time to choose an expert geomancer who would advise upon the exact location of one's tomb and the purchase of one's coffin.

But this was America.

And Trinh had heard that in this country, the elderly were often left to die alone, or else were transported to homes where people other than family would reluctantly tend to their needs. So who could say that his son had not wearied of supporting an old man who could contribute nothing but legendary tales to the family's wealth? Who could say that the move to Orlando was not merely a ruse to rid themselves of him? So, yes, he'd been extremely worried on that night a week ago . . .

Mai Chim said something to him in Vietnamese, apparently correcting him, because he nodded at once, and said, "Yes, eight days ago, that is so. I was worried, as I told you . . ."

. . . because it had been a while now since his son left for Orlando, and there are people here in the community who have telephones (although there is none in this house), and they are willing to take messages, so why has he not called to say they are having difficulty finding a suitable home, or else there is some problem with acquiring the restaurant, or what*ever* the circumstances may be? Why leave an old man here to worry and wonder?

He thinks he hears a scream.

He thinks it is perhaps the scream that awakens him.

But perhaps not. He has been tossing and turning ever since ten o'clock, when he went to bed. Perhaps it is only his own restlessness that at last nudges him awake to the sounds of the night. A faraway train whistle. A dog barking. A scream?

In the darkness, he looks at the luminous dial of his wristwatch, which he purchased at the U.S. Army PX in Honolulu before beginning his long journey to the mainland, a journey that has taken him to four states and seven cities, a journey that may yet end in prosperity in Orlando, Florida, the second home of Mickey Mouse.

His watch reads ten minutes past midnight.

The night is sticky and hot.

His sheets are soggy with the moisture of the night and the dampness of his own anxiety. He throws back the top one and then swings his thin legs over the side of the narrow bed, goes to the door of the house, peers out through the screen door, and sees . . .

A man.

Running.

"Through the screen?" Matthew asked. "Did he see this man through the screen?"

Mai Chim asked the question in Vietnamese. Trinh answered.

"Yes," Mai Chim said. "Through the screen."

Then it's possible his view was distorted, Matthew thought.

"I could see him sharply in the moonlight," Mai Chim said, translating as Trinh spoke again. "He was wearing . . ."

. . . a yellow cap and a yellow jacket.

A tall, broad man.

Running toward the curb.

There was an automobile parked at the curb. The man ran around to the driver's side of the car, opened the door . . .

"Did he see the man's face?" Matthew asked.

Mai Chim translated this, and then listened to Trinh again.

"Yes," she said. "A white man."

"Was it Stephen Leeds?"

She translated this into Vietnamese, listened to Trinh's answer, and fed it back to Matthew in English.

"Yes, it was Stephen Leeds."

"How does he know that?"

Again she translated, and again she listened.

"He identified Leeds in a lineup."

And now the dialogue seemed to flow back and forth between her and Matthew, the necessary translations forming only a singsong counterpoint to the main theme — which happened to be this matter of positive identification.

"How many men in the lineup?"

"Seven altogether."

"All of them white?"

"Three white, three black, one Asian."

Loaded, Matthew thought. Only two other whites besides Leeds.

"They didn't have him wearing that yellow jacket and hat, did they?"

"No. All of the men were wearing jailhouse clothing."

Then the lineup had to have taken place between Leeds's arrest on Tuesday, August fourteenth, and Trinh's departure for Orlando on Thursday, the sixteenth. Matthew himself had read about the witnesses in Friday morning's *Herald-Tribune*.

"When did this lineup take place?" he asked.

"The day before I left for Orlando. A Wednesday."

"The fifteenth."

"Yes, I think that was the date."

"Prior to that time, had you seen any pictures of Leeds in the newspaper? Or on television?"

"No."

"Do you *watch* television?"

"Yes. But I did not see any pictures of the white man who killed my countrymen."

"How do you know Leeds killed them?"

"It is said he killed them."

"Said by whom?"

"Said in the community."

"Said in the community that a white man named Stephen Leeds killed your countrymen?"

"Yes."

"But is it said in the community that the white man you identified is the one who killed your countrymen?"

"Yes, this is also said."

"Was this said *before* you made identification?"

"I do not understand the meaning of your question."

"I'm asking if prior to the lineup you discussed Stephen Leeds with anyone who may have seen pictures of him in the newspaper or on television?"

"I discussed the murders, yes."

"With anyone who'd seen a picture of Leeds?"

"Possibly."

"And was he *described* to you? Did anyone tell you what he looked like?"

"No, I don't think so."

"Do you know a man named Tran Sum Linh?"

"I do."

"Prior to the lineup, had you discussed the murders with Tran Sum Linh?"

"I may have."

"Did he tell you he'd seen a man wearing a yellow hat and jacket entering the house where the three murder victims lived?"

"No, he did not."

"Before the lineup, then, no one had described Stephen Leeds to you, from pictures they'd seen in the paper or on television . . ."

"No one."

"And Tran Sum Linh did not mention that he'd seen a man in a yellow hat and jacket earlier that night?"

"He did not."

"So the first time you saw this man was at ten minutes past twelve . . ."

"Yes."

"On the night of August thir — well, actually the morning of August fourteenth, is that right?"

"Yes."

"Running to the curb, where an automobile was parked."

"Yes."

"Running from *where*?"

"From the house where my three countrymen lived. My countrymen who were murdered."

"You actually saw this man coming *out* of their house?"

"No. But he was coming from the *direction* of their house."

"I see. And running to this automobile."

"Yes."

"What kind of automobile?"

"I am not familiar with American cars."

"Are you familiar with Italian cars?"

"No. Not those, either."

"What color was this car?"

"Dark blue. Or green. It was difficult to tell in the dark."

"But there was a moon."

"Yes, but the car was parked under a tree."

"So it was either a dark blue car or a green car."

"Yes."

"Not a red car."

"It was not a red car."

"Was it a sports car?"

"I do not know what a sports car is."

Mai Chim translated this to Matthew and then went into a lengthy dissertation in Vietnamese, presumably explaining what a sports car was. Trinh listened intently, nodding in understanding, and finally said, "No, this was not a sports car. It was just an ordinary car."

"Two-door or four?"

"I did not notice."

"But you *did* notice Stephen Leeds's face."

"Yes. I am better with faces than with cars."

"What else did you notice?" Matthew asked.

Trinh answered the question in Vietnamese.

Mai Chim nodded. Her face was noncommittal.

"What?" Matthew said.

"He noticed the license-plate number," she said.

They were lunching at Kickers. Sitting on the deck outdoors, under one of the big green umbrellas. Patricia Demming and her investigator, Frank Bannion. Bannion was thinking they made a nice couple. He was wondering if she had a boyfriend or anything. He was feeling very attractive after last night. Last night, he had taken Sherry Reynolds to bed. He always felt attractive after he'd scored. Made him feel he was devastating. Especially if the woman was on the youngish side.

Sherry had told him in strictest confidence that she had just celebrated her thirtieth birthday two weeks ago. This was while she was blowing him. In order to prove that older women knew how to do certain things better than teenage girls. To Bannion, thirty was young. He told her so. He also told her that

he was forty-two years old and still had his own hair and teeth. She seemed to find this quite impressive.

Today was Sherry's day off.

She had told him last night that she had all day off tomorrow and they could do whatever they wanted all night long or even all day tomorrow since she didn't have to be back at work till ten-thirty Wednesday morning. Bannion told her he had to be back at work at nine tomorrow, but they'd give it their best shot anyway. It was now twelve-thirty tomorrow, actually today already, actually Tuesday already, and here he was at a table overlooking the water, sitting with a very good-looking blonde who happened to be his boss, but about whom he was nonetheless entertaining libidinous thoughts. The weather down here did that to you. Down here in this sticky heat, it was very easy to get horny and to feel devastating.

"This is where the boat pulled in," he said.

"What time?" she asked.

"About a quarter to eleven."

"Which would've been about right, wouldn't it?" Patricia said.

"Coming out of Willowbee at ten-thirty, sure, Leeds could've made it here easy in fifteen minutes."

"Did she actually see it coming down the channel?"

"Yep. And she knows the water. She didn't see it coming off marker 72, that's too far north. But she picked it up on its approach to the dock here."

"Saw it from where?"

"The bar there. Clear shot of the channel."

Patricia looked.

"Okay," she said. "Did she describe the boat?"

"Down to the cleats."

"Saw the name on the transom?"

"No. He pulled in bow first."

"Which slip?"

"Second from the end. On your right."

Patricia looked again.

"Still a clear shot from the bar," Bannion said. "And even though she didn't see the name . . ."

"*Felicity,*" Patricia said, and shook her head.

"Sucks, don't it?" Bannion said, taking a chance. Nothing crossed her face. He considered that a good sign. "But even if she couldn't see it 'cause the transom was away from her, she knows boats, all kinds of boats, and she can describe this one in court. Better yet, she can describe *him.*"

"Leeds?"

"Maybe, I don't know, we'll have to run a lineup for her. But certainly a guy in a yellow jacket and hat."

"Driving the boat?"

"Driving it, tying it up, going up the steps on the side of the dock there, and walking straight into the parking lot."

"This was at what time?"

"Let's say ten to eleven."

"That checks out. When did she lose him?"

"When he got in the car and drove off."

"What kind of car?" Patricia asked, leaning forward intently.

"A green Oldsmobile Cutlass Supreme."

"And the license plate?"

"She couldn't see it from the bar."

"Shit," Patricia said.

Which Bannion found not only exciting but also terribly promising.

"Shall we order?" he asked, and smiled his most devastating smile.

"There's yet another way to look at this," Mai Chim said.

She and Matthew were sitting in a restaurant some seven miles from Kickers, where Bannion had just identified the make

of the automobile Trinh Mang Duc had been able to describe only as an ordinary dark blue or green car. But Trinh had seen the license plate. A Florida plate, he'd said. Very definitely a Florida plate. And Matthew had written down the number on that plate. 2AB 39C. Find the car, he was thinking, and we've got the man in the yellow jacket and hat.

"Another way of looking at what?" he asked.

He'd been surprised and pleased when she'd accepted his lunch invitation, and he was satisfied now to see her enjoying the meal so much. He'd frankly wondered whether Italian cooking would appeal to a woman who'd spent the first fifteen years of her life in Saigon. But she ate as if famished, first demolishing the linguine al pesto, and now working actively — and with seemingly dedicated intensity — on the veal piccata.

"The murder," she said. "The rape. Whether or not they're linked."

"Do you think they're linked?"

"Not necessarily. I think those men raped her, yes, but that doesn't mean . . ."

"You do?"

"Oh, yes. Mind you, the Vietnamese immigrants in this city would prefer having it the other way round. They were very pleased when the verdict came in. Not guilty was what they'd been praying for. There is not a single Buddhist temple in all of Calusa, did you know that? It makes it difficult for many Asians coming here."

"Are you Buddhist?" Matthew asked.

"Catholic," she said, shaking her head. "But many of my friends were Buddhist when I was growing up. What are you?"

"Nothing right now."

"What were you?"

"Whitebread Episcopalian."

"Is that good?"

"I guess if you're going to be anything in America, it's best to be a Wasp, yes."

"What's that?"

"Wasp? White Anglo-Saxon Protestant."

"Is Episco — could you say it again for me, please?"

"Episcopalian."

"Episcopalian, yes," she said, and then tried it again, rolling the word on her Asian tongue. "Episcopalian. Is that a form of Protestant?"

"Yes," Matthew said.

"And is Whitebread a form of Episcopalian?"

"No, no," he said, smiling, "Whitebread is . . . well . . . Wasp," he said, and shrugged. "They're synonymous."

"Ah," she said.

"Yes," he said.

"Then Whitebread Episcopalian is redundant," she said.

"Well, yes."

"I like that word. It's one of my favorite English words. Redundant. How old are you?" she asked abruptly.

"Thirty-eight," he said.

"Are you married?"

"No. Divorced."

"Do you have any children?"

"One. A daughter. She's up in Cape Cod this summer. With her mother."

"What's her name?"

"Joanna."

"How old is she?"

"Fourteen."

"Then you were married very young."

"Yes."

"And is she quite beautiful?"

"Yes. But all fathers think their daughters are quite beautiful."

"I'm not sure my father felt that way about me."

"He got you on that helicopter."

"Yes, he did," she said.

"And you are," Matthew said. "Quite beautiful."

"Thank you," she said, and fell silent.

He wondered if she knew this. How very beautiful she was. Or had she lost all sense of self during those war-torn years in Vietnam? Or in all those years of constant move and change since her father had lifted her into the arms of that black Marine sergeant? Was there in Mary Lee the bookkeeper any semblance of the little Vietnamese girl Le Mai Chim once had been? He wondered.

"Who do you think killed them?" she asked, shifting ground quite suddenly, as if wanting to distance herself from whatever thoughts their immediate conversation had provoked. Her eyes shifted, too. Away from his. Avoiding contact. He felt awkward all at once. Had she mistaken his sincere compliment for a clumsy pass? He hoped not.

"It's not my job to find a killer," he said. "I only have to show that my man didn't do it."

"And do you believe he didn't do it?"

Matthew hesitated for only an instant.

"Yes, I do," he said, but at the same moment Mai Chim said, "You don't, do you?" so that their words overlapped.

"Let's say I'm still looking for evidence," he said. "To support my belief."

"Will the license plate help?"

"Maybe."

"Provided Trinh was seeing correctly."

"I have no reason to believe he wasn't. Unless . . . are your numbers the same as ours?"

"Oh, yes, our numbers are Arabic. And for the most part, our alphabet is the same, too. Give or take some missing letters and a million diacritical marks."

"What's a diacritical mark?" Matthew asked.

She looked at him.

"I don't know what it is," he said.

"You could have bluffed, you know," she said, and smiled.

"Sure. But then I'd *never* know. What is it?"

"It's a tiny little mark that's added to a letter to give it a different phonetic value."

"Ah-ha."

"Do you understand?"

"Yes. Like the cedilla in French or the umlaut in German."

"I don't know what those are."

"You could have bluffed, you know," he said.

"Yes, but what are they?"

"Diacritical marks," Matthew said.

"Okay."

"I think," he said, and smiled.

He liked the way she said *okay*. She made it sound foreign somehow. Okay. This most American of words.

"The Vietnamese language is very difficult for a foreigner to learn," she said. "This was one trouble when the American soldiers were there. It is not a language you can easily pick up. And where there is no common language, there is suspicion. And mistakes. Many mistakes. On both sides."

She shook her head.

"This is why the Vietnamese here were so happy with the verdict. If these men were not guilty, then there would be less suspicion of the foreigners, less abuse."

"Is there? Abuse?"

"Oh yes. Sure."

"Of what sort?"

"Everyone in America forgets that everyone here once came from someplace else. Except the Indians. Maybe they were here to begin with. The rest came from all over the world. But they forget this. So if ever an argument starts between an American and someone who is new here, the first thing the American says is, 'Go back where you came from.' Isn't this so?"

"Yes," Matthew said.

Go back where you came from.

He wished he had a nickel for every time he'd heard those words tumbling from the lips of a so-called native American.

Go back where you came from.

"Which is what I meant earlier," Mai Chim said.

"About what?"

"About another way of looking at this," she said.

"And what's that?"

"That the rape and the murder are totally unrelated."

"That's what our approach has been, actually."

"Then you believe as I do," she said. "That someone was telling the Vietnamese in Calusa to go back where they came from."

He looked at her.

"This *is* the South, you know," she said.

He kept looking at her.

"Where I understand crosses are sometimes burned on lawns."

It took the jailer ten minutes to get Stephen Leeds to the telephone. When finally he picked up the receiver, he sounded cranky and irritable.

"I was napping," he said.

Matthew looked at his watch. Three-twenty. He had left Mai Chim at two-thirty, and then had driven home to pick up his Sony tape recorder. It was sitting on his desk now.

"I'm sorry I woke you," he said, "but there are a few more questions I'd like to ask."

"Have you been reading the papers?" Leeds said. "They've already tried and convicted me."

"That may work in our favor," Matthew said.

"I don't see how."

"Change of venue," he said.

"Meanwhile, everyone in this town thinks I'm a murderer."

"That's exactly what I mean. How can you pick a jury when everyone's already made up his mind?"

"Yeah, well," Leeds said dubiously.

"Mr. Leeds, I want to check some things you told me. If I remember correctly, your own car is a Cadillac, is that right?"

"That's right. A Cadillac Seville."

"What color is it?"

"It's got a black top and silver sides."

"Could the color be mistaken for a dark blue? Or a green?"

"I don't see how."

"At night, I mean."

"Even so. The silver is . . . well, it's silver, it's metallic. Dark blue or green? No. Definitely not."

"What's the license-plate number, do you know?"

"I'm not sure. W something. WR . . . I don't remember. I always have to look at this little tag I have on my key ring."

"Would the number be 2AB 39C?"

"No. Definitely not. It starts with a W, I'm sure of that. And I think the second letter is R. WR something."

"Not 2AB . . ."

"No."

". . . 39C?"

"No. Why?"

"One of the witnesses says he saw you getting into a car with that license plate."

"When? Where?"

"Outside Little Asia. At a little past midnight on the night of the murders."

"Good," Leeds said.

"I gather it wasn't you."

"Damn right, it wasn't. Do you know what this means?"

"Yes, of course," Matthew said.

"If we can track down that car, we've got whoever killed them! Jesus, this is the first good news we've *had* on this case! I

can't wait to tell Jessie. The minute you hang up, I'm going to call her."

"I'll let you know what we come up with. Meanwhile, I want you to repeat something after me."

"Huh?" Leeds said.

"First listen to all of it, and then repeat it when I give you the signal, okay?"

"Sure," Leeds said, but he sounded puzzled.

"Hello," Matthew said, "this is Stephen Leeds. I'll be . . ."

In Calusa, Florida, you paid for your license plate in the Tax Collector's office, either by mail or in person. And, similarly, you either picked up the plate or else it was mailed to you. The Tax Collector's office was on the second floor of the new courthouse building, adjacent to the Public Safety Building and the city jail. At four o'clock that Tuesday afternoon, Warren Chambers was telling Fiona Gill — whose official title was Supervisor of Motor Vehicle Taxation — that his boss was looking for an owner identification on a license-plate number in his possession.

"Who are you working for these days?" Fiona asked.

She was an extremely good-looking black woman, her eyes the color of anthracite, her skin the color of mocha, her lips painted with a ruby-red gloss that caused them to shine wetly and invitingly here in the dim drabness of this unusually grim government office. She was wearing a bright yellow dress that Warren guessed was linen, buttoned up the front to the third button down, gold loop earrings, a gold chain hanging around her neck, the letter *F* nestling in the clefted shadow of her breasts, partially revealed in the open V of the dress. Warren thought she was an altogether fine piece of work. He wondered if she thought he was too young for her. Many women her age

— he guessed she was forty-two or thereabouts — found men his age immature.

"Summerville and Hope," he said. "Do you know them?"

"No," she said. "Should I?"

"Not unless you've been in trouble lately," he said, and smiled.

Fiona took this as innuendo, which it was.

She had worked with Warren Chambers before and had found him lacking in only one quality: age. Fiona was forty-six years old, and she guessed that Warren was in his mid-to-late thirties. But other than his callow youthfulness, she could find no fault with him. Except perhaps his new haircut, which made him look even younger than she suspected he was. But now — innuendo. Well, well, well.

"Not the kind of trouble requiring a lawyer," she said. "Or a real estate agent, if that's what they are."

"No, you were right the first time."

"Last time I needed a lawyer was when I got my divorce," Fiona said.

Warren considered this unsolicited and welcome information.

"How long ago was that?" he asked.

"Fourteen years," she said.

"And now you're happily married again," he said.

Which Fiona considered a fishing expedition.

Which it was.

"Nope," she said. "I'm happily playing the field. Though, to tell you the truth, Warren . . ."

This was the first time she'd ever used his given name.

". . . all the available men in Calusa are either married or gay."

"Not me," Warren said.

Fiona arched an eyebrow.

"Good-looking fella like you must be involved, though,"

she said, and decided to lay her cards on the table. "With a woman more your own age."

"I'll tell you the truth, Fiona," he said, using *her* given name for the first time. "I find most women my age a bit adolescent."

"You do, huh?"

Eyes meeting.

"I prefer more mature women," he said.

"Indeed," she said.

"Indeed," he said.

Both of them nodding. Slow nods in the afternoon stillness. Somewhere in the dim recesses of the room, a typewriter began clacking. And then fell abruptly silent again. Warren was wondering whether he'd get shot down if he asked her out to dinner. She was wondering whether she should suggest discussing his age preferences over a drink later this afternoon. Neither said a word. The opportunity hung there expectantly, hovering on the air like a Spielberg spaceship, all shining with promise. And then, unassailed, it drifted off into a galaxy of glittering dust motes, and the distant typewriter began clacking again, shattering the stillness, destroying the moment. It was Fiona who, embarrassed, broke eye contact.

"So what kind of license plate has your boss come up with?" she said.

Warren dug into his pocket and fished out his notebook. He leafed through it until he came to the page upon which he'd scribbled the number Matthew had given him on the phone.

"Here you go," he said, and handed it across the counter to her. Fiona looked at it.

"No such animal," she said.

"What do you mean?"

"We don't have plates beginning with a number. Not here in Florida."

"This is what the man saw," Warren said.

"Then the man saw wrong. Here in Florida, we use three letters, two numbers, and then a single letter. The computer chooses the letters and numbers at random, automatically eliminating any already-designated sequence. You can have, oh, CDB 34L, or DGP 47N, or AFR 68M, or whatever. But what you *can't* have is the sequence here on this paper."

"You're sure about that, huh?" Warren said.

"Am I sure that my unlisted phone number is 381-3645?" she asked, and arched her eyebrow again.

7

The police gym was the size of a good college gym, well equipped, air conditioned, and relatively empty at five o'clock that Tuesday afternoon. Save for Matthew and Bloom, there were only two other people in the vast, echoing room: a runner tirelessly circling the overhead track and a bare-chested man in blue trunks, pumping iron. Late-afternoon sunlight streamed through the long, high windows. It had not yet rained today. It had not rained at all yesterday. Everybody in Calusa was saying that the Russians were monkeying with the weather. This in spite of *glasnost*. Some ideas were slow to take hold in the state of Florida.

Bloom was wearing grey sweatpants and sweatshirt, the Calusa P.D. seal in blue on the front of it. Matthew was wearing black warmup pants and a white T-shirt. Both men were wearing sneakers. Bloom had an inch or so on Matthew, in height and in reach, and some forty pounds in weight. But he was here to teach him tricks that automatically rendered physical superiority meaningless.

"You put on some weight," he said.

"Ten pounds," Matthew said.

"That's a lot. You got a little paunch, Matthew."

"I know."

"You ought to come here every afternoon, run the track."

"I should."

"Those two cowboys catch you with a paunch, they'll roll you down 41 all the way to Fort Meyers."

He was referring to Matthew's private spectres, two Ananburg cowboys who'd once made chopped liver of him in a Calusa bar, and whom he'd later caught up with and all but crippled. His nightmare was that they would find him again one day and next time he wouldn't be quite so lucky. Bloom kept telling him it wasn't a matter of luck, it was skill. Knowing how to break the other guy's head before he broke yours. Bloom said that learning to maim somebody was merely a matter of how much fear you had inside you. If you didn't care whether two cowboys beat the shit out of you and maybe buggered you, then forget learning how to fight dirty. For Matthew, the personification of fear was Two Cowboys. This was fear incarnate. Beat the Two Cowboys, and you vanquished fear. But to beat them, you had to know how to gouge out an eye or crack a man's spine.

"You want to dance around a little before we start?" Bloom asked.

The men moved onto the mat. Bloom was very fast for a man his size. Matthew, with his paunch — well, it wasn't *quite* a paunch — was slower, and therefore more susceptible to the open-handed slaps Bloom kept landing. Puffing, out of breath, he danced around Bloom, caught him with a good left-handed slap to the jaw —

"Good," Bloom said.

— and then followed up with a right-handed slap to Bloom's biceps, which, had it been a punch, would have hurt him badly.

"So we're on opposite sides again, huh?" Bloom said, mov-

ing away, feinting, and then slapping a fast one-two to Matthew's face. The slaps stung. Matthew backed off, circling, circling.

"You took the Leeds case, huh?"

"I took it."

"You're getting a reputation," Bloom said.

"For what?"

"Defending sure things."

Bloom was smiling. This was a joke. The last three had been anything but sure things.

"We make these wonderful arrests we think'll stick," Bloom said, "and then you come along and knock us on our asses. Tell me, Matthew, why don't you make my life simple?"

"How?"

"Run for State Attorney. Then we can work these cases together."

"Oh?" Matthew said. "Is Skye quitting?"

Across the gym, the weight lifter had begun working out on the punching bag. A steady rhythmic background patter now accompanied their dance over the mat, both men moving around each other, constantly jabbing, slapping, moving in again, backing away, circling, great blots of sweat staining their shirts, rivulets of sweat running down their faces.

"Skye's looking northward to Tallahassee," Bloom said.

"What's this big one he's sitting on, Morrie?"

"What big one?" Bloom asked innocently.

"I hear something's in the wind."

"Who told you that?"

"A little yellow bird."

"Me, I'm deaf, dumb, and blind," Bloom said.

"Supposed to break in the paper. I'm still waiting."

"Maybe we're still waiting, too."

"For what?"

"Ask your little yellow bird. You had enough of this?"

"Sure," Matthew said.

They walked over to where they'd put their bags against the wall, took out towels, wiped their faces and necks. Both men were breathing hard.

"Can I ask you some questions?" Matthew said.

"Not about that."

"No, about the Leeds arrest."

"Sure."

"Tell me what happened that morning."

"Nothing. We went there with a wallet we found at the scene. Unmistakably Leeds's. He was in his pajamas when we talked to him. He identified the wallet as belonging to him, and we asked him to come along. Interviewed him in the captain's office, pulled Skye in when we figured we had real meat."

"When was that?"

"You mean when we knew we had him?"

"Yes."

"When we got the call from Tran Sum Linh."

"Saying?"

"Saying he'd seen the man who'd murdered his friends."

"And?"

"We ran a lineup for him. He identified Leeds as the man he saw going into the house that night."

"When did you get your other witness?"

"The next day. After Leeds was already charged."

"Wednesday."

"Whenever."

"The fifteenth."

"I'm winging this, but the dates and times are pretty much okay," Bloom said. "911 clocked the call in at six-fifty on the morning of the fourteenth, a Tuesday. From this guy whatever his name was, these fucking Vietnamese names drive me crazy, he'd gone over there to pick up his pals and drive them to work, found all three of them dead. They were working two jobs, the victims. A factory during the day, the restaurant at night. I guess you know that. Anyway, the dispatcher sent Charlie car

over, which radioed back with a confirmed triple homicide. The captain called me at home, and I met Rawles over there, it must've been eight, a little after. The minute we found the wallet, we drove out to the Leeds farm. I didn't know farmers were so rich, did you?"

"Some of them."

"Mmm," Bloom said, and picked up the life vest he'd carried into the gym with him. Orange, with orange ties, stamped across the back with the words PROPERTY OF U.S. COAST GUARD. "Anyway, Tran identified him that same afternoon, and we zeroed in on the second witness the next day. So you're right, it was Wednesday the fifteenth. You know why I'm putting on this life jacket?"

"Because the gym is about to sink," Matthew said.

"That's very funny," Bloom said, but he didn't laugh. "I'm putting this on because it's padded around the shoulders and neck, and that's where you're going to hit me a lot."

"Tell me something, Morrie. When you went out to the farm, did you see any signs of forced entry?"

"We weren't looking for a burglar, Matthew."

"But did you see any marks around any of the doors or windows?"

"I told you. We weren't looking for any."

"I'm going to send somebody out there to do a check."

"Sure. Just let Pat know if you find anything."

"Better not call her Pat, Morrie."

"But I'll tell you, Matthew, you'll be wasting your time. Look, I know just where you're heading, you think somebody may have broken in there and stolen that jacket and hat, don't you? And then returned them to the closet, right? But did somebody *also* steal Mrs. Leeds's car keys? And then return *them* to her handbag in the upstairs closet? Or the duplicate set of keys Leeds was using, which were then returned to the top of the bedroom dresser? Because as I'm sure you already know . . ."

"Yes, Charlie Stubbs saw . . ."

"Yes, he saw Leeds drive up in the Maserati at around ten-thirty that night."

"*If* it was Leeds."

"Then who was it if *not* Leeds?"

"It was a man in a yellow hat and a yellow jacket."

"Which Leeds just happens to own."

"The hat was a giveaway item, and the jacket came from Sears. There could be a hundred people in this town with that same damn jacket and hat."

"And are there a hundred people in this town who *also* have keys to the Maserati this person in the yellow jacket and hat was driving?"

"Well, I admit . . ."

"*And* keys to the boat?"

Matthew sighed.

"Yes," Bloom said. "Matthew, I know I was wrong the last time around. But this time, there's too damn much. Cop a plea, Matthew. Demming's new and eager, she'll make it easy for you. Do me that favor, will you? Save yourself a lot of embarrassment. Please?"

Matthew said nothing.

"Come on," Bloom said. "I'll teach you how to paralyze me."

There were two messages on Matthew's answering machine when he got home that night. The first was from Warren Chambers, telling him what he'd learned about the number on the license plate.

"Shit," Matthew said.

The second was from Jessica Leeds, asking him to call back as soon as he could. Standing in his workout clothes, wanting nothing more than a shower, he opened his directory to the *L*'s, found the number at the farm, and dialed it. Jessica picked up on the third ring.

"Mrs. Leeds," he said, "Matthew Hope."

"Oh, hello, I'm so glad you got back to me," she said. "Stephen phoned me this afternoon, right after you left him. He was *so* excited."

The goddamn license plate, he thought.

"Well," he said, "it turns out we were a bit premature."

"What do you mean?"

"There's no such number in the state of Florida."

"Oh *no*," she said.

"I'm sorry."

"This is *so* disappointing."

"I know."

"Could it possibly have been an out-of-state plate?"

"Trinh is sure it was a Florida plate."

"This'll *kill* Stephen, it'll positively *kill* him."

"Did he tell you what the number was?"

"Yes, he did."

"Does it mean anything to you?"

"Mean anything?"

"You wouldn't have seen a car with that plate driving past the farm . . . or cruising the neighborhood . . . anything like that? Looking over the place?"

"Oh. No, I'm sorry."

"Because if someone *did* break in there . . ."

"Yes, I know exactly what you mean. But we're so isolated here . . . I think I would've noticed something like that. A car driving by slowly . . ."

"Yes."

". . . or making a turn in the driveway . . ."

"Yes."

"But no, there was nothing."

"Incidentally," Matthew said, "I'll be sending someone there to check your windows and doors. His name's Warren Chambers, I'll ask him to call you first."

"My windows and *doors*?"

"For signs of forced entry."

"Oh, *yes,* what a good idea."

"He'll call you."

"Please."

She was silent for a moment.

Then she said, "I don't know how to tell this to Stephen."

Neither did Matthew.

"I'll do it," he said. "Please don't worry about it."

Warren's photographic memory had served him well for the better part of his life. In high school — and later during his short stint in college — while students everywhere around him were scribbling crib notes on their shirt cuffs or the palms of their hands, he was memorizing pages and pages of material that he could later call up in an instant. In its entirety. A photograph of the page suddenly popping into his mind's eye. Exactly as it had appeared when he'd read it. Phenomenal. The trick worked beautifully for faces as well. When he was on the St. Louis police force, he'd look at a mug shot once and only once, and there it was in his head, recorded forever. See that same cheap thief on the street two years later, he'd follow him for blocks, trying to figure out what no-good mischief he was up to now.

If Warren had seen that license plate on the night of the murders, you could damn well bet he wouldn't have remembered it wrong. It would have registered on the camera of his eye, *click,* and it would have been etched on his mind forever, in living color, orange and white for the colors of the state's plates.

Mr. Memory, that was Warren Chambers.

Except for tonight.

Tonight, he could not for the life of him remember Fiona Gill's unlisted telephone number.

Am I sure that my unlisted phone number is 381-2645?

Was what the lady had said.

Wasn't it?

But when he dialed 381-2645, he got a man who sounded like a caged beast, spitting and snarling because Warren had woken him up in the middle of the night. Except that it was only eight-thirty. So he'd dialed the number a second time, certain that his renowned memory could not be at fault, thinking he'd merely made an error punching out the numbers, and lo and behold, the same roaring monster telling him to quit calling this number or —

Warren hung up fast.

He knew he wasn't wrong about the 381 because that was one of Calusa's seven prefixes and none of the others — 349, 342, 363, and so on — came even close. So 381 it had to be. So how had he goofed on the last four numbers? Had he remembered them in improper sequence? If so, how many possible combinations of the numbers 2, 6, 4, and 5 could there be?

Calling up a page from a long-ago college textbook chapter on permutations and combinations, he conjured the formula $4 \times 3 \times 2 \times 1 = X$, and came up with $4 \times 3 = 12 \times 2 = 24 \times 1 = 24$, and calculated that there were twenty-four possible ways of arranging the numbers 2, 6, 4, and 5. He had already dialed 2645 — twice, no less — so that left twenty-three possibilities.

He started with 2654, and went from there to 2564 and 2546, and next to 2465 and 2456.

No Fiona Gill.

So he moved on to the next sequence of six, this time starting with the number 6 itself, and dialing first 6245 and then 6254, and on and on and on until he ended the sequence with 6542, and still no Fiona Gill.

It was now almost nine o'clock.

He figured it was taking him about thirty seconds to punch out each telephone number, let the phone ring three, four, however many times, discover there was no one named Fiona

Gill at that number, thank the party, and then hang up. Six different phone numbers in each sequence. A hundred and eighty seconds altogether. Three minutes, give or take, depending on the length of each conversation. It was five after nine when he finished the sequence beginning with the number 5. Still no Fiona. He went on to the last sequence.

381-4265.

Brrr, brrr, brrr . . .

"Hello?"

"May I speak to Fiona Gill, please?"

"Who?"

"Fiona Gill."

"Nobody here by that name."

And then 381-4256 . . .

And 381-4625 . . .

And down the line till he came to the last possible combination, 381-4562, the phone ringing, ringing, ringing . . .

"Hello?"

A black woman.

"Fiona?"

"Who?"

"I'm trying to reach Fiona Gill."

"Man, you got the wrong number."

And *click*.

He sat there despondently, his pride in his fabled memory considerably shaken. Now listen, he thought, there has got to be some mistake here. Maybe she *gave* me the wrong number. Maybe she was so excited, she forgot her own telephone number, that is a distinct possibility. So how can I get the *right* number if it's an unlisted one? He picked up the receiver again, punched the O for Operator, let the phone ring once, twice . . .

"Operator."

"Detective Warren Chambers," he said, "St. Louis Police Department."

"Yes, Mr. Chambers."

"We're trying to locate the sister of a homicide victim here . . ."

"Oh, my, a homicide," the operator said.

"Yes, her name is Fiona Gill, her number seems . . ."

"The victim."

"No, the sister. She lives down there in Calusa. I was wondering . . ."

"How's the weather up there?"

"Terrific. Lovely. Lovely summer weather. Fiona Gill, that's G-I-L-L. I don't have an address."

"Just one moment, sir," the operator said. She was off the line for what seemed ten seconds. When she came back, she said, "I'm sorry, sir, that's an unpublished number."

"Yes, I know that."

"We're not per —"

"This is a homicide here," Warren said.

Which always worked.

"I'm sorry, sir, it's our policy not to give out unpublished numbers."

"Yes, I realize that. May I speak to your Service Assistant, please?"

"Yes, sir, one moment, please."

Warren waited.

"Miss Camden," a woman said.

"Detective Warren Chambers," he said. "We're working a homicide here in St. Louis, and I need to get in touch with a woman named Fiona Gill in your city. Can you please ask your Floor Manager to . . . ?"

"Working a homicide *where?*" Miss Camden said.

"St. Louis," Warren said.

"You've got to be kidding," she said, and hung up.

Warren looked at the mouthpiece.

Okay, so sometimes it *didn't* work.

He put the phone back on its cradle, thought for a moment, and then opened his personal directory. On the last case

he'd worked for Matthew, he'd hired two rednecks from the Calusa P.D. to do some moonlight housesitting. One of them had got himself killed on the job, but the other one was still alive, and he and Warren still shared a sort of tentative relationship, the only kind a redneck could offer a black man in this town. He looked up Nick Alston's home number, glanced at his watch — twenty past nine — and dialed.

"Hello?" a voice said.

"Nick?"

"Yeah?"

"Warren Chambers."

"How you doin', Chambers?"

Just overjoyed to be hearing from him again.

"I need a favor," Warren said.

"Yeah?"

Still wildly enthusiastic.

"A phone number," Warren said. "This case I'm working."

"Where?"

"Here. Calusa."

"The number, I mean."

"That's what I'm talking about, the number. It's unlisted."

"No shit? When do you need it?"

"Now."

"I ain't at work."

"Can't you get somebody up there to call it in for me?"

"Maybe. Where are you?"

"Home."

"Where's that? Newtown?"

Naming the colored section of Calusa.

"No, here on Hibiscus."

"Give me the number there," Alston said.

Warren gave him the number.

"What's this person's name?"

"Fiona Gill," Warren said.

"She's in the Tax Collector's office, ain't she?" Alston said.

"That's right."

"Motor Vehicles, right?"

"Right. I'm trying to get a line on a license plate."

"So you have to call her at home, right?"

"Right," Warren said.

"Yeah, right, shit," Alston said. "I'll get back to you."

He got back some ten minutes later.

"The lady's number is 381-3645," he said.

"Ahhhh," Warren said.

"Yeah, ahhhh," Alston said. "Ahhh *what?*"

"A three. Instead of a two."

"Which is supposed to make sense, huh? I don't usually run a dating service, Chambers. I hope you realize that."

"I owe you one."

"You bet you do."

"I won't forget. Thanks a lot, Nick, I really app —"

"You remember my partner?" Alston said. "Charlie Macklin? Who got shot when we was sittin' that house on the beach?"

"I remember him, yes," Warren said.

"I still miss him," Alston said.

There was a silence on the line.

"Let's have a beer sometime," Warren said.

"Yeah," Alston said.

There was another silence.

"I'll talk to you," Warren said. "Thanks again."

"Yeah," Alston said, and hung up.

Warren put the receiver back on the cradle. It was twenty-five minutes to ten; he wondered if it was too late to try her. While he was debating this, the telephone rang. He picked up the receiver.

"Hello?" he said.

"Warren?"

"Yes?"

"Hi," she said. "This is Fiona Gill."

*

In Calusa, Florida, the beaches change with the seasons. What in May might have been a wide strand of pure white sand will by November become only a narrow strip of shell, seaweed, and twisted driftwood. The hurricane season here is dreaded as much for the damage it will do to the condominiums as for the havoc it might wreak upon the precious Gulf of Mexico shoreline.

There are five keys off Calusa's mainland, but only three of them — Stone Crab, Sabal, and Whisper — run north-south, paralleling the mainland shore. Flamingo Key and Lucy's Key are situated like massive stepping-stones across the bay, connecting the mainland first to Sabal and then to Stone Crab — which normally suffers most during autumn's violent storms, precisely because it has the *least* to lose. Stone Crab is the narrowest of Calusa's keys, its once-splendid beaches eroded for decades by water and wind. September after September, Stone Crab's two-lane blacktop is completely inundated, the bay on one side and the Gulf on the other joining over it to prevent passage by anything but a dinghy. Sabal Beach historically suffers least — perhaps because there *is* a God, after all. It was on Sabal that the law-enforcement officers of the City of Calusa looked the other way when it came to so-called nude bathing.

Well, not *quite* the other way.

The women on Sabal were permitted to splash in the water or romp on the beach topless. But let one genital area, male *or* female, be exposed for the barest fraction of an instant, and suddenly a white police car with a blue City of Calusa P.D. seal on its sides would magically appear on the beach's access road and a uniformed minion of the law would trudge solemnly across the sand, head ducked, eyes studying the terrain (but *not* the offending pubic patch) to make an immediate arrest while citing an ordinance that went all the way back to 1913, when the city was first incorporated.

Tonight, Warren's old Buick was the only car on the access road. The main parking lot was far off down the beach, adja-

cent to the public pavilion, where each night Calusa's teenagers gathered to practice their peculiar tribal rites. Someone off there in the distance was playing an acoustic guitar; tattered snatches of an unintelligible tune drifted listlessly on the humid air. Not a breeze was stirring. Warren was very nervous.

The last time he'd been this nervous was in St. Louis, when a sniper up on the roof was shooting down into the street and Warren and four other police officers in vests went up there and kicked in the metal fire door and barged on out there into a spray of rifle fire. That was when the nervousness turned to sheer terror. Man behind the rifle looked like a raving idiot. Hair sticking up on top of his head, eyes wild. Blue. Blue eyes flashing in the sunshine. Man. He had been the most frightening human being Warren had ever seen in his lifetime up till then. He had since met even more frightening people — the world was full of lunatics who caused your heart to stop cold — but his definition of terror would always be linked to that blue-eyed white man spraying bullets across a sunwashed black rooftop.

Tonight, he wasn't terrified, he was merely nervous.

Because . . .

Well . . .

On the telephone, Fiona had apologized for calling so late, and then had told him how nice it had been, seeing him again this afternoon, and then she mentioned how hot the weather was . . .

"I don't recall it *ever* being so hot down here, do you?"

"No, I don't," Warren said.

"No rain the past two days," she said. "Must be the Russians."

"Must be."

He was wondering why she'd called.

"This would be a lovely night for a swim," she said, "except that I don't have a pool. Do you happen to have a pool?"

Warren told her he was living in a studio apartment on the

second floor of a converted bank on Hibiscus, and no, he did not have a pool. She told him it was too bad neither of them had a pool because this was such a splendid night for a swim, although it was probably too late for —

"No, I don't think it's too late," he said.

And glanced quickly at his wristwatch.

"No, it's only nine-forty," he said.

"Little moonlight swim," she said.

"Yes, that might be nice," he said.

"Yes, mightn't it?" she said.

There was a silence on the line. Like that silence in the Tax Collector's office this afternoon, when the air had crackled with possibilities about to be lost.

"So," Fiona said at last, and he would never know the kind of courage this had required, "do you think you might like to come on down here and . . ."

"Yes," he said at once.

". . . pick me up . . ."

"Yes, I would," he said.

"And we can drive over to Sabal together?"

Sabal, he thought.

Which is when his heart had begun pounding and his hands had got all clammy.

Because Fiona *might* have suggested any one of the other beaches in Calusa for their moonlight swim — and there *was* a moon tonight — but she had chosen Sabal. And Sabal was the one and only topless beach.

She was wearing sandals and a blue jumpsuit zippered up the front. She took off the sandals as Warren locked the car and held them in one hand, dangling from the straps. He was wearing jeans and a cotton sweatshirt, loafers without socks. He went around to the trunk, unlocked it, and took out towels, a blanket, and a cooler on a strap. Resting on the ice inside the cooler, there was a capped orange juice bottle filled with martinis, a can of country pâté Warren had bought at The French Château on

Gaines Street, a box of water biscuits, some paper plates, plastic cups and utensils, and a Colt .38 Detective Special.

"Help you with anything?" Fiona asked.

"If you could take the towels," he said.

"Sure," she said. "Let me have the blanket, too."

"No, that's okay," he said, and handed the towels to her. Slamming the trunk shut, he noticed his own license plate as if for the first time:

DTU 89R.

Three letters, two numbers, and then another letter.

Just as the lady had told him.

He set the cooler down for a moment, took off his loafers, and then threw the blanket over his shoulder like a serape. Picking up the cooler again, slinging it from the strap, he followed Fiona out onto the sand. The tide was just coming in. Not a hint of surf tonight, the waves gently nudging the shore, whispering in. They found a spot on dry sand some twenty feet back from the shore and spread the blanket. There was no need to anchor it; there was not a semblance of a breeze. Warren looked up and down the beach. Not a soul anywhere in sight.

Fiona was unzipping the jumpsuit.

"I was just about to call you," he said, "but you beat me to it."

"Liar," she said.

"No, really."

Unzippered to the waist now. She shrugged it off her shoulders, lowered it, stepped out of it. She was wearing a skimpy green bikini.

"I was going to ask you to have dinner with me," he said.

She looked spectacularly beautiful.

"This is much better," she said, and grinned, white teeth flashing in the moonlight, and then turned suddenly and ran toward the water. He watched her go. So beautiful, he thought, and wondered how many hours she put in at aerobics. He unbuckled his belt, took off the jeans and then the sweatshirt. He

felt suddenly foolish wearing boxer trunks. He should have put on something sexier tonight, one of those Italian-made swimsuits that looked like a jock and came in fire-engine red, midnight black, and navy blue. But he didn't own one.

She watched him from the water.

Tall and wiry, the body of an athlete.

So beautiful, she thought.

He came running across the beach, long strides, sand splashing up behind him, entered the water running, knees pumping, took a long, shallow dive, and surfaced grinning some ten feet from where he'd gone under.

"Water's even warmer than the air," he said.

"Yes," she said.

"Lovely," he said.

He was talking about her.

"Lovely," she said.

She was talking about him.

"I didn't call because I forgot your number," he said.

They were treading water, facing each other. Moonlight rippled the surface, silver coins floating everywhere around them.

"Shame on you," she said.

"My memory is usually very good."

"Maybe you wanted to forget it."

"No, no, why would I want to forget it?"

"I don't know. Maybe you're scared of me."

"No, no."

"Because I'm an older, more experienced woman."

"I'll bet," he said.

"I'll bet," she said, and smiled mysteriously.

"You're very beautiful," he said.

"So are you."

They kissed in the moonlight.

Only their lips touching.

Floating on that sea of coins, lips touching. Gently.

She said, "Mmmm."

He said, "Yes."

They swam for some ten minutes, the memory of that single kiss lingering, the night laden with expectation.

"So how were you about to call me?" she asked. "If you'd forgotten the number?"

"Oh. I got it from a friend of mine in the Calusa P.D."

"Went to all that trouble."

"Yes."

"My my," she said.

"381-3645," he said.

"That's it, all right."

"Emblazoned," he said, and ran a forefinger across his forehead.

"All that trouble," she said, and kissed him again.

They were standing in shallow water this time. He put his arms around her, drew her closer to him. She lifted her arms, circled his neck. Kissed him harder. His hands cupped her buttocks. She moved in closer to him.

"Oh my," she said.

They walked out of the water hand in hand. He looked up and down the beach again. Still empty. A crescent moon in the star-drenched sky. They were alone in the night, alone in the universe.

"I mixed martinis," he said.

"So thoughtful," she said.

He removed the lid from the cooler, reached in for the tin of pâté, snapped off the key fastened to its top, inserted it into the groove, said, "These things never work," and then swiftly and without difficulty peeled back the top. "A miracle," he said. She was watching him. She was thinking how very handsome he looked in his boxer trunks and his high-top fade. She was wondering if she should take off the top of her bikini, this was a topless beach. No, she thought, let *him* take it off.

He opened the box of biscuits, and then took from the

cooler a white plastic knife and a pair of translucent plastic cups. "I'll pour if you fix," he said, and handed her a white paper plate. She began spreading pâté on the biscuits. He watched her, thinking how long and slender and elegant her fingers were, how studious she looked with her head bent, concentrating on the biscuits, evenly spreading the pâté, moonlight catching her high cheekbones and perfect nose. You're the most beautiful woman I've ever seen, he thought.

"You're the most beautiful woman I've ever seen," he said.

"That's very nice of you," she said softly, and looked up at him.

"These aren't the best glasses for martinis," he said. "Plastic."

He seemed suddenly embarrassed.

"They're fine," she said.

"I forgot to bring olives," he said.

"Who needs olives?" she said.

He poured the drinks.

"I love martinis," she said.

"So do I."

"Silver bullets," she said.

"Mmm," he said.

They put the lid back on the cooler, using it as a low table, the plate with the crackers on it, the orange juice bottle with what was left of the martinis. Moonlight touched her hair. Moonlight touched the sloping tops of her breasts above the skimpy green bikini top. He wondered if she would take off that top, this was a topless beach. He thought he would die if she took off the top. He hoped she would not take off the top. Somehow, that would be cheap, and Fiona Gill was not a cheap woman.

"Did you see *From Here to Eternity*?" she asked.

"I think so. The movie, do you mean?"

"Yes."

"Yes, I saw it on television."

"I don't mean the mini-series they made . . ."

"No, no, the movie. With Burt Lancaster and Deborah Kerr."

"Yes. These are very good, Warren."

"Thank you."

"Strong but good. This reminds me of that movie."

"It does?"

"The scene in that movie."

"Which scene, Fiona?"

"Where they're on the beach making love," she said, "and the waves are rushing in."

His heart began pounding hard again.

"The waves rushing in," she said, and looked out over the sea. "Have you ever noticed," she said, "that there aren't too many scenes with black people making love? In the movies, I mean. Well, *forget* television, can you imagine Bill *Cosby* making love? But you'd think in the *movies* . . ."

"Well, I think I've seen love scenes," Warren said.

"Where'd you see them?" she asked. "These scenes."

"I think I saw Gregory Hines doing some love scenes. I think."

"Did you ever see Eddie Murphy kissing anybody?"

"I think so, yes. In the one where he's this African chief coming to find a bride here. I think he kisses her."

"Kisses her."

"Yes."

"Why don't you kiss me?" she said.

He kissed her. Long and hard. They put down their drinks. He lowered her to the blanket and kissed her again.

"I love kissing you," she whispered.

"I love kissing you," he whispered.

His hand moved under the flimsy green top, found her naked breast. The nipple was hard. From the water, he guessed. But the water wasn't cold.

"It's because they're afraid of it," she said.

"Of what?" he said.

"Of showing sex between two black people," she said.

"I'll bet that's it," he said.

"They're afraid we'll incite the populace to riot," she said, and laughed softly.

He kissed the laughter from her mouth. And untied the top of her suit. Her breasts spilled free.

"Yes," she said.

He kissed her nipples.

Her hand slid down inside his trunks.

"Do you suppose it's true what they say about black men?" she asked.

Which meant she'd never been to bed with a white man, and had no basis for comparison. He hoped. For that matter, he hoped she'd never been to bed with anyone but her ex-husband, hoped she was a virgin except for him, knew this was impossible, almost asked her if it was possible, but didn't. Instead his hand moved flat over her belly and down into the bottom of the green bikini, his fingers questing.

"It must be true," she said, "what they say."

"Mm-huh," he said.

"About black men," she said.

"Mm-huh."

Finding her.

"That must be why they're so afraid of doing a *real* sex scene," she said.

"Mm-huh," he said.

Touching her.

"They're afraid black men'll run out into the streets with their big *cocks* . . ."

Grabbing him hard as she said this, illustrating her point.

". . . and rape all the white women in the nation."

"I'll bet that's it," he said again, breathlessly.

"Don't you want to kiss me again?" she asked.

He kissed her again.

He got dizzy kissing her again and again.

"I think you'd better be careful," he said.

"Mmm," she said.

"What you're doing," he said.

"Yes," she said.

"Because . . ."

"They'll do all these steamy sex scenes between two *white* people," she said, her hand moving recklessly, "but never between two blacks, yes, there it is, now you've got it, mmm. Oh maybe a little kissy-facy, mmm, yes, but never the real thing, oh no, oh *yes*, right there, oh God, yes, never a real sex scene, oh *Jesus!*" she said, and suddenly lifted her hips to him. He yanked the bikini pants down over her thighs and her knees. She kicked them away onto the sand and spread herself wide for him on the blanket. He was naked in an instant, rolling onto her.

"Never anything like *this*," she said, "oh Jesus, *never!*"

8

You came down into the marina on a dirt road behind the Toys "Я" Us warehouse off Henley Street on the South Tamiami Trail, skirting the Twin Tree Estates development along the wetlands bordering Willowbee Creek, the pampas grass moving gently in the welcome early-morning breeze. You saw first the fenced-in boats up on trailers under the storage sheds, their tin roofs rusting in the sunshine. Beyond the sheds was the asphalt-shingled house in which Charlie Stubbs lived with his wife and a pet golden retriever named Shadrach. The house was on the water, and it commanded a good view of the twenty-one slips he rented to boaters. On the night of August thirteenth, Stephen Leeds was supposed to have climbed onto a boat named *Felicity* at a slip numbered twelve and cruised off into the night to do multiple murder.

"We had three of them, one time," Stubbs told Matthew. "A female named Meshach and another male named Abednego."

He was bending over to stroke, tug, scratch, and twist the ear of the big golden, who sat loving it all, his tongue hanging out and his eyes closed, his giant lion paws solidly planted on the wooden planks of the dock. They were standing just outside the marina office. Through the open marina door, Matthew could see boat keys hanging on hooks, each key identified by a slip number crudely painted onto the wooden rack. He wondered if the office door had been locked on the night of the murders.

"This was when we were still living up north, you familiar with a little town in Vermont called West Dover? Pretty country up there, but you can freeze your butt in the wintertime. Me and my wife come down here in 'forty-seven, looking to buy ourselves a motel, ended up with a marina, didn't know a damn thing about boats. Anyway, one winter up there in Vermont the two other ones disappeared, Meshach and Abednego. We figured some skier up from New York had kidnapped them, there's a big market in pedigreed dogs, you know. They were beauties, too, the pair of them. Figured they'd been stolen. My wife was broken-hearted. She loved them dogs, especially the bitch. Anyway, come springtime, I get a call from the caretaker at one of the lodges up there, he tells me he was cleaning some fallen branches and such out of the lake, and he looked down and saw what he thought was a couple of deer on the bottom, but it turned out to be two big dogs. He knew to call me 'cause of the tags on their collars. It was them, all right. The way we figured it, they must've been playing on the ice, you know, just frisking, and crashed on through. Couldn't find a way to get up again, couldn't find their way *out*, you know. It must've been a bad way to die, don't you think?"

Matthew wondered if there were any good ways to die.

"My wife loved them two dogs," Stubbs said.

The way he said it, the forlorn sound of his voice, the way he kept working the dog's ear, caused Matthew to believe that

Stubbs himself had loved those dogs more than his wife had.

"Mr. Stubbs," he said, "I'm sorry to bother you this way . . ."

"No bother at all."

"But there are just a few more things I'd like to go over."

"Sure."

"First, can you tell me . . . those *are* boat keys, aren't they? Hanging on the rack there inside the office door?"

"Yes, they are."

"Identified by slip number, isn't that right?"

"Twenty-one of them, that's right."

"Mr. Stubbs, was the office locked . . ."

"It was."

". . . on the night you saw Stephen Leeds take his boat out?"

"It's locked *every* night. Owners have their own keys, all we keep in there's the spares, for when we have to move the boats, one reason or another."

"Then Stephen Leeds would've had his own key when he took the boat out that night?"

"*Had* to've had his own key. The spare was right there in the office, and the office was locked."

"Mr. Stubbs, would you mind if I sent someone around to check the office doors and windows?"

"For what?"

"For signs of forced entry."

"Be my guest," Stubbs said, and shrugged. "Wasn't anyone broke in there, though, I'd've noticed. What is it, boy?" he said to the dog. "You gettin' hungry again? Your mama just fed you this morning, didn't she? Old Shad here'd eat us out of house and home, we'd let him," he said to Matthew, and then turned to the dog again and said, "Come on then, 'fore you die of starvation."

He walked into the marina office, Matthew and the dog following. From a shelf in one of the wall cupboards, he took

down a big bag of dog food and poured generously into a plastic cup bigger than the dog's head.

"There you go, boy," he said, and patted him on the head and watched appreciatively as the dog began eating. Outside, a fifty-foot Sea Ray with a sedan bridge was pulling into one of the slips. Stubbs turned his attention from the dog.

"Man there's learning how to drive a boat, bangs my dock up every time he comes in. Watch him now."

Matthew watched. There was on the captain's face a look of panic Matthew had seen a hundred times before, a look that had been on his own face all too often. The look said that an irresistible force was about to strike an immovable object and there was nothing that could be done about it. Absolutely nothing. Twist the wheel, tug at the gearshift levers, pull back on the throttle, nothing could stop this damn boat from —

"There she goes," Stubbs said, and winced.

The starboard side of the boat slammed into the slip piling, bounced off it with a thudding lurch. The captain threw his gears into reverse, panicked again, twisted the wheel in the wrong direction, and whapped into the piling yet another time. A young blond girl in a black bikini — either the captain's daughter or his girlfriend, you never could tell down here in southwest Florida — stood on the bow trying to keep her balance as the boat whacked the piling once again. There was an astonished look on her face, as if she were trying to understand whether this was the way you were *supposed* to dock a boat. The captain finally got the boat alongside and yelled for the girl to jump ashore. She hesitated a moment, and then leaped the two feet to the dock, popping one of her breasts out of the scant bikini top, recovering it quickly and without embarrassment, and then bracing herself to catch the line the captain tossed to her.

"Better go help him," Stubbs said, "before that nitwit falls in the water."

He stamped out of the office and walked swiftly to the

dock. Gently, he said, "I'll take that, miss," and accepted the line from her and then swiftly and automatically looped it around the piling in a series of half-hitches. "Let me have the other one," he called to the captain, and then went through the same routine on the port side of the boat.

"Think I'll need lines aft?" the captain asked.

"'Less you want her banging around all day," Stubbs said.

It took him some ten minutes to make the boat secure. The girl watched him all the while, trying to learn something. Matthew figured she was in her early twenties. Seven or eight years younger than Mai Chim. He wondered why Mai Chim had suddenly popped into his mind. Perhaps because the girl on the dock looked so indigenous to Florida, and Mai Chim looked like a total stranger.

Stubbs came stamping back up the dock. He looked at the captain and the girl as they walked off toward where their car was parked, and then he came back into the office again.

"He'd spend less time screwing that little girl and more time learning how to park, he'd be a better seaman all around," Stubbs said. "First thing you learn when you come down from the north is there's only two things to do here in Florida. Screw and drink. He's from Michigan and he's learned how to do both real well."

Stubbs shook his head.

"When's this door-and-window man gonna show up?" he asked.

"I'll talk to him when I get back to the office," Matthew said. "His name's Warren Chambers, he was here . . ."

"Right, last week," Stubbs said. "Nice young feller. Smart as a whip, too. Anybody gonna find anything here, it'll be him. Look at that dog go, will you? Think he hadn't been fed in a month." He shook his head again and watched the dog in silent amazement. Then he looked up at Matthew and said, "Well, if that's it, I got work to do."

"Just one other thing," Matthew said. "I wonder if you could listen to something for me."

"Listen?"

"Yes, sir," Matthew said, and took from his pocket the small Sony tape recorder he'd carried to the office yesterday.

"What is it?" Stubbs asked.

"A tape I made."

He pressed the rewind button to make sure the tape was fully rewound, said, "Listen," and then hit the PLAY button. The tape began unreeling.

"Hello, this is Stephen Leeds," a man's voice said. "I just wanted to tell you I'll be taking the boat out again for a little moonlight spin, around ten, ten-thirty, and I don't want you to be alarmed if you hear me out there on the dock."

Stubbs looked at the recorder.

There was silence now.

The reel kept unreeling.

"Was that the man who called you last Monday night?" Matthew asked.

"Can you play it back for me?" Stubbs said.

"Happy to."

Matthew rewound the tape. He hit the PLAY button again.

"Hello, this is Stephen Leeds. I just wanted . . ."

"Sure as hell *sounds* like Mr. Leeds."

". . . to tell you I'll be taking the boat out again for a little moonlight spin, around ten, ten-thirty, and I don't want you to be alarmed if you hear me out there on the dock."

Stubbs was nodding now. "Yep," he said, "that's Mr. Leeds, all right."

"That's not what I asked you," Matthew said. "I asked if that was the man who called you last Monday night."

"Oh," Stubbs said. "Play it again, willya?"

Matthew played it again.

"Hello, this is Stephen Leeds. I just wanted to tell you . . ."

"No," Stubbs said.

Matthew stabbed at the STOP button.

"That's Mr. Leeds, all right," Stubbs said, "but that ain't the man who called me last Monday."

At *last,* Matthew thought. One for our side.

More damn doors here than you could find in a Broadway farce. Windows, too. Everyplace you looked. A burglar's paradise. You told your average junkie burglar there was a farm out here on Timucuan with no burglar alarm system and all these windows, he'd wet his pants in glee. Even your sophisticated burglar would appreciate a vacation from having to work so hard getting into a place.

Your junkie burglar went for the windows. All he knew was crack, man. Got to get the crack, man. Smash, grab, got to get the crack. Even if he *knew* how to pick a lock or loid a door, which he didn't, he couldn't waste time fooling around with such things. Easier to smash the window with a brick or a hammer, climb on in, take all the shiny stuff, and split to the crack house.

Your sophisticated burglar knew locks and alarms. There wasn't a door he couldn't open or an alarm he couldn't circumvent. Break a window? No way. Everybody knew the sound of breaking glass. Guy asleep in his bed five miles away, snoring to beat the band, he hears breaking glass he jumps up in bed, knows right away something's happening, reaches for the phone. You broke a window, it was like banging a pair of cymbals together, announcing to the world at large that a burglary was in progress. Your sophisticated burglar went in and out through *doors.* Warren had once read a book with that title. Doors. About a burglar. He forgot who wrote it.

Here at the Leeds farm, you didn't have to be *any* kind of burglar to get in. A two-year-old kid still learning to walk could

get into this house. Not a single one of the windows was locked. The front door and the two other doors on the entrance side of the house had Mickey Mouse locks on them, the kind with the little buttons you pushed in to lock them, what you usually saw on the inside of a bathroom door, worthless against forced entry. The sliding doors on the back of the house were equipped only with thumb locks fitted to their handles. You could open them from the outside with a screwdriver. Warren was looking for tool marks that would conclusively show forced entry, but he knew he wouldn't find any. You didn't need tools to get into this place. All you needed was determination. And not much of that, either.

He was trying a door he'd missed at the side of the house . . .

More damn doors.

. . . twisting the knob, unsurprised when the door opened without the slightest re —

"Help you?" the voice behind him said.

Warren turned.

He was looking at a very big, very good-looking white man in bib overalls and high-topped work shoes. Six feet two inches tall, he guessed. Two hundred and twenty pounds at least. Twenty-six, twenty-seven years old, in there. Bulging biceps showing where his short-sleeved blue denim shirt ended. Tattoo of a mermaid on his right forearm, all bare-breasted and scaly-bottomed. Shock of red hair hanging on his forehead. Glittering green eyes. A wide grin on his face. The grin was not friendly, but it was reasonable. It was saying a thief had been caught in the act. Maybe it was even saying a *nigger* had been caught in the act. Sometimes you couldn't tell from grins alone, however reasonable they appeared. Not down here, anyway, where everyone was oh so friendly and polite.

"Mrs. Leeds knows I'm here," Warren said at once.

"I'll bet she does," the man said.

"My name is Warren Chambers, I work for Matthew Hope, the lawyer who's defending Mr. Leeds."

The man kept looking at him, still grinning reasonably.

"Ask your boss," Warren said.

"I will. Want to come along with me?"

The look added, *Or I'll break your arm.*

Like two old buddies out for a short morning stroll, they ambled around to the back of the house together. Not half an hour earlier, Warren had talked to Jessica Leeds on the terrace here. She'd been having her morning coffee at a round glass-topped table overlooking the pool. Wearing a jungle-green nylon wrap, short nightgown under it. Barefooted. Legs crossed. She'd offered him a cup of coffee. He'd politely declined, saying he wanted to get to work right away. That was when he thought he'd be busy with tool marks. That was before he learned the house was a cracker box. Mrs. Leeds was no longer at the table. Even the breakfast things were gone.

"I spoke to her right here," Warren said.

"Uh-huh."

"I'm a private investigator," Warren said. "Let me show you my license."

"I'd sure like to see it," the man said.

He watched Warren as he fished into his side pocket. His look said, *You'd better not pull a knife or anything.* All Warren pulled was a wallet. He opened it, found his plastic-encased ID card, and showed it to the guy in the overalls. The card, together with a class-A license to operate a private investigative agency in the state of Florida, had cost him a hundred bucks and was renewable each year at midnight on the thirtieth day of June. He had also posted a five-thousand-dollar bond for the privilege of being allowed to investigate and to gather information on a wide range of matters, public or private. The guy in the overalls seemed singularly unimpressed.

"Why were you going in the house?" he asked evenly.

A field *nigger's supposed to stay in the* fields, his look said. *Only a* house *nigger's allowed to go in the house.*

"I wasn't going in the house," Warren said. "I was trying the door. May I have that back, please?"

The guy in the overalls handed the card back.

"Why were you trying the door if you weren't going in the house?" he asked reasonably. His reasonable grin was back, too. Warren was already figuring out his defense. With somebody this size, you went immediately for the balls.

"I'm checking for forced entry," he said.

"Uh-huh."

"We're trying to find out if someone got in here on the night of the murders."

"Uh-huh."

"Look, get Mrs. Leeds, will you? She'll straighten this out in a . . ."

"Oh, I'm sure she will. But I think maybe I ought to get the cops instead, don't you?"

"Sure, do that," Warren said, and sighed heavily.

"Ned?"

Her voice. Our Lady of Redemption. Calling from inside the house.

"What's the trouble, Ned?"

"No trouble at all," he called over his shoulder.

Ned. Perfect name for an asshole in bib overalls. What's the trouble, Ned? No trouble at all. Just going to break this man's arm, is all.

"Mrs. Leeds?" Warren called. "Can you please come out here a minute?"

Silence from within.

Had she forgotten the private investigator was here?

Had she mistaken him for someone here to cut back the palms? Do your trees, lady? Ten bucks a tree? Well, okay then, my second price is six-fifty.

"Just a moment," she said.

They waited.

Ned grinning.

Warren looking out over the fields.

It did not take a moment, it took more like ten moments. When finally she appeared, she was wearing tailored jeans and an emerald-green T-shirt that echoed the color of her eyes. Green was the lady's color, Warren guessed. He also figured that the reason she'd taken so long was that she'd been dressing. But she was still barefooted. And there was no bra under the thin cotton shirt.

"Did you need some help?" she asked him.

Paraphrasing what young Ned here had asked not ten minutes ago.

"Ned thinks I'm a burglar," Warren said.

"Oh?"

She seemed amused.

Green eyes twinkling, smile forming on her lips.

"Saw him trying the side door," Ned said.

"I knew he was here, Ned."

"Well, just thought I'd make sure," he said, and shrugged. "Strange man trying a door to the house."

Strange *black* man was what he meant.

"This is Warren Chambers," Jessica said. "Ned Weaver."

"Delighted to meet you," Warren said, but did not offer his hand. Neither did Weaver.

"Warren's trying to find out if anyone broke into the house," Jessica explained.

"Tell me, Mrs. Leeds," Warren said, "do you ever lock any doors around here?"

"We're safe here in the country," she said. "Aren't we, Ned?"

Something passed between them.

A look?

No, nothing quite that blatant.

Something, though.

"Very safe," Weaver said.

The something again.

Ineffable.

But there.

All at once, Warren wondered if young Ned here was diddling the farmer's wife.

The eye contact — or whatever it had been — between Jessica and Weaver broke like delicate crystal. Weaver brushed the lock of hair from his eyes, the mermaid on his forearm catching the sun as if she were breaking the surface of shining water. Warren glanced at the tattoo. Weaver caught the glance.

"Nice tattoo," Warren said.

"Thanks," Weaver said.

The eyes grazed again, his and hers, green brushing green, touching, veering away.

Press it, Warren thought.

"Navy?" he asked.

"Nope," Weaver said.

"I've always wanted a tattoo," Warren said. "Did you get that here in Calusa?"

"San Diego," Weaver said.

But not Navy, Warren thought.

"Big Marine base there, right?" he said. "San Diego?"

"I wouldn't know," Weaver said. "I've never been in the service."

Which left only one other thing Warren could think of.

"You'll excuse me, won't you?" Jessica said, and turned and went back into the house.

"I just want to check a few more doors," Warren said to her green-shirted back.

"I got work, too," Weaver said, and left him standing there in the sun, still wondering.

*

Patricia Demming was sitting in Matthew's outer office when he got back at three that afternoon. She was wearing a dark-blue tropical suit with a white silk blouse and medium-heeled blue leather pumps. She was thumbing through what looked like the Calusa telephone directory but which was only *Vogue*'s Fall Preview issue. The window behind her was running with rain-snakes. The rains had returned, and with them the Assistant State Attorney. She put down the oversized magazine.

"Hi," she said, and smiled. "I've been waiting for you."

Matthew remembered how Andrew Holmes had described her courtroom style: flamboyant, seductive, aggressive, unrelenting, and unforgiving. He wondered what she was doing here.

"Come on in," he said.

"Sure."

She rose, smoothed her skirt, followed him past Cynthia Huellen's desk — Cynthia giving her the once-over as she went by — and then down the corridor to Matthew's office.

"Have a seat," he said.

"Thanks."

"Coffee?" he asked. "Soft drink? Anything?"

"Nothing, thanks."

"So," he said.

"So," she said.

"To what do I owe the honor?"

Patricia crossed her legs. Blue pantyhose. Sleek legs. Long blond hair, electric blue eyes. A beautiful woman altogether.

"I thought you might be ready to talk a deal," she said.

Matthew looked at her.

"Am I wrong?"

"You are wrong," he said.

"That's not the impression I got."

"From whom?"

"I won't play games, okay? Morris Bloom told me you'd discussed the case with him . . ."

"I didn't discuss a deal."

"I know that. But he told you that *I* might be ready to make one, isn't that so?"

"He mentioned something like that, yes. We're friends."

"I know that, too."

"He was afraid I might not have a case."

"Didn't want to see his friend get burned by the Wicked Witch of the West, huh?"

"He never once called you that."

"But you know the nickname, don't you?"

"I've heard it."

"Because you had someone research me, didn't you?"

"Yes."

"And you learned that my first job was in Los Angeles with Dolman, Ruggiero . . ."

"Yes."

". . . where I was called the Wicked Witch of the West."

"Apparently."

"Because I was such a mean bitch," Patricia said, and smiled. "I've had you researched, too, by the way. I can tell you anything you want to know about yourself."

"Uh-huh."

"Graduate of Northwestern, where you also got your law degree, married quite young to a nice Chicago girl, divorced her several years ago, picked up again with her sometime later, ended it yet again sometime after that. You've got a fourteen-year-old daughter who's said to be a quote Brainy Beauty un-quote and who now attends a private school in Massachusetts. You came to the practice of criminal law rather late in your career, having specialized before then in real estate, divorce, and what-have-you."

"Right, what-have-you," Matthew said.

"Right. But from what I understand, you've had a remark-able string of successes till now . . ."

Matthew did not miss the "till now."

". . . defending murderers like Stephen Leeds."

"Objection," he said, and smiled.

"Sustained," she said, and returned the smile. "In fact, there are people in town who say you're even better than Benny Weiss."

"I take that as a compliment."

"You should. He's a shark. But so am I."

"So I understand."

"In which case, you should consider yourself fortunate," she said.

"About what?"

"My presence here. To offer you a deal."

"My man's innocent."

"No, no, Matthew."

"Yes, yes, Patricia."

"Ah, he remembers my name. Hear me, will you, please? You know what I've got, you've seen all the discovery material."

"Yes."

"Well, now I've got even more."

"Want to tell me?"

"Sure. I've got a witness who saw Leeds parking his boat at a restaurant named Kickers . . ."

"I'm assuming I'll be receiving . . ."

"Yes, all in due course, name, statement, bra size," she said, and rolled her big blue eyes. "She also saw Leeds getting into the car one of my Vietnamese witnesses described. A green Oldsmobile Cutlass Supreme."

"He didn't know the make."

"But he described it accurately otherwise."

"No, he wasn't sure about the color, either."

"He said dark blue or green. And my new witness nailed it as green."

"Did she also nail that nonexistent license plate?"

Patricia looked at him.

"There's no such plate in the state of Florida," he said.

"I assume you've checked."

"Oh, yes."

"You're better than I thought," she said.

"I try," he said.

"But I've still got enough to cook him."

"Maybe."

"Take my deal, Matthew."

"Why? If your case is so wonderful . . ."

"I want to save the state money."

"Please," he said. "No bullshit."

"Okay. Skye wants this one put away fast."

"Why?"

"Ask *him*."

"Me? *I'm* still waiting for the morning edition to break."

"Here's the deal," she said. "You plead your man guilty to . . ."

"I don't even want to hear it."

"Come on, Matthew," she said, and smiled again. "I got caught in the rain walking over here, the least you can do is hear me out."

"You always seem to be getting caught in the rain."

"Bad failing, I know. What do you say? Give me a break, huh?"

Blue eyes wide. Little Miss Innocence.

"If I hear your deal, I'd be obliged to report it to my client."

"If you know I'm *ready* to deal, you're obliged to report *that*, too."

Matthew looked at her.

"Let me hear it," he said.

"You plead him guilty to three counts of murder one, we agree to waive the penalty proceeding."

"Meaning?"

"Meaning your man gets life and becomes eligible for parole in twenty-five years."

"Times *three*," Matthew said.

"Oh dear," she said, "that's right. There *are* three separate counts, aren't there?"

As if just discovering this.

"But we can always stipulate that the sentences be served concurrently, can't we?" she said, and smiled.

"Uh-huh," he said.

"Which would make him eligible in twenty-five, wouldn't it? How does that appeal to you, Matthew?"

"What makes you think a judge would grant a proceeding waiver?"

"The State Attorney herself pleading clemency for the *defendant*? Reeling off mitigating circumstances? No significant history of prior criminal activity . . . under the influence of extreme mental or emotional disturbance . . . oh, yes, it would fly, Matthew."

"Maybe," he said.

"I could *make* it fly, believe me."

"Uh-huh."

"I'm good, Matthew."

"And modest, too."

"Tell your client, okay?"

"That you're good?"

"No, that I'm offering him an opportunity to breathe fresh air again before he's an old man."

"In twenty-five years, he *will* be an old man."

"Which is better than being a *dead* man."

"Unless he's innocent," Matthew said.

Stephen Leeds was eating his dinner when Matthew got there that evening. In the Calusa jail, they served dinner at five-thirty. Lights-out was at nine.

"The routine gets to you more than anything else," Leeds said.

He was moving some amorphous-looking stuff around on his tray. It stuck to his fork like glue. "You'd think in jail," he said, "they'd figure since there's nothing to do, they might as well let you go to bed late, sleep late in the morning. But, no, there has to be a routine. So they turn the lights out at nine, and they wake you up at six. On the farm, the only people who are up at that hour are the people who work for me. Look at this stuff, will you?"

He held up the fork.

The Thing From Another Planet clung to it tenaciously. It was green. It might have been spinach.

"One of the prisoners here, he's been in and out of jail all his life," Leeds said, "he told me they're only allowed three dollars and sixty-five cents a meal. That's what the city gives them to spend. What can you get for three sixty-five nowadays? Look at this stuff," he said again, and put down the fork. It seemed to move across the tray of its own volition, but perhaps he'd only set it down crookedly.

"My stockbroker was here yesterday," he said. "He comes every day, just the way I used to go to his office every day. Except that he can only come see me during visiting hours, which are from eleven to twelve in the morning and three to four in the afternoon. The routine again, right? You can come anytime you want, of course, but you're my attorney. Bernie usually comes in the morning, before lunch. Lunch is at least edible. They get it from McDonald's, there's no way anyone can screw up a hamburger and fries. Breakfast isn't bad, either. But dinner? Look at it," he said again, and shook his head.

Matthew looked at it.

The fork seemed to be corroding.

But perhaps it had been rusty to begin with.

"Anyway; Bernie comes here, and we discuss my portfolio," Leeds said. "But it isn't the same as when I was going there every afternoon at two, two-thirty, it just isn't the same. I sit there listening to him telling me how Motorola is doing now

that they're supplying telephones to Japanese car makers, and I wonder if I'll ever make a call from a car telephone again. There's a telephone in the Caddy, I had it installed after I had a flat out near Ananburg one night, not a garage open, not a phone booth anywhere on Timucuan, I figured the hell with this. Had a phone put in the next morning. Bernie sits there and tells me about car telephones, and I'm wondering if they'll let me make a last call from the electric chair."

"You're not going to the electric chair," Matthew said.

This would have been a good time to tell him about the deal Patricia Demming had offered, but he held back because his man was talking and he wanted to *keep* him talking. When they talked, they sometimes came up with something they hadn't thought of earlier, information that often could blow the prosecution's case out of the water. Matthew hoped Leeds would come up with that elusive something now. Let him talk, let him ramble, and meanwhile listen hard. Benny Weiss had taught him this. But that was before they'd become such fierce competitors.

"I keep forgetting things," Leeds said. "From my real life. The routine here becomes a life in itself, you see. So you remember things from *this* life — wakeup at six, roll call at six-ten, showers at six-fifteen, breakfast at seven, exercise in the yard at eight, and so on — but you start to forget the *important* things, the things from your *real* life. I've been meaning to tell Jessie for the past three days now that my car is ready. The Caddy. It was supposed to be ready Monday morning, and this is already late Wednesday, three days have gone by. But I keep forgetting to tell her. Somebody's got to pick it up, either her or Ned. I don't want it sitting there at the garage, it might get banged up or vandalized. There's a lot of that stuff going on in Calusa these days, there's dope everywhere in America, and where there's dope, there's crime. Did you ever think it would come to this? Did you ever in a million years imagine an America that

could sink so deep into the slime? It makes me ashamed. It makes me want to cry."

He fell suddenly silent.

It seemed possible that he would, in fact, begin crying in the very next moment.

Keep them talking, Benny Weiss had advised Matthew.

And if they stop talking, prod them.

"I played that voice tape for Stubbs early this morning," he said. "He told me it wasn't the voice he'd heard on the telephone the night of the murders. Which confirms that someone else took your boat out. Or at least that someone else called to *say* he was taking the boat out."

"Which still doesn't distance me too very far from the chair, does it?" Leeds said. He was on the edge of tears now. Keep him talking, Matthew thought. Listen for that one sharp note sounding in the mist.

"Who knows where you keep your boat?" he asked.

"Dozens of people."

"Tell me about each and every one of them."

"All of our friends know the marina I use," Leeds said. "Most of them have been on the boat with us. But none of them would set me up for murder."

"How do you know?"

"A person knows his friends. They're not his friends if he doesn't know them."

"I'll want a list of their names anyway. Before I leave. All the people who've been on the boat or who know where you keep it."

"Sure," Leeds said. But there was total despair in his voice; he was thinking this would be a worthless exercise.

"My investigator tells me you can get into your house with a can opener. Correction. Even *without* a can opener. Were all the entrance doors locked on the night of the murders?"

"I don't know."

Again the sound of defeat. They were already strapping him into the chair. A man with a black hood over his head was standing near the wall, his arms folded across his chest, waiting to step into the other room where he would look through a glass panel and throw the switch.

"Do you *normally* lock the doors before you go to sleep?" Matthew asked.

"Not always. We're in the country, there's never been any trouble out there. Besides, Ned sleeps in the guesthouse just down the road, he'd hear anything that . . ."

"Ned?"

"Jessie's brother. Our manager. Ned Weaver."

"Your manager is . . . ?"

"Yes, my brother-in-law. My wife's maiden name was Weaver. Jessie Weaver. Ned's been working for us ever since . . ."

There was a slight pause. Hardly long enough to notice — unless you were listening for that single sharp, piercing note.

". . . last summer," Leeds said.

Matthew looked at him.

Their eyes met.

What? Matthew thought.

What's here?

"So you feel it isn't necessary to lock the doors," he said. "With your brother-in-law living in the guesthouse."

"He's a very big man," Leeds said.

"How far away is the guesthouse?"

"Down the end of the road."

"How far is that?"

"Two, three hundred yards."

"Then . . . if the doors were unlocked . . . someone *could* have got in, isn't that so? Without Ned hearing them?"

"Well, I suppose so. But you don't think something like that's going to happen, you know. Someone breaking into the house . . ."

"Or just *walking* in, actually, if the doors were unlocked."

"Yes, but you don't think of that out in the country."

"I suppose not. Mr. Leeds, when you took your car in for service . . . the Cadillac . . ."

"Yes?"

"Did you leave them your keys?"

"Yes, I did."

"Which keys?"

"Well, my key chain."

"Were your house keys on that chain?"

"Well . . . come to think of it, yes, I suppose they were."

"You left your *house* keys at the garage?"

"Well . . . yes. I've been taking it to the same place for the past God knows how long. I trust those people completely."

"You trust them with your *house* keys?"

"I'm sure Jimmy doesn't leave keys out in the open. I'm sure he's got this metal box he puts them in. Hanging on the wall. With a lock on it."

"Jimmy who?"

"Farrell. He owns the garage."

"What's the name of the garage?"

"Silvercrest Shell. On the Trail near the Silvercrest Mall."

"Any other keys on that ring? Beside your car keys and your house keys?"

"Well, the keys to Jessie's car, too, I guess."

Matthew looked at him.

"It's a hard ring to get keys on and off of," Leeds said.

Matthew kept looking at him.

"Well, it is."

"So what we've got here," Matthew said, "is a situation where anyone could have taken those keys from the garage . . ."

"No, I'm sure Jimmy locks them up."

"But if someone *did* get hold of them, he could have got into your house even if the doors *were* locked . . ."

"Well, yes, I . . ."

". . . and then driven away in your wife's Maserati."

"Yes. I suppose so."

"How many people knew you'd taken your car in for service?"

"I really don't know. I spoke about it, I guess . . ."

"To friends?"

"Yes, I suppose so."

"I really do want that list, Mr. Leeds. Who else would have known?"

"Well, everyone on the farm. The people who work for me. They'd have known the Caddy was gone. But I don't think they'd have known *where* it was. The garage I took it to. They couldn't have known that."

"Your boat key wasn't on that key ring, was it?"

"No, no."

"I didn't think it'd be. What have you got? One of these little flotation key chains . . . ?"

"Yes, shaped like a buoy . . ."

"The kind that comes apart?"

"Yes."

"So you can put your registration inside it."

"Yes. Red and white."

"Mine's green and white. Where do you keep that key, Mr. Leeds?"

"In my study. At the farm."

"Where is that? The study?"

"Just to the left of the entrance door. You take two steps down, and you're in the study."

"And the key would be where?"

"On a brass key holder fastened to the wall. Alongside the door leading out to the garage. We keep the car keys on it and also the boat keys."

"Any spares to that boat key?"

"One."

"Where?"

"At the marina. In case they have to move the boat."

"And those are the only boat keys? The one on the wall in your study and the one at the marina?"

"Yes."

"After you took the boat out on the afternoon of the murders . . . did you put that key back in your study?"

"Yes."

"Would you know if it's still there?"

"How could I? I was arrested the next morning."

"Would Jessica know where to find that key if I asked her?"

"I'm sure she would. It's right on the wall."

"Who *else* knows where you keep that key?"

"You have to understand . . ."

"Yes?"

"Whenever we invited friends on the boat, they'd come to the farm first. We'd gather there, do you see?"

"Yes?"

"And the last thing I'd do before we left for the marina was take that key off the wall. I'm sure any number of people saw where I kept it. It wasn't a secret. It was just the key to the boat." Leeds shrugged. "I mean . . . you don't expect something like this to happen."

"No, you don't," Matthew said.

You don't expect murder to happen, he thought. Only when it happens do the keys to a boat and a house and a red Maserati become important. Only when it happens do you realize that any *number* of people could have gained entrance to a house as accessible as the Gulf of Mexico. And taken a boat key *and* a car key from that house. And driven off to the Riverview Marina in the red Maserati Stubbs later saw. Any number of people. Which was the same thing as saying *anybody*. And when you had *anybody*, you had *nobody*.

Matthew sighed heavily.

"Mr. Leeds," he said, "Patricia Demming came to . . ."

"Patricia Demming?"

"The State Attorney who's . . ."

"Oh, yes."

"She offered a deal," Matthew said. "I'm obliged to tell you what the offer was."

Leeds nodded, said nothing.

"You plead guilty to three counts of murder one . . ."

"I didn't kill those men," Leeds said.

"You plead guilty and the state will consolidate the three indictments and ask for a waiver of the penalty proceeding."

"What does that mean?"

"They'll agree to life imprisonment. If the judge goes for it."

"I didn't kill those men."

"You'd be eligible for parole in twenty-five years."

"I'd be sixty-six years old."

"You'd be alive."

"But I didn't kill those men."

"What shall I tell her?"

"Tell her to go to hell."

"That's what I wanted to hear," Matthew said. "Thank you."

From a phone booth outside the Calusa Safety Building, Matthew dialed the State Attorney's office number from memory and asked for Patricia Demming. It was several moments before her voice came on the line.

"Hi," she said pleasantly.

"Hello, Patricia," he said. "I just talked to my client."

"And?"

"He says to tell you he didn't kill those men. He doesn't want your deal."

"I'm sorry he feels that way," she said.

She did sound genuinely sorry.

"It's not what he *feels*," Matthew said, "it's what he *knows*. He did *not* kill those men."

"We think otherwise," Patricia said.

"Yes, that's why there are courts of law," Matthew said.

"Well, fine," she said, her voice going suddenly harsh. "You prove it in a court of law, okay?"

"You've got it backward, Patricia. You're the one who has to prove . . ."

"Which I will," she said. "Goodbye, Matthew."

There was a click on the line. Matthew looked at his watch. He opened the telephone directory hanging from a plastic-shielded metal cord — miraculously still here in this day and age of pointless vandalism — found the number for Silvercrest Shell, deposited a quarter, and dialed it. The young kid who answered the phone told him that Jimmy Farrell was gone for the day and wouldn't be back till tomorrow morning. Matthew left his name and said he'd call again.

He looked through the directory again.

He dug into his pocket for another quarter.

He hesitated.

What the hell, he thought, and dialed.

The old man was in the habit of taking a little stroll after dinner. Tradition. Gobble your rice, vegetables, and fish, and then take a little stroll along the levee. Look off to the mountains beyond Saigon. Except that this was Calusa, Florida, and the nearest mountains were in North Carolina. Plenty of water, though. If you walked the block and a half from Little Asia to the Tamiami Trail, and then took a left and followed U.S. 41 where it curved northward past the Memorial Gardens, you suddenly caught a view of Calusa Bay that was enough to make your heart stop dead. Sailboats out there on the water or in the slips at Marina Lou's, the Sabal Key Causeway stretching out toward the bar-

rier islands and the Gulf, the setting sun staining the sky and the burgeoning massed clouds — breathtaking.

The old man had to die.

Tonight.

"Actually, I was glad you called," Mai Chim said.

"I'm glad you weren't busy," Matthew said.

"Oh, I'm never busy," she said.

They were sitting at a window table in Marina Lou's, not four or five blocks from where Trinh Mang Duc was walking northward on U.S. 41, his hands behind his back, his head turned to the left as he looked out over the bay, a wistful smile on his face. Matthew and Mai Chim were looking out over this same vista, the short peninsula of the city park in the near distance, the bay beyond festooned with the colors of sunset and busy with evening boat traffic. The sun was just dipping behind the nearest barrier island, man-made Flamingo Key. Within the half hour, darkness would claim the bay and the night.

Matthew was wearing one of his Third World Outfits, the label his partner Frank gave to the assorted cotton trousers and shirts he bought in a shop not far from the house he was renting. Made in Guatemala, or Korea, or Malaysia, or Taiwan, the clothes were casual and lightweight, perfect for the summer heat. They were also loose-fitting and therefore perfect for a man who'd gained ten pounds stuffing his face with pasta in Venice, Florence, and Rome. This morning the scale showed that Matthew had lost two of those excess pounds. He hoped to get down to his fighting weight within the next two weeks. Tonight he had ordered a simple grilled fish. Low in cholesterol, fat, and calories.

Mai Chim was digging into a steak the size of her native country. She was wearing a pink skirt, low white sandals, and a pastel blue blouse cut in a V over her breasts. Her long black

hair fell loose on either side of her face. Long silver earrings dangled from her ears. A thick silver bracelet circled her right wrist. She looked very American and very Asian. She also looked very beautiful. And she was eating like a truck driver. Her appetite continued to astonish him. But what astonished him even more was the fact that she was so slender. He wondered if she ate anything at all when she wasn't with him. He wondered, too, what she'd meant about never being busy. A woman as beautiful as she was?

"It took me a long time to learn how to use a knife and fork," she said. "I've learned pretty well, don't you think?"

Commenting on her own voracious appetite, making a joke about it. He suddenly wondered if she'd ever gone hungry in Vietnam. Or afterward.

"I'm a pig, I know," she said cheerfully, and forked another slice of steak into her mouth. Chewing, she said, "I was going to call *you*, in fact."

"Oh?" Matthew said. "Why?"

"To teach you some Vietnamese," she said, and smiled mysteriously.

The old man had been off by only a hair, but it wouldn't be long before someone got him talking about that license plate he'd seen, got him rambling, and bingo! Someone would make the connection.

Seeing the car hadn't been part of the plan.

The car was supposed to remain the big secret, pick it up at Kickers, drive it to Little Asia, park it in the shadows under the big pepper trees lining the street, and then go in all yellow and bright to do bloody murder. The car wasn't meant to be seen. Only the yellow jacket and hat. In and out, slit your throats, good night, boys, sleep tight. Put out your eyes, cut off your cocks, oh what a horrible sight.

But the old man had seen the license plate.

Seen it wrong, as it happened, but seen it nonetheless, close but no cigar. So now the old man had to go. No witness, no license plate, no tracing it back to you know who. Goodbye and good luck, please give my regards to your recently departed countrymen.

There.

Walking past the marina entrance now.

Getting dark out there on the bay.

Wait.

Wait for blackness.

"Do you remember my telling you about diacritical markings?" Mai Chim said.

"Yes. The cedilla and the umlaut."

"Which, by the way, I looked up. And you were right, that's what they are."

"Yes."

"Yes, you told me. But I thought *our* marks would be easier to understand if you could *see* them. Some of them, anyway. So I Xeroxed the Vietnamese alphabet from an old grammar I have. Which is why I was going to call you," she said, and smiled. "Would you care to have a look?"

On her tongue, the words *care to have a look* seemed foreign somehow. Just a trifle off the money.

"Sure," he said.

She put down her fork and knife and reached for the handbag hanging over the back of her chair. She unclasped the bag, took out a folded sheet of paper, unfolded it, said, "I copied it at work," and handed it to him:

a ă â b c d đ e ê g h i k l m n o ô ơ p q r s t u ư v x y

The alphabet seemed foreign, too, just a trifle off, even though the letters were written just as in English. Perhaps the marks accounted for that.

"Of course, this only shows the basic order," she said. "There are also marks for *tonal* distinctions. I can draw them for you, if you like, but they would only look like chicken tracks."

"Hen tracks," he said.

"Yes," she said. "It's a very complicated language, I told you. A million marks in it. Well, not that many. But plenty. You can keep that, if you like."

"Thank you," he said, and refolded it and slipped it into his pocket.

"For your next visit to Saigon," she said, and rolled her eyes heavenward to show how remote a possibility this was. She picked up her utensils again, cut another slice of steak, and was raising it to her mouth when she asked with sudden and genuine concern, "Is the fish okay?"

Okay.

The way she said it.

The lilt of it.

A bit strange. A bit foreign. Like everything else about her.

"Only so-so," Matthew said. "My partner says it's impossible to get a good fish anywhere in Florida. The boats have to go out too far for it, and by the time they come back in, the fish isn't really fresh anymore. So speaks the oracle."

"I never eat fish here," she said. "In Vietnam, I ate fish all the time, but never here. The fish is not so good here. I think your partner is right."

"So do I, actually. But please don't tell him."

"Do you like him, your partner?"

"Oh, yes. Very much."

"Is he married?"

"Yes."

"Happily?"

"Well . . . let's say they're still working on it."

"Were you happily married?"

"No."

"Which is why you got divorced."

"Actually, it was more complicated than that."

"That means there was another woman."

"Yes."

"And is there a woman now? In your life?"

"No one serious."

"Someone *un*serious?"

"Just a few women I enjoy seeing."

She had finished her steak and now she placed her fork and knife horizontally on her plate, the way someone had undoubtedly taught her to do here in America, and sat sipping her beer and looking out over the bay, where the sky had turned a violent purple. In moments, the sun would drop into the sea, and it would be dark. She was silent for what seemed a long time, the color of the sky growing steadily deeper behind her.

"You see," she said at last, still staring out over the blackening water, "I've been wondering why you called."

"Because I wanted to know you better," he said.

She nodded.

And was silent again.

And then she turned to him and said, "Does that mean you want to go to bed with me?"

Her gaze demanded honesty.

He risked honesty.

"I guess so," he said. "Eventually."

"When is eventually?" she asked. "Tonight? Tomorrow? Next month? Next year?"

"Whenever," he said. "*If* ever."

"And when is that?"

"Only if and when we both want to."

"And if I don't want to?"

"Then we won't."

"And then we'll never get to know each other better."

"No, I didn't say that."

"I'm Asian," she said.

"I know."

"Is that why you want to go to bed with me? Because I'm Asian?"

"I haven't asked you to go to bed with me," he said. "I asked you to dinner. And that had nothing to do with your being Asian."

"Because there are men who want to go to bed with me for that reason alone, you know. The fact that I'm Asian."

He felt as if he'd been led down a jungle path by a beautiful woman who'd suddenly turned Vietcong, raising her hands high over her head to reveal primed hand grenades tucked under her arms.

He said nothing.

"I hope that isn't the case with you," she said.

He still said nothing.

"Because I've never been to bed with anyone in my life," she said, and turned away again as blackness completely devoured the bay.

The old man was standing by the sidewalk railing some ten feet from the street lamp, looking out over the boats in their marina slips. On one of the boats, someone was playing a ukulele. The instrument sounded tinny on the night, something from another time and place, like the old man himself. There were lights on many of the boats. The lights reflected in the black water. There were soft voices on the night. The ukulele kept plinking its notes onto the sticky night air. The old man stood listening in seeming fascination, his head bent. Then, at last, he turned away from the railing and began moving away from the lamppost . . .

This way, come on.

. . . his hands behind his back again, head still bent, leaning slightly forward, moving well beyond the marina's lighted orbit . . .

Yes, come on.

. . . coming closer and closer, the street lamp behind him now, the sidewalk ahead of him as black as the night, moving into the blackness of the night, moving into the blackness where the knife waited, where the knife . . .

Yes!

9

Framed photographs of the detective squad he'd commanded up north in Nassau County lined Morris Bloom's office in the Public Safety Building. They shared the wall space with a citation plaque from the Nassau County Chief of Detectives; a pair of laminated front-page stories from the *New York Daily News* and Long Island's *Newsday*, headlining the daring capture of two bank robbers in Mineola, Long Island, by a police officer named Morris L. Bloom; and several framed photographs of his wife. A boxing trophy he'd received while serving in the U.S. Navy sat on top of his bookshelf, alongside a Snoopy doll his nineteen-year-old son had given him last Father's Day. Hanging around the beagle's neck was a hand-lettered sign that read *To the best bloodhound in the world. Love, Marc.*

Bloom was looking at the headline of that morning's *Calusa Herald-Tribune.*

The headline read:

**BIGGEST FLORIDA
DRUG BUST EVER**

"I thought World War III was starting," Matthew said.

"Mmm," Bloom said.

"The size of that type."

"Mmm."

The bylined story under the headline went on to reveal, somewhat hysterically, that the largest cocaine seizure ever made in southwest Florida had taken place yesterday morning, August 21, and that the arrests of twelve men in the so-called Bolivian sector of Calusa might very well have put an end to all trafficking in this part of the state. The article went on to say that the four-month-long investigation had been initiated by Skye Bannister, the State Attorney, and that detectives from his office had worked in conjunction with the DEA, the Calusa P.D., and the Calusa Sheriff's Department to bring about a successful conclusion to the covert operation. Together they had confiscated in the early-morning raid thousands of kilos of cocaine, millions of dollars in cash, and enough handguns, rifles, and automatic weapons to start a war in Central America. Skye Bannister was quoted as saying, "If you do drugs, you will be caught. And when you're caught, you will be punished. These men will be going away for a long, long time. I'll see to that personally. We will not tolerate drugs in this city. We will not tolerate drugs in this state."

"So this is what was cooking," Matthew asked.

"This is what was cooking," Bloom said.

"Skye's rocket to Tallahassee."

"Let's say it couldn't hurt," Bloom said.

"Which is why he wants to sweep the murder case under the rug."

"So to speak."

"Make an offer, get his conviction fast, and dance on home with Mama."

"Uh-huh."

"Because if he *loses* this one . . ."

"Big one to lose, Matthew."

"Oh yes."

"He loses this one, it's goodbye, Tallahassee."

"I'm going to make sure he loses it, Morrie."

"*Ahuvai*," Bloom said. "But I don't think you have a chance."

"No, huh? Was my man out of jail and roaming the waterfront last night?"

"A copycat murder, Matthew. Plain and simple."

"The party line," Matthew said.

The murder was buried on page fourteen of the paper, in a brief story that ran for half a column on the left-hand side of the page, adjacent to an almost-full-page ad for the Curtis Brothers Department Store. The story reported that Trinh Mang Duc, sixty-eight years old, an unemployed immigrant from Vietnam, residing at 1224 Tango Street, had been found dead on the North Tamiami Trail, near Marina Lou's, at five minutes past two A.M. by the motorized police officer patroling that sector.

When certain apparent similarities were pointed out to Patricia Demming — the Assistant State Attorney prosecuting the sensational case involving the murder and mutilation of three Vietnamese immigrants recently acquitted of rape charges — the young prosecutor told reporters that such incidents were not uncommon. "It's extremely unfortunate that so many murders are imitated by impressionable people who commit the same crime in the identical manner," she said. "We call them copycat murders. The slaying of Mr. Trinh is just such a horrible tragedy. He was the innocent victim of a twisted person seeking dubious fame through the repetition of a previous murder — or murders, as the case happens to be here. There is no doubt in my mind, however, that the murders are related only in that way. We already *have* the man who committed the earlier murders, and I'm certain the Calusa police will find the man or woman who committed this most recent outrage."

"Some mouth on her," Bloom said.

"Some *baloney*," Matthew said. "Who was responsible for burying the story?"

"Not me," Bloom said.

"I didn't think you."

"I didn't even catch the squeal. Palmieri was on last night."

"Was the body mutilated in the same way?"

"Identical."

"To make *sure* we think copycat, right?"

"I *do* think copycat."

"The murderer just happened to pick one of Demming's witnesses, right?"

"No, he *deliberately* picked him."

"Why?"

"Who knows why? Maybe because Trinh *was* related to the previous murders. Who knows what goes on in a copycat's head, Matthew? These people are *nuts,* do you think they *know* what they're doing? They don't know what they're doing, believe me. I had a copycat in Nassau, when I was working up there, he went around killing old ladies because some *other* poor lunatic had killed his eighty-year-old mother the week before. Made headlines all over New York. But the copycat picked only grey-haired ladies. Because his *own* mother had grey hair. So never mind the first guy's mother had hair even blacker than yours. The *copy*cat's mother had *grey* hair, so he went looking for grey-haired victims. A *meshuggener*," Bloom said.

"No motive, is that what you're saying?"

"Fame maybe, Demming was right about that. A lot of them do it 'cause they think it'll make them as famous as the guy they're imitating."

"How about this for a motive, Morrie? Trinh saw the license plate on the murderer's car."

"There's no such plate in Florida," Bloom said, and shook his head.

"I know. But do you think I'd have left it there? Do you

think I wouldn't have gone after him till he *remembered* what he saw?"

"I guess you would have," Bloom said, and shrugged.

"And you don't think the murderer realized that?"

"I don't know what he did or didn't realize, if it's a he to begin with. Murderers don't think the way you or I do. In murders, there's nothing neat, take my word for it. Murders are messy. And the people who commit murders don't read Agatha Christie. They're not all crazy, Matthew, but this one is, believe me. This is a classic copycat murder. And the person responsible will do another one, and maybe another one after that, and he'll keep doing them till we catch him. We'll catch him, Matthew, wait and see. And he'll be a copycat. And him and your man'll be sitting together on death row."

"I promised him otherwise," Matthew said.

"You shouldn't have," Bloom said.

They were both drinking coffee and eating scrambled eggs and bacon in a Sabal Key joint called The Miami Deli. There was something wrong with the air conditioning today, the waitress explained. This meant that the temperature inside the place was something like a hundred and four Fahrenheit. Warren had wanted to leave at once, find another place, but Nick Alston said he didn't mind the heat. A fat lady in pink shorts and a pink tube top sat near the windows, fanning herself with a laminated menu. On the road outside, an occasional car went by, heading north toward Sabal's public beach. Alston was enjoying his eggs.

"What is it you want this time?" he asked.

"Computer work," Warren said.

He had always operated on the theory that if you were going to ask a favor you asked it straight out, without doing a little tap dance around the mulberry bush. Saved a lot of time all around. And maybe generated a little respect. He had told

Alston on the phone that he needed another favor. Alston had sourly agreed to meet him and had hinted that this time there'd be a price tag. But now, seeing the man, Warren wasn't so sure he wanted to get down to business quite so fast.

Alston didn't look too terrific.

He had never been what anyone would call handsome, but his brown eyes were now shot with red, and his craggy face looked puffy and bloated, and his straw-colored hair looked stringy, and there was a beard stubble on his face, and it was plain to see he'd already been drinking this morning. Only ten o'clock, and the smell of alcohol on his breath was overpowering. He had told Warren that today was his day off, but now Warren wondered if he drank even on the days he was working.

"How have you been, Nick?" he asked.

"What kind of computer work?" Alston said.

"You been all right?"

"Well, you know."

He kept his eyes on his plate, cutting into the eggs with the edge of his fork, lifting the fork to his mouth, repeating the operation.

"There's a new guy in Frank sector," he said.

"How is he?"

"Okay, I guess."

He kept eating. Warren signaled to the waitress for more coffee. She was a plain-looking blonde with spectacular legs. She wore her skirt very short, to show off the legs. Both Warren and Alston noticed the legs. It would have been impossible not to notice those legs.

"Throw a flag over her face," Alston said, "fuck for Old Glory."

An old joke, but Warren smiled.

"He's the other car in the sector," Alston said. "The car that used to be Charlie Macklin's. We ride solo, you know. But there's two cars in each sector, we can get pretty quick backup if

we need it. I don't know him too good yet, but he ain't no Charlie Macklin, I can tell you that."

"How long had you known Charlie?"

"Oh, Jesus, we go back for years."

Present tense. As if he were still alive.

"Must be difficult," Warren said. "Losing a partner."

"Yeah. Well, you know, we really got along good together. I'da trusted Charlie with my life — well, hell, that's exactly what I *did* do, more times'n I can count. It ain't the same without him, Chambers, I can tell you that," he said, and nodded, and picked up his coffee cup.

Warren watched him for a moment.

Go on, he thought, take a chance.

"You been drinking much?" he asked.

"A little," Alston said.

"You should try to cut back."

"What business is it of yours?"

"None."

"Then butt out."

"I thought maybe I could help," Warren said.

Alston looked across the table at him.

"Come on," he said.

"I'm serious. If there's anything I can do to . . ."

"Come on, I hardly know you. Why should it matter to you?"

"I don't like to see anyone in trouble."

"I'm not in trouble."

"You've been drinking already this morning, haven't you?"

"Nothing to speak of. What are you, a minister?"

"I'd like to help, Nick. Call me, okay? You ever feel like talking, give me a call."

"Come on," Alston said, embarrassed.

"Instead of turning to the bottle," Warren said.

"I guess I have been drinking some," Alston said, and

shrugged, and looked away. Across the room, the waitress was leaning over the fat lady's table, refilling her coffee cup.

"You ever see wheels like that?" Alston asked.

"Never."

"Competition-class wheels, those are."

"Indeed," Warren said.

"Man," Alston said, and shook his head in admiration.

Both men were silent for several moments, looking at the girl's long, splendid legs.

"It's just I sometimes start thinking about what happened," Alston said. "I didn't think I'd miss him this much, you know? Charlie. I mean . . . we used to have breakfast together every morning before we went out in the cars . . . and we'd stop for coffee two, three times during the shift, and then grab a bite when the tour was over, and we'd . . . we'd talk about all different kinds of things. Women, the job, places we been, things we wanted to do, it was good to be able to talk to somebody like that. Because this job, you know, it gets to you after a while. All the stuff you see. All the stuff that goes down in this city, especially nowadays with drugs calling the tune. You read the papers this morning? What bullshit! The S.A. makes one lousy drug bust, he thinks that's the end of it. He oughta come ride the sector with me some night, I'll show him the end of *nothing*."

"They think they can nickel and dime the drug lords out of business," Warren said.

"The drug budget is a laugh," Alston said. "I try to explain that to my girlfriend, she's a dispatcher down the Building, she understands police work a little. But not the underbelly, you know? What you have to deal with day in and day out. You need a partner to talk to about that."

"Somebody who knows the work," Warren said.

"Sure. Otherwise, you're out there, you start thinkin', what am I doing here? Who even *cares* whether I'm here or not?"

"I used to be in the job, you know," Warren said.

"No, I didn't know that."

"Yeah. St. Louis P.D."

"So then you know."

"Oh sure."

"That's interesting," Alston said. "You being a St. Louis cop."

"Ever been to St. Louis?"

"No, but I hear the women there got diamond rings," Alston said, and smiled.

"They've got other things, too."

"But not legs like this one's got," Alston said. "I'd like to lick my way up those legs all the way to the crotch, starting with the toes."

She was coming back to their table now. High heels clicking on the asphalt tile floor. Long stride on her. Proud of those magnificent legs.

"Anyone for more coffee?" she asked.

"You got a sister for my friend?" Alston asked, and winked at Warren.

The girl smiled. She didn't know quite how to handle this. Salt-and-pepper team at the table here, what could she say? She played it safe.

"Anyone for more coffee?" she asked again.

"You might want to hotten mine a bit," Alston said, and winked at Warren again.

"Mine, too," Warren said.

The girl poured coffee into both cups. She was truly very plain except for those legs. And those legs probably had brought her the wrong kind of attention ever since puberty. Men equated legs like those with sexuality. It was a fact of life, not entirely discouraged by television commercials and magazine ads. But she sure knew she had those legs. Head high, she clicked away from the table like a racehorse.

They watched her go.

"Mmmm-*mmmm*," Alston said.

"Indeed," Warren said.

They sat there sipping their coffee. The fat lady got up and walked to the cash register.

"I like mine better than yours," Alston said.

Both men grinned like schoolboys.

"I meant what I said, you know," Warren said.

"Okay."

"You ever feel like talking to somebody, give me a call."

"Okay, I'll keep that in mind."

"I mean it."

"I hear you."

"Good."

"What do you need from the computer?" Alston asked.

"What does a tattoo mean to you?"

"Armed robber," Alston said at once.

"A lot of them, anyway," Warren said, nodding.

"*Most* of them," Alston said. "In fact, every one of them I ever come across had a tattoo one kind or another."

"I'm looking for whatever you've got on a man named Ned Weaver. San Diego may be a place to start."

"What else can you give me? The computer likes the more the merrier."

"He's in his late twenties, big guy around six two, two twenty or thirty, looks like he's done some weight lifting. Red hair, green eyes, no visible scars. The tattoo's on his right forearm. Big-titted mermaid with a long, fishy tail. He says he wasn't in the service, but you may want to check the FBI files anyway."

"I'll go down the Building soon as we finish here."

"Let me know how much time you put in, will you?"

"Why?"

"So we can figure out . . ."

"Don't be a jackass," Alston said.

"On the phone, you told me . . ."

"That was then, this is now."

Warren looked at him.

"Okay?" Alston said.

"Okay," Warren said.

Jimmy Farrell was bent over the open hood of a Chrysler LeBaron convertible when Matthew came into the garage at eleven that morning. He had called ahead, and Farrell was expecting him. But he took his own sweet time straightening up. Matthew disliked him at once. It had to have been his looks because the man hadn't yet opened his mouth.

He was bearded and bald, five-ten or -eleven inches tall, a bit shorter than Matthew, but much more solidly built. He was wearing a red T-shirt with the Shell company's yellow scallop logo across its front. The shirt rippled with well-defined pectorals, and muscular biceps bulged below the short sleeves, one of which was rolled up around a package of cigarettes. He had dark brown eyes and shaggy brows that matched the full beard, altogether a very hairy fellow except for the entirely bald and undoubtedly shaven head. He looked as if he ate spark plugs and spit out pistons. He looked like one of those phony wrestlers on television. Matthew was willing to bet he went hunting a lot.

"Matthew Hope," he said. "I called."

He did not extend his hand; Farrell's hands were covered with grease.

"Does he know the Cad's ready?" Farrell asked.

"Yes. He was going to talk to his wife about it. Or his brother-in-law."

"*That* turd," Farrell said, but did not amplify. "When's somebody gonna pick it up? I got limited space here, and also I wouldn't mind getting paid for work already done."

"The man's in jail," Matthew said evenly.

"Tough," Farrell said. "He shoulda been more careful, he wouldn't be in jail."

"Mr. Farrell, I wonder if you can show me where you keep the keys to the cars you service."

"Why?"

"It might be important to Mr. Leeds's case."

"He thought he was still in the jungle, didn't he?" Farrell said. "Where it didn't matter shit what he did. He forgot he was back in civilization."

A Vietnam vet, Matthew realized. Just about the right age — thirty-nine or forty — and in his eyes a look Matthew hadn't noticed earlier. A bitter, cynical look that said he and others like him had done things luckier mortals hadn't been forced to do.

"I don't think he killed those men," Matthew said.

"If he didn't, he should've," Farrell said. "Only with a little finesse. I still don't know why you want to see the key box."

"*Is* there a box?"

"Hanging right there on the wall," Farrell said, and pointed to a long grey metal box screwed to the wall just inside the door that led to the office. The panel door of the box was standing wide open, a key jutting out of its lock. There were perhaps half a dozen sets of car keys hanging on hooks inside the box.

"Is the box open like that all day long?" Matthew asked.

"Nobody here but us," Farrell said.

Plus whoever wanders into the garage, Matthew thought.

"When do you lock it?"

"When we leave at night."

"But all day long the key just sits there in the lock, is that it?"

"Safest place for it," Farrell said. "Might get lost otherwise."

"Where do you put that key when you lock the box at night?"

"In the cash register."

"What time do you normally leave here?"

"Around six."

"Everybody?"

"Usually. Every now and then, somebody'll be working on a car, he'll stay a little later. But we stop pumping gas at six. That's it. Life's too short."

"Do you know what night the murders took place?"

"Couple of weeks ago, wasn't it?"

"The thirteenth. A Monday night."

"Uh-huh."

"Do you remember what time you left here that night?"

"Around six, I guess. Same as usual."

"Did you lock that box when you left?"

"I did."

"Was Leeds's key ring in that box when you locked it?"

"I guess so. No reason to have taken it out."

"Do you know what keys are on that ring, Mr. Farrell?"

"Yep. I called about it, in fact. Spoke to that dumb fuckin' brother-in-law of his, told him I wasn't gonna be responsible for all those keys on the ring, looked like a house key and what-not. He said he'd stop by to pick them up. Do you see him here?"

"Mr. Farrell, who *else* knows there's a house key on that ring?"

"You mean people working here?"

"Yes."

"If you're thinking somebody *used* that key to get into the Leeds house . . ."

"I'm thinking that's a possibility, yes."

"I'm thinking it ain't."

"I'd still like to talk to anyone who had access to those keys."

"There's only three of us here," Farrell said. "The high-school kid I got pumping gas don't come in till after school, three, three-thirty. He's sixteen years old, and he didn't break into anybody's house."

"How big is he?"

"Why?"

"Because somebody big was wearing Leeds's jacket and hat on the night of the murders."

"Danny's five-seven, and he weighs around a hun' sixty," Farrell said. "So I guess he ain't the one who broke into Leeds's house and stole his goddamn clothes."

"Who said his clothes were stolen?"

"If somebody was wearing them, then they were stolen."

"Who else works here?" Matthew asked.

"I got a mechanic helping me out, that's all. And he's six-two, which I guess makes you happy."

"Where is he?"

"Out gettin' some coffee for us."

"I'll wait for him," Matthew said.

The computer's name was Bessie. Alston wondered why somebody had named it Bessie. He also wondered if computers everywhere in the world had women's names. *Fat* women's names. The girl with the legs back there in the deli wouldn't be caught dead with a name like Bessie. Face that could stop a clock on that girl, but legs he would never forget in his entire lifetime. You didn't name any computers after a girl with legs like that. Bessie. All right, let's go, Bessie, let's see what you've got on Mr. Ned Weaver.

He was sitting alone in the Computer Room of the Public Safety Building, the computer screen not a foot and a half from his face, his big hands hovering over the keyboard, the forefingers poised to type. Like a man playing "Chopsticks" on a toy piano, he pecked out the letters that opened the file, and then hit the RETURN key.

The screen asked him which of several categories he wanted searched.

He tapped out the letters CR, for "criminal."

The machine whirred.

The screen said SELECT ONE:

1) CITYWIDE

2) STATEWIDE

3) NATIONWIDE

4) OTHER SPECIFIC STATE

He knew that if he hit the numeral 3 for the nationwide search, Bessie would tap into FBI files and he'd be sitting here all day. He hit the numeral 4 instead, calling for a specific state search outside Florida, and at the next prompt he typed in the letters CA for California.

The machine whirred again.

A single word appeared on the screen:

YEAR?

He typed ? for "unknown."

SEARCH SPAN?

Chambers had told him the subject was in his late twenties. Alston knew there were kids who got in trouble before they could tie their own shoelaces, but the longer the span, the longer he'd be here. He figured a ten-year search was long enough. Weaver would've been sixteen, seventeen years old back then, nice age to run afoul of the law, and the search would continue on up to the current year. He typed in the numerals 1-0, and then hit the RETURN key again.

LAST NAME?

He typed in W-E-A-V-E-R.

FIRST NAME?

He typed in N-E-D.

MIDDLE NAME?

He typed ? again.

The screen asked IS NED AN ALIAS? TYPE "Y" OR "N"

He typed N. For no.

The machine whirred.

The words NO CRIMINAL RECORD NED WEAVER STATE OF CALIFORNIA, and then immediately and again asked IS NED AN ALIAS? TYPE "Y" OR "N"

This time he typed Y.

The screen said SELECT ONE:

1) NED FOR EDMUND
2) NED FOR EDWARD
3) NED FOR NORTON
4) ALL OF ABOVE

He typed 4.

A hundred goddamn Edmund, Edward, and Norton Weavers popped up on the screen.

Alston had his work cut out for him.

Farrell's mechanic was indeed six feet two inches tall. Wrinkled and sun-browned, swinging his arms, he came ambling past the gasoline pumps toward the office. There was a brown paper bag in his right hand. A cigarette dangled from his mouth. A peaked baseball cap was perched on his head. He was tall for sure. But he was also a scarecrow of a man in his early sixties, and he could not have weighed more than a hundred and fifty pounds. Access to house keys or not, it was impossible to believe that this man could have overpowered and murdered — with a *knife*, no less — three young men.

"This is Avery Shoals," Farrell said. "Ave, the man here'd like to ask you some questions."

"Sure thing," Shoals said. He put the brown paper bag on the counter alongside the cash register, dragged on his cigarette, eyes squinted, and said, "Only bought two coffees, though. Didn't know we had company."

"That's okay," Farrell said, and smiled. "I don't think Mr. Hope'll be staying very long."

Warren Chambers was waiting for him when he got back to the office at one that afternoon. Neither of the men had yet had lunch. They walked up Main Street toward the new little mall in the reconstructed Burns Building. The size of a tennis court, the mall occupied the street-level floor of a four-story office building, one of the oldest in downtown Calusa, surrounded now by the city's modest version of skyscrapers. The mall's restaurants were of the takee-outee variety, except that you didn't take the food home with you. Instead, you lined up at various counters for your hamburgers or hot dogs or pasta or Mexican or Chinese food, and then you carried the food and your beer or soda or milk shake to these little round tables in a sort of open courtyard. Canned music piped through hidden speakers relentlessly flooded the courtyard, but it was impossible to tell which songs were being played. There was only a *sense* of music, a constant, low-key, muted background din.

Warren had good news.

Depending upon how you looked at it.

He told Matthew first about the tattoo on Ned Weaver's arm, and how a large percentage of armed robbers wore tattoos. This happened to be a fact, he said, even though it was news to Matthew. Weaver's reluctance to discuss his sexy mermaid had piqued Warren's curiosity, so he had asked a friend of his on the Calusa P.D. to crank up the computer and see if there was anything on a Ned Weaver in San Diego, because this was where Ned Weaver said he'd picked up the tattoo.

What he'd also picked up in San Diego was twenty-two thousand dollars and change from a bank he'd robbed with a buddy of his named Sal Genovese, who was wheelman on the job. Actually, the holdup would have been a great success if, first, one of the bank guards hadn't been silly enough to draw

his pistol while looking down the muzzle of a .44-caliber Magnum. Naturally, Weaver had to shoot him. The man missed death by an ace. The several rounds from Weaver's weapon ripped into the guard's left biceps some three inches from his heart and almost tore off his arm.

Even so, and in spite of this slight setback, the job still might have worked out well if, second, the getaway car hadn't got stuck in downtown traffic. There was another unfortunate shootout between the fleeing bank robbers and the San Diego police, which this time the police won. Norton (which was Ned's full given name) and his good buddy Salvatore (which was his) both went to prison for a long, long time. The prison's given name was Soledad. Last summer . . .

Here it is, Matthew thought.

Last summer, Weaver was paroled and he moved here to Florida.

Exactly what Leeds had told him yesterday. But only after a slight hesitation.

Ned's been working for us ever since . . . last summer.

Had he been about to say "ever since he got out of prison"?

Possibly. Which knowledge might have pleased Matthew — as it pleased him now — especially since he already knew that Jessica Leeds had contemplated hiring someone to kill the three men who'd raped her. Her brother hadn't *quite* killed that bank guard, but not for lack of trying.

"I wonder where young Ned was on the night of the murders, don't you?" Warren asked.

"Indeed I do."

"Because there may be wheels within wheels here, Matthew. As for example, suppose Weaver didn't like the idea of those three Vietnamese punks getting away with the rape of his sister, and suppose he decided to *do* something about it. A man spends nine years in prison . . ."

"Was that it?"

"He was nineteen when he went up. Nine years is a long

time behind bars, Matthew, especially for somebody who's a hothead to begin with. So now he's out, and he sees these three punks getting away with rape, he thinks 'Hey, man, this is my *sister* here!' This isn't a bank guard getting in his way, this is three punks who raped his *sister*. So maybe — I'm only saying maybe — maybe he got it in his head to go after them."

"Especially if his sister suggested it," Matthew said.

"Well, we don't know that she did," Warren said.

"She explored the possibility with her husband."

"She did?"

"Yes."

"Mmm."

"Mmm is right," Matthew said.

"So let's say young Ned *did* do the job . . ."

"No, Warren, it won't wash."

"Why not?"

"Leeds's wallet was at the scene."

Both men were silent for a moment. Warren was eating enchiladas and drinking beer. Matthew was eating a hamburger and drinking a Diet Coke. At a nearby table, two young women were trying to eat with chopsticks. Food kept dropping back onto their plates. They giggled each time another morsel escaped the chopsticks.

"One thing you learn in prison," Warren said.

Matthew looked up.

"It ain't good to get caught."

"Meaning?"

"Meaning how did Weaver get along with his brother-in-law?"

"Good question."

"Because if, let's say, he didn't *like* him so much . . . then why *not* set him up? Juke the three punks and make it look like Leeds did it."

"That would be hurting his sister, too. I don't think . . ."

"The man did time," Warren said. "In the slammer, you

learn a code, Matthew, you learn a different kind of law. This law says you rape my sister, I'm gonna get you. This law says I hate my brother-in-law, I'm gonna get *him*, too. That's the kind of law you learn in jail, Matthew, and it's got nothing to do with the kind of law you practice."

"I'll talk to Leeds . . ."

"I'm only saying it's possible."

". . . try to find out what kind of relationship they had," Matthew said.

"Because here's a man can go in and out of that house at will," Warren said. "Take Leeds's jacket and hat, he wants to, grab his sister's car keys, the boat keys, whatever the hell he needs to do the murders and pin a rose on his brother-in-law. But I may be wrong."

"Can you get me a tape of his telephone voice?" Matthew asked.

It kept bothering Bannion.

The license plate the old gook had seen on the getaway car.

2AB 39C.

No such plate in the state of Florida. But that hadn't stopped somebody from killing him. Bannion wished he could see eye to eye with his boss on this one, but he just couldn't accept her belief that this was a copycat murder. Not when the victim was one of the state's witnesses, nosir. Bannion had been in police work too long not to know the difference between a crazy and a *crazy* crazy. To his way of thinking, anyone who committed murder was crazy. But the ones who did it without rhyme or reason, those were the *crazy* crazies.

The person who had killed Trinh Mang Duc did not strike Bannion as a certified nut. A copycat murderer wouldn't have gone to all the trouble of seeking out Trinh in Little Asia, and then following him all the way up to Marina Lou's. Your

garden-variety lunatic copycat murderer would've settled for *any* gook walking the streets of Calusa, never mind a witness who had seen the murderer getting into a car with a license plate that did not exist in this state. Any gook would've satisfied the need, short, tall, fat, skinny, old, young, it wouldn't have mattered to the copycat. Grab him from behind, slit the poor bastard's throat, poke out his eyes, cut off his cock and stick it in his mouth.

But *this* guy had deliberately sought out Trinh Mang Duc.

Had to've read his name in the paper, that was the first mistake, you didn't go putting a witness's name in the paper. Unless, of course, you already had your alleged murderer behind bars, which happened to be the case here. *If* he was the right man.

Bannion wasn't paid to make trouble for his own boss. His job was to compile information that would help her prove beyond a reasonable doubt that the man they'd charged with three counts of murder was the man who'd actually committed those murders. But it was also Bannion's job — or so he saw it — to make sure Patricia Demming didn't make a damn fool of herself. And if she had the wrong man in custody while the real murderer was still out there someplace killing a witness who had seen the license plate on his auto —

But there *was* no such plate.

Not if it was a Florida plate.

Trinh Mang Duc had said it was a Florida license plate.

2AB 39C.

Which he had seen through a closed screen door. At night. Well, the moon was still almost full. But the car was parked under a leafy pepper tree. Some distance from where he was standing inside his house looking out through a screen door.

2AB 39C.

So either it wasn't a Florida plate . . .

Which was a fairly distinctive plate, orange letters on a white field . .

Either it *wasn't* a Florida plate, or else Trinh had seen it wrong. Read the numbers and the letters wrong. In which case, why kill him? If he had it wrong, then as a witness he wasn't worth a rat's ass. So why bother with him? Let the man live. Unless . . .

Unless he'd been damn *close* to what the numbers and letters on that plate actually were. In which case, he might have remembered them correctly if prodded long enough. And if he'd eventually remembered them, those letters and numbers might have led not to the man Patricia Demming had in jail, but to the man or woman who'd actually slit those gooks' throats. In which case, Trinh had to go. Now. *Before* he remembered. So long, sir, it was nice having you here in Florida, may your ancestors welcome you with joy and your descendants mourn you eternally.

2AB 39C.

What *could* he have seen instead?

Bannion picked up a pencil and began writing the numbers and letters over and over again . . .

2AB 39C
1AB 39C
2AB 39C
2 A B 39C
2 A B 39C
2 A B 39C

. . . and all at once he realized what it was that Trinh Mang Duc had actually seen, and knew in that same instant why it had been necessary to kill the old man.

He pulled the telephone to him and began dialing.

10

The pallor had set in. And so had the gloom.

This was Stephen Leeds's tenth day in jail, and the routine he had earlier described to Matthew was taking its toll on him. Send this man to prison for any extended length of time, and he would be destroyed as surely as if he were strapped into the electric chair.

He was sitting at the far end of a long table in what was called the P.C.R., the letters standing for Private Consultation Room, a bleak cubicle set aside for prisoner-lawyer conferences. There was a single barred window set high up on the wall behind him. It was raining steadily at nine o'clock that Friday morning. You could hear the rain pelting the fronds of the palm trees that lined the sidewalk outside the jail. The small, tight room felt almost cozy with the rain beating down outside. Leeds's big hands were clasped on the table in front of him. He was listening intently to Matthew, who was asking him if he and his brother-in-law got along well, or was there —

"I hate his guts," Leeds said.

"Why?"

"I'm a farmer and he's a convicted felon. That'd be reason enough, even if there weren't *other* things."

"Why'd you hire him?"

"Jessica wanted him here."

"Why?"

"To keep him out of trouble, was what she said. If you ask me, he's the kind who'll *always* be in trouble of one sort or another. That bank robbery wasn't the first crime he committed, you know. It was just the first one he got sent away for."

"What were the others?"

"You name them, he did them."

"Like what?"

"Drugs, assault, rape, burgla —"

"Rape?"

"Rape."

"When was this?"

"Which?"

"Start from the beginning."

"The first dope arrest was when he was thirteen, fourteen, in there. Judge took pity on him, gave him a suspended sentence. He looks so damn clean-cut, you know, so apple pie, American boy next door, it's hard to believe he's a vicious son of a bitch."

"Tell me about the assault and the rape."

"The assault was when he was sixteen. He mugged an old lady in the park, ran off with her purse. Jessie says the old lady identified the wrong man. Maybe she did. They searched high and low for her handbag, threw the apartment and especially Ned's room upside down, but they never did find it."

"How about the rape?"

"Ned was seventeen, the girl was thirteen. And retarded."

"And he got *away* with it?" Matthew asked.

"Jessie says he didn't do it. The jury said so, too. His lawyer had five witnesses who claimed Ned was out bowling with them at the time of the rape, and the jury believed them."

Wheels within wheels, Warren had said.

Ned Weaver charged with rape when he was seventeen years old. And an acquittal.

His sister the victim of multiple rape all these years later. And another acquittal.

"He wasn't so lucky the next time around," Leeds said. "That was the bank holdup. Jessie claims he was forced into it. Ned owed this Italian fellow some money, the man forced him to go along on the robbery, to square matters, you know? That's what Jessie says it was. Just a matter of trying to settle a bad debt. Which doesn't explain why Ned *shot* that bank guard, does it?"

"No, it doesn't."

"He shot him because he's a vicious son of a bitch, is why. But even so, look at the sentence he got. Out in nine years. He's been lucky all his life when it comes to kindhearted judges and pushover juries."

"But your wife doesn't feel that way, does she?"

"Oh, no, according to her, he's Mr. Clean. Just had a string of bad luck, is all. He'll get in trouble again, though, you wait and see. And next time I hope they lock him up for good."

"Were all of these arrests in California?" Matthew asked.

He was wondering why the computer had located only the one arrest and conviction.

"The early ones were in South Dakota," Leeds said, "while he was growing up. Growing up *rotten*. It's hard to believe him and Jessie are from the same stock. She's seven years older than he is, you know, she's thirty-six. Her parents were killed in a car crash, she's like a mother to him. Which I guess is why she wanted him here on the farm. But they didn't move to San

Diego till he was eighteen, after the rape episode. Just in time to get in trouble all over again, right? Clean slate in a new town, might as well shit all over it."

"Is that where you met her? In San Diego?"

"No, no, we met right here in Florida. She used to model, you know."

"No, I didn't know that."

"Oh, yes. She was doing a trunk show here at the Hyatt. We started talking, I asked her out . . . and that was it, I guess."

"When was this?"

"We've been married for almost six years now."

The gloom settled over his face again.

Marriage. Memories. A shining past.

And a future that seemed as dark as the rain outside.

"Didn't even know she *had* a brother," he said. "He was in prison when I met her, she never once mentioned him. The first I knew of him was when he showed up on our doorstep last summer. It was one of the hottest days of the year, I remember . . ."

. . . the sun sitting in the sky like a ball of fire, the sprinklers going in the fields, a Yellow Cab from town coming up the road and throwing dust a mile into the sky. Leeds is in the barn doing something, he doesn't remember what just now, perhaps stitching a torn cinch on a saddle, he has always been very good with his hands, even when he was a kid, and he loves repairing things. He can't imagine why a taxi has come out here to Timucuan Point Road, and he has no idea who the man getting out of the cab might be.

He puts down the saddle girth — that's what he'd been working on, he now remembers clearly — and goes out to where the young man is paying the driver, the driver making change, the dust still rising on the air around them. It occurs to him that the young man has the same coloring as his wife. Green eyes, red hair — well, hers is a bit more on the brown side, a reddish-brown. But this is just a fleeting observation, and

he makes no real connection, he never once thinks they might be brother and sister.

The young man turns and extends his hand.

He is wearing a short-sleeved shirt open at the throat, blue jeans, Western boots.

There is a mermaid tattoo on his right forearm.

The mermaid has long yellow hair and blue eyes and bright red lips and red-nippled breasts and a blue-scaled tail.

I'm Ned Weaver, the stranger says, hand still extended.

Which, of course, is Jessica's maiden name, Jessica Welles Weaver, the Welles for her mother's maiden name — is this young man a cousin or something?

But no, he is not a cousin.

Because a cry of joy sounds from within the house, and Jessica comes bounding out in cutoff shorts and a green T-shirt, barefooted, running toward the young man, who drops the duffel he's been holding in his left hand, and turns to her and opens both arms wide to her, and clasps her to him, her long reddish hair — she was wearing her hair long then — cascading over his arms behind her back, showering the mermaid's yellow hair and red-nippled breasts. Oh, Ned, she cries, oh God, how *happy* I am to see you!

"She'd been writing to him all the while he was in prison," Leeds said now. "Had herself a P.O. box in town, he'd send his letters to her there. I didn't know she'd offered him a job till all the introductions and the laughing and the oh my Gods were out of the way and we were sitting around the pool drinking. I didn't know he was a jailbird until that night in bed when she told me his sad, sad history. Always the innocent victim, that brother of hers, dear little Ned, pure as the driven snow. Norton Albert Weaver, named for Jessica's father, who'd been lucky enough to die long before his only son turned rotten. Norton Albert Weaver, a vicious son of a bitch if ever there was one, but I didn't know that until the day with the dog. This must've been . . ."

. . . late October last year, the hurricane season all but gone, Ned settling into his duties on the farm. The man has a thumb can turn a ripe tomato blue, but he's now one of the foremen around here, barking out orders, strutting like a peacock for the women in the fields, making pass after pass at pretty little Allie in the kitchen, who loves her husband to death and who's so flustered by Ned's unwanted attentions that she's tempted to give up the only good job she's ever had. She speaks to Jessica about it, and Jessica promises to talk to her brother. But privately, she tells Leeds that their housekeeper has been flirting with Ned.

That day with the dog . . .

The dog belongs to Allie and her husband, Pete, who before Ned took over as foreman was doing a fine job of running things by himself. Pete is a Vietnam vet, thirty-five years old — it's difficult to realize that anyone who was a veteran of that war would now have to be at *least* thirty-three, but that is actually the case. He is a soft-spoken man who lowers his eyes whenever he's addressed, as though he is fearful a person might look into those eyes and see reflected there all the things he has seen — and done. It is difficult to imagine this man ever killing anyone. But he is alive today. And if you were in combat in Vietnam, as was Pete, and you did not kill people, then you would not be alive today. The equation is a simple one.

Whenever he drives his truck out there in the fields, his dog is sitting beside him on the front seat. The dog's name is Jasper. He is a spotted something-or-other; no one has ever been able to determine his ancestry with any accuracy, but it's reckoned he is at least part Dalmatian, a dog with a somewhat sappy look on his face and a manner as gentle as his master's.

On that day in October . . .

It is one of those crisp, glistening days that infrequently bless this part of Florida, causing all those settlers who moved from colder climes to thank their lucky stars all over again for the wisdom of their decision and the beneficence of the Lord

Almighty. The cloudless sky stretched taut over the bountiful acres of the farm is as blue as Monday, and a fair wind is blowing in off the Gulf and carrying inland. There is a man-made pond on the farm, stocked with trout, stalked by water birds that take immediate wing whenever an alligator puts in a sudden and unwanted appearance.

It is against the law to shoot alligators in the state of Florida.

Alligators are a protected species.

Occasionally, a farmer or an orange grower will take a shot at one, and occasionally alligator steaks will appear on the dinner table — but no one talks about that much. In the state of Florida, there are a great many things that people don't talk about. Rainy weather is one of those things. Cold weather is another. Shooting alligators or ospreys is yet another. But over the years, Leeds has shot and killed and later grilled and eaten three alligators that decided to make a home in his trout pond. A fourth alligator is in that pond on this bright, shining day in October.

"We all heard Jasper screaming," Leeds said. "Sounded like a human being. A baby. Screaming and screaming. And then the screaming stopped. We were all on our way down to the pond by then. The alligator was still gnawing on that poor dog. Snout all covered with blood — have you ever seen the teeth on an alligator? Someone had tied Jasper to an old oak tree near the edge of the pond. The rope was still wound around the trunk of the tree. Jasper had circled and circled the tree trying to get away from that 'gator, and then he'd run out of rope and the 'gator just took him." Leeds shook his head. "It was my brother-in-law who tied that dog to the tree."

"How do you know that?"

"He all but said so."

"When?"

"Right after the trial. We were all pretty upset about that verdict, you know, letting those men go free after what they did

to Jessie. Ned said if he had his way, he'd go after all three of them and drag them down to the pond and tie them to that old oak, the way someone had done with Jasper. That's when I knew he was the one who'd done it. I'd suspected it all along — we *all* did — but that was when I knew for sure it was him. I could see it right there in his eyes."

"So what he said, in effect, was that he wanted to *kill* those men."

"Well, yes. But the point is he wanted to kill them the way Jasper had . . ."

"Yes, I understand that. Did he sound serious when he said this?"

"As serious as any of us," Leeds said. "We *all* wanted them dead."

"Yes, but what I'm asking . . . do you think this was more than just an idle threat? What your brother-in-law said?"

"About going after them, do you mean?"

"Yes. Do you think he did, in fact, go after them?"

"Well, I . . ."

"Do you think he killed them?"

It was evident that the thought had never once entered Leeds's mind. Ned Weaver as his sister's avenger? Ned Weaver as the Midnight Vigilante? But if so . . .

"Do you mean . . . ?"

He was sorting out the implications. If indeed Ned had gone after those men, if indeed Ned had killed them, then Ned had also dropped his wallet at the scene, Ned had set him up.

"The son of a bitch," he said.

"*Could* he have done it?" Matthew asked.

"He's mean enough, that's for sure," Leeds said.

"Did you see him at any time on the night of the murders?"

"Yes, he stopped by right after dinner."

"Was he in the habit of stopping by?"

"Well, yes. Jessie's his sister, you know. They're very close."

"Stopped by for what reason?"

"Just to say good night. This must've been a little before eight, we'd just finished dinner. We were getting ready to watch the movie."

"How long did he stay?"

"Just a few minutes. Jessie offered him a drink — we were having an after-dinner drink outside — but he said no, he had some things to do."

"What things?" Matthew asked.

"Didn't say."

"What time did he leave?"

"Eight o'clock? A little after? No later than that. We were still sitting at the table out back, by the pool."

"Did someone show him to the front door?" Matthew asked.

"No. What do you mean? He knows the way, he's in and out of our house all the time."

"Went to the door by himself then?"

"Yes."

"Did he go through the house?"

"I believe so, yes."

"Went through the house to the front door."

"Yes."

"And you and Jessie stayed out back."

"Yes."

"How long did it take him to leave?"

"I'm sorry, I don't know what you mean."

"He said good night to you out back and walked through the house to the front door . . ."

"I assume he did."

On the night of the murders, someone had driven Jessie's Maserati to the marina and boarded Leeds's boat. The someone had been wearing a yellow jacket and hat and he was seen later that night both at Kickers and in Little Asia. Leeds's yellow jacket and hat had been hanging in the hall closet, just inside the entrance to the house. The study was off to the left, two

steps down. The keys to Jessie's Maserati had been hanging on a brass holder fastened to the study wall. The keys to Leeds's boat had been hanging on that same wall.

"Did you hear the front door close behind him?" Matthew asked.

"I . . . really can't say."

"Then you don't know how long he was in the house *after* he'd said good night."

"No, I don't," Leeds said.

Matthew nodded. It was at least possible.

But the look of gloom had settled on Leeds's face again, clouding his eyes, causing his mouth to go slack. He knew what Matthew was thinking, but he wasn't buying it. Not any of it. His eyes revealed only despair.

"We don't *have* to find the real murderer, you know," Matthew said.

"I know," Leeds said, and clasped his hands in front of him on the table again.

"We only have to show you couldn't have done it."

"Yes."

"And we're well on the way to doing that."

"Are we?"

"Well, sure," Matthew said. "We've got a witness who saw a license plate that doesn't ex —"

"A *dead* witness," Leeds said.

"What Trinh said is still on the record. We have his statement. And his murder only helps our case."

"I don't see how."

"Because whoever killed him may have killed the others as well."

"The papers are saying it was a copycat."

"The papers are saying what the State Attorney *wants* them to say."

"They hate my father," Leeds said. "Because he tried to buy them out."

"I know that. So don't worry about what the papers are saying. The papers aren't a judge and jury."

"It feels like they are."

He looked down at his clasped hands. Head bent. Behind him the rain kept riddling the palm fronds. His gloom was palpable. Matthew didn't know what he could say to dispel it.

"We've also turned Stubbs around," he said.

No answer.

"He's ready to testify that the man who called him wasn't you."

No answer.

"Which is very good news. He was one of their best witnesses."

No answer. Just sat there looking at his hands, the rain falling behind him. And then, without looking up, in a voice so low that Matthew had trouble hearing him, he said, "Be nice if it *was* Ned, wouldn't it? But when I think of the victims he picked for himself" — and now he was shaking his head — "not the bank guard, that was just someone who got in his way. But the others" — still shaking his head, looking down at his hands — "an old lady . . . a retarded girl . . . that sweet, gentle dog . . ."

He looked up at last.

His eyes were brimming with tears.

"No, Mr. Hope," he said. "I don't think it was Ned. He just doesn't have the balls."

There was a message that Mai Chim Lee had called. Matthew looked at his watch. It was a little before noon. Hoping he'd catch her before she left for lunch, he dialed the number she'd left, let it ring six times, and was about to hang up when a woman's voice said, "Longstreet and Powers, good morning. Or afternoon. Whichever it is."

"Morning," Matthew said. "For the next five minutes."

"Thank God *someone* has the right time. Is your power still on?"

"Yes," he said. "Well, I don't know, just a minute." He snapped on his desk lamp. "Yes, it is," he said.

"There are some lines down, we've been out since ten this morning," she said. "But enough of my troubles. How can I help you?"

"May I speak to Miss Lee, please?"

"Mary? Sure, just a minute."

Mary, he thought, and waited.

"Hello?"

The singsong voice. The somewhat sorrowful lilt of it.

"Mai Chim? It's Matthew."

"Oh, hello, Matthew, how are you? I'm so happy you called back."

"Is everything all right?"

"Yes, fine, thank you. Did you read about Mr. Trinh?"

"I did, yes."

"Such a nice old man," she said.

"Yes."

"Matthew, I feel very bad about the other night."

"Why should you?"

"Because I behaved so foolishly."

"But you didn't."

"So very foolishly."

"No."

"Like a child."

"I didn't think so at all. Really, Mai Chim . . ."

"I'm almost thirty-one years old, Matthew."

"I know that."

"That's not a child."

"I know."

"Matthew, would you care to have dinner with me tomorrow night?"

"I'd love to have dinner with you," he said.

"Please understand that *I'm* the one who's asking you."

"Yes, I realize that."

"Good, then that's settled. I think I know a very nice place. Can you pick me up at eight?"

"Eight sounds fine."

"Perhaps we will get to know each other better," she said, and hung up.

Matthew looked at the mouthpiece.

Warren Chambers's answering machine had a recording capability that made it relatively simple to tape a conversation without the knowledge of the person on the other end of the line. All you had to do was hit the PLAYBACK button, dial your number, and — when your party started talking — hit the RECORD and START buttons simultaneously. No beeps would sound to alert the party on the other end. The operation was what was known as covert.

He was making his call from the small office that used to belong to Samalson Investigations before Otto Samalson himself went out of business. Otto went out of business because someone shot him dead. Getting shot dead in the private-eye business usually happened only in novels and movies, but Otto had somehow managed the trick in real life. The Chinese lady who'd worked for him — Warren couldn't remember her name, but she'd been damn good — left for Hawaii shortly afterward, and the office had remained unoccupied until Warren recently took over the lease and bought all the furniture from the man to whom Otto's children had sold it.

The frosted-glass door to the Chambers Detective Agency opened onto a reception room that measured six by eight feet, into which were crammed a wooden desk with a typewriter on it and a wooden chair behind it, an upholstered easy chair opposite it, green metal filing cabinets and bookshelves, and a Xerox

machine and a coatrack, all enclosed by walls now hung with photographs of Warren's mother and his two sisters and their families back in St. Louis. Warren figured that if someone wasn't going to hire you because you had pictures of your black family on the walls, then maybe he ought to look across the desk and discover that *you* were black, too.

Warren did not as yet have a receptionist; his answering machine served that purpose. Whenever he put on temporary help, whichever investigator he hired normally worked out of the reception area. His own private office was larger than the outer office — eight by ten as opposed to six by eight — but just as cluttered. It enjoyed the advantage of a window, however, which, combined with its few extra feet, made it seem spacious by comparison, even if the only view from it was of a bank building across the street.

Rain streaked that window as Warren dialed the number at the Leeds farm. Jessica Leeds herself answered on the third ring. Warren told her who was calling, and they exchanged some small talk about the awful weather, and then he asked if he might speak to Mr. Weaver, please. He did not say, "May I speak to your *brother*, please?" He felt that allowing her to assume he didn't yet know this fact was the safest course to follow. She asked him to wait, please. He waited. While he waited, he hit both the RECORD and START buttons. He was now recording dead air. But better that than any telltale click when Weaver came on the line. Rain slithered down the windowpane. He looked across at the bank building. Everything looked grey and bleak and dismal. He kept waiting.

"Hello?"

You're on the air, he thought.

"Hello, Mr. Weaver?"

"Yes?"

"It's Warren Chambers, I hope I'm not catching you at a bad time."

"Nope."

"I wanted to apologize, first of all, for our little misunderstanding the other day. I can see how . . ."

"Okay."

The man was a monosyllablist.

"I can see how a person who looked as if he was trying to break into the house . . ."

"I said okay."

Three words this time. Not bad. Warren wondered if he'd like to try for four.

"If you've got a minute . . ."

"Sure."

" . . . there are a few questions I'd like to ask you."

"Sure."

"Mr. Weaver, had you ever known Mr. Leeds to take his boat out for a little moonlight spin?"

"A what?"

"A little moonlight spin."

"Sure. All the time."

"You understand what I mean, don't you?"

"Sure. A little moonlight spin."

Good. He'd repeated the exact words Stubbs had heard on the telephone. *A little moonlight spin.* He was making remarkable progress, having come as far as five full words in a row. If Warren could get him up to six, or maybe seven, or maybe even a complete sentence with a subject and a predicate, and from there to a full paragraph — the possibilities were limitless, the horizons boundless.

"What time would you say he went out for these little spins?" he asked.

"Varied."

Back to single syllable utterances again.

"Seven-thirty?"

"Later."

"Eight-thirty?"

"Sometimes."

"What time *would* you say?"

Say ten, ten-thirty, Warren thought. Say the words *ten, ten-thirty.*

"Eleven, eleven-thirty," Weaver said. "That'd be a moonlight spin, around that time. If there *was* a moon, of course."

Little bit of humor there. Little bit of jailhouse jokery. And certainly more words than Warren had heard from him since they'd started talking. But Weaver hadn't said the words Warren wanted to hear, which would have been nice, since ten, ten-thirty was the e.t.a. the caller had given Stubbs on the telephone.

"You weren't worried when he took the boat out at night, were you?"

"Nope."

"It being dark and all."

"Not with a moon."

More jailhouse jollity. Must've been a card out there on the yard, young Ned.

"But when there *wasn't* a moon, if he took the boat out for a little moonlight spin when there *wasn't* a moon — would that have alarmed you?"

Say the word, Warren thought.

"*Alarmed* me?"

Bingo.

"Yes. Would that have alarmed you?"

"Nope."

"How come? You know what I'm saying, don't you?"

Say it again for me, Warren thought.

"Sure," Weaver said. "Would I be alarmed."

Thank you, Warren thought.

"Yes," he said. "Him being out in the dark and all."

"Man knows how to run a boat, don't he?" Weaver said, and Warren could visualize him shrugging on the other end of the line.

"Well, thanks for clearing that up," he said. "We were a little concerned about it."

"Why?" Weaver asked.

"Something in the papers the State Attorney sent over," Warren said.

"Oh," Weaver said.

"So thanks again, you've been a big help."

"Yeah," Weaver said, and hung up.

Now, you little prick, Warren thought, let's see if you were making any phone calls on the night of August thirteenth.

In Chicago when he was a boy, Matthew used to run along the lake, hoping one day to be fast enough to qualify for the track team at school. He'd never got fast enough. Too light for football, too slow for track, he'd opted instead for ice hockey and had broken his leg — or, rather, had it broken *for* him — during the first game of the season. The leg still hurt when the weather was bad. Like today. Running around the track at the police gymnasium, undisputed and unlimited admission courtesy of Detective Morris Bloom, the leg hurt like hell. But he could feel the pounds melting away.

This morning at eight, after he'd swum a hundred laps in the pool — *and* in the rain — he'd weighed a hundred and eighty-four pounds. That was close to eighty-four kilos in Rome, where he'd put on some of the weight, and a bit more than thirteen stones in London, where he'd stopped on the way home to see a lawyer friend of his who now spent much of the year in Hawkhurst, Kent. Tomorrow morning, if it didn't rain, he had another tennis lesson with Kit Howell, who had demolished him last Saturday. This time, Matthew hoped to be at *least* six pounds lighter and a lot faster on his feet.

The steady pounding of his sneakers on the track's synthetic surface, rather than lulling him to sleep, provided a rhythmic background to his thoughts. It worked the same way

whenever he was at a concert. He wondered why this should be so. Why mindless physical exertion stimulated thought as effectively as sitting in a concert hall with wave after wave of sound washing over him. There were two other runners on the track ahead of him, one a tall, hefty man wearing a black warmup suit, the other a slender man some five feet nine inches tall, wearing a grey sweatshirt and sweatpants, a blue watch cap pulled down over his ears. Matthew did not try to pass either of them. Nor did either of them seem intent on breaking any speed records. The hefty man was out in front, the smaller man some thirty feet behind him, Matthew some thirty feet or so in the rear. They kept up the steady pace, the regular distance between them, like strangers in a big city on a cinder track in a park. But this was indoors at the police gym, with the rain still drilling the streets outside.

He wondered why Trinh had been killed.

This was the single most significant development in the case, the murder of the man who had seen the killer entering an automobile parked at the curb outside Little Asia. This information had been reported in Calusa's own lovely rag, the *Herald-Tribune*: *Trinh Mang Duc, one of the key witnesses in the Stephen Leeds murder case, is reported to have seen the license plate on the automobile allegedly driven by the murderer*. There it was. An invitation to slaughter. And good enough reason to petition for a change of venue.

But then why hadn't the murderer also gone after Tran Sum Linh, who'd shared a smoke on his front step with one of his many cousins, and who'd seen a man in yellow running through the moonlit night toward the house the victims shared? He, too, was a witness, the essential *before* to Trinh's *after*. Why go after one and not the other? Or was Tran next on the killer's list?

The runners ahead were picking up the pace.

Matthew increased his own pace, keeping the same steady distance between himself and the nearest runner; the man in

the blue woolen cap was now drenched with sweat, great black blots spreading over the back of his grey sweatshirt and the backs of his thighs in the grey sweatpants, sneakered feet pounding the track. Matthew was similarly soaked, contentedly awash in perspiration. Tomorrow morning, he would step out on that tennis court as svelte and as swift as Ivan Lendl. *Whack*, his racket would meet the ball, and *swissssssh* the ball would zoom over the net — and it's yet another ace for Matthew Hope, folks, the fourth in this exciting set, Fat Chance Department.

It had to have been the license plate.

Trinh seeing the plate.

Seeing it erroneously, as it turned out, but seeing it nonetheless. Because otherwise, if the killer was covering his tracks, he'd be going after *all* the witnesses: Tran, who'd seen him at a little after eleven, and the woman they'd named in yesterday's paper — this time *after* Matthew had received from the S.A.'s office her name and sworn statement, thank God for small favors — someone named Sherry Reynolds who worked at Kickers and who claimed to have seen the ubiquitous man in the yellow jacket and hat getting off a fifty-foot Mediterranean, which happened to be the very sort of boat Leeds owned. Saw him disembarking at ten-thirty that night and getting into a green Oldsmobile Cutlass Supreme, which later on turned up in Little Asia, bearing the license plate Trinh and only Trinh had seen, which was an impossible plate in the state of Florida.

So why kill him?

The plate he'd seen simply did not exist.

But the killer couldn't have known this because the newspapers hadn't revealed the numbers and letters on the plate; Patricia Demming had at least kept back that much.

So the killer did not know Trinh had made a mistaken identification.

The killer knew only that Trinh had seen the license plate, Trinh had identified the car, and if the State Attorney knew this then the police *also* knew this, and the ball game was over.

But then why kill Trinh?

Why not get the hell out of Calusa as fast as his feet could carry him, run to China, run to the North Pole, get out of town before they traced the license plate directly to his front door?

Something was wrong here.

Because . . .

If the killer thought the State Attorney and the police were in possession of his correct license plate number, then the cat was already out of the bag, and he would have run for his life. Or given himself up, one or the other. What he would *not* have done was go after Trinh Mang Duc to shut him up after he'd *already* revealed what he'd seen. There was no sense to that.

So maybe Bloom and Patricia were both right, maybe this *was* a copycat murder.

Or maybe the killer *knew* — but how could he? — that Trinh had given them the wrong numbers and letters, and maybe he figured he had to get *rid* of Trinh before he remembered the *right* ones.

Damn it, that had to be it.

The killer had to have known —

The collision came suddenly and unexpectedly.

One moment Matthew was running along at a steady pace, lost in thought, losing weight and minding his own business, and the next minute the sweat-stained man ahead of him stopped dead, and before Matthew could stop his own forward momentum, he crashed into him. They went tumbling down together in an awkward embrace, Matthew pushing out with his arms in a vain attempt to prevent the crash, the other man partially turning when he realized he'd been hit from behind, meeting the full force of the blow with his hip, the track coming up fast to meet them both. "Oh shit!" the other man said, and Matthew recognized the voice and realized that the tangle of arms and legs in the grey sweatshirt and sweatpants was none other than Assistant State Attorney Patricia ("Do Not Call Me Pat or Even Trish") Demming, even *before* she rolled over into a

sitting position and yanked the blue woolen watchcap from her head to reveal a mass of sodden blond hair.

"You," she said.

"We keep colliding," Matthew said.

They were sitting in the center of the track now, both of them out of breath, facing each other, knees up, sneakered feet almost touching. Her sweatshirt was drenched.

"This time it was *your* fault," Patricia said.

"No, you stopped dead."

"My shoelace was untied."

"You should have signaled."

"I didn't know anyone was behind me," she said, and got to her feet. Matthew got up, too. The other runner had already circled the track again and was bearing down on them. He was red-faced and puffing hard, wearing headphones and flapping his arms at them like a swimmer doing a frantic breaststroke, urging them to clear the track before there was yet another collision. He went by like a locomotive on the way to Albuquerque, New Mexico, wherever that was, sweat flying from his face and his neck, feet pounding the track, while Patricia and Matthew crowded the rail for dear life.

"You're soaking wet," she said.

"So are you."

"Seems like old times," she said, and grinned.

He was remembering her in the red silk dress. Her nipples threatening the red silk. Both of them standing in the rain.

"I think I know why Trinh was killed," he said.

"Don't you ever sleep?" she said.

"Want to discuss it over a drink?"

"No, Counselor," she said, "it was nice seeing you again," and slapped the woolen watchcap against her thigh and walked swiftly toward the door leading off the track, shaking her head.

The 6:01 express was coming around again.

Matthew got out of its way.

*

Policemen standing in the rain look the same all over the world. Especially when they're standing there looking down at a corpse. You won't see an umbrella anywhere in evidence. The uniformed cops may be wearing rainslickers, and the plain-clothesmen may be wearing trenchcoats, but blues or suits, it doesn't matter, you'll never see an umbrella. There were eight policemen, some of them suits, most of them blues, standing around the corpse in the drainage ditch.

This was still only nine o'clock that Friday night, the weekend hadn't yet begun in earnest. None of the cops had been expecting a corpse quite this early. Anyway, in this city, the corpses were few and far between. Oh yes, several more per month now that crack was on the scene, but crack was on the scene everywhere in America, crack was the shame of the nation, a thousand points of light shining down on cocaine you could inhale from a pipe, this was some shining city on a hill, this nation.

Detective Morris Bloom was one of the cops standing around the corpse. He was wearing a blue suit and a white shirt, dark-blue tie with a mustard stain on it. The rain had tapered off to a slow, lazy drizzle. He stood hatless and coatless in the light rain, looking down at the corpse. An assistant Medical Examiner was kneeling beside the corpse. The drainage ditch had a curved bottom. The corpse was lying on its side facing the rear of the ditch, away from the road. No one had touched the body yet. No one wanted to. The skull was all crushed in. There was blood all over the ditch, blood on the shiny black road where the body had been dragged before it was dumped.

The assistant M.E. was having trouble with the curving sides of the ditch. The ditch was slippery, and he kept losing his footing as he tried to examine the body. No one had yet looked for any identification of any kind. They were all waiting for the M.E. to finish here. Or better yet, to get *started* here.

Cooper Rawles walked over from where he'd been talking to the officer who'd first responded. Like Bloom, he was hatless

and coatless. But he'd just come off a plant at a homosexual bar where crack was allegedly being sold over the counter like jelly beans, and he was wearing tan tailored slacks, tasseled brown loafers, a pink V-necked cotton sweater over a bare chest, and a gold earring in his right ear.

"You look stunning," Bloom said.

"Thanks," Rawles said drily. "The man in George car says the motorist was gone when he got here."

"What motorist?"

"The one who called it in. Gave the location and then split."

"Small wonder," Bloom said. "It's the earring that does it, you know."

"I thought the earring was a nice touch, too," Rawles said.

The captain in command of Calusa's detective bureau — a new man called Rush, for Rushville, Decker — came walking over from the Criminalistic Unit's mobile van. He'd only recently replaced the bureau's Captain Hopper, whom Bloom used to call His Royal Shmuck. Behind his back. Decker seemed like a good man. So far.

"How we doing here?" he asked the M.E.

"Can you get me some more light?" the M.E. said.

The cars were angled so that their headlight beams were pointed at the scene, and they had also set up a generator and some lamps — the road out here near the fairgrounds was normally pitch black — but there still wasn't enough illumination. The men milled about the spot where the corpse had been dumped, casting long shadows, the light refracted by the falling rain.

"Let's get the Doc some more light here," Decker said, and two of the blues in orange rainslickers walked over from the knot of police cars and shined their long torches into the ditch and onto the corpse. A car with a State Attorney's office seal on the door pulled to a stop behind the other vehicles, and a man Bloom hadn't met before walked over and introduced himself

as Dom Santucci, Assistant S.A. Decker shook hands with him and in turn introduced him to both Bloom and Rawles.

"Messy one," Santucci said.

Bloom had seen worse.

"Any idea what did it?" Decker asked the M.E.

"Some kind of blunt instrument," he answered. He was still kneeling over the body, seemingly more comfortable with his position now. The two officers in the orange slickers kept their torches shining at the back of the stiff's head, where the hair was all matted with blood around the craters in the skull.

"Like what?" Decker asked. "A hammer?"

"Hard to say. Whatever it was, it was wielded with considerable force. Can someone give me a hand here, help me roll him over?"

No one seemed eager to give him a hand.

"Give the Doc a hand there," Decker snapped to the two officers in the orange slickers.

Both men put down their torches and straddled the ditch. Lying on the roadway, the torches cast a crazy kind of splayed light into the blackness. Legs widespread, the officers tested for purchase and then looked for a place to grab the body; neither of them wanted to get blood on his hands.

"One, two, three, *ho!*" one of them said, and they rolled the body over.

"Light, please," the M.E. said.

The officers picked up the torches, shined them on the corpse's face.

The man from the S.A.'s office let out a short, sharp gasp.

"That's Frank Bannion," he said.

11

His scale this morning had read a hundred and eighty-two pounds; he'd been hoping for a hundred and eighty. He'd swum another hundred laps before breakfast, and now, at twenty minutes to eight, he was in his tennis whites and ready to drive to the club, feeling somewhat more fit than he had *last* Saturday, when Kit Howell had taught his devastating left-handed lesson.

There was something immensely satisfying about getting up at the crack of dawn, awake with the sun and the birds, and breakfasting before there was any sound of life in the streets. The front lawn was sparkling with dew as he backed the rented car out of the garage. There went Mrs. Hedges across the street, walking in her robe to get the newspaper from the mailbox. A wave. Morning, Mrs. Hedges. Morning, Mr. Hope. Long pink robe, floppy pink slippers, he wondered what Patricia Demming looked like at a quarter to eight in the morning. If she looked terrific sopping wet in the rain or dripping sweat in a running suit, how bad could she look in the morning? Don't you

ever sleep? she'd asked him. But that was before Frank Bannion's skull got crushed with something blunt.

There was a peaceful calm to the club's parking lot. Matthew wondered if the early-morning players walking from their automobiles had read the headlines today. He wondered if they even knew who Frank Bannion was. The morning was sunny and bright after yesterday's rain, not too terribly hot as yet, it was going to be a lovely day. Who wanted to think about dead investigators on a day like today? He wondered if Patricia Demming was thinking about her dead investigator. He wondered if she still thought a copycat murderer was on the loose while Stephen Leeds languished in jail.

He went into the men's locker room to pee one last time, washed his hands afterward at the sink, looked at himself in the mirror, and thought, You can do it, Hope. You can beat Kit Howell. He nodded at his own image, dried his hands, picked up his racket, and strode confidently to the teaching court.

"The trouble with your game," Kit was saying, "is that you don't plan ahead. You have to plan at least two, three moves ahead. Otherwise, you'll always be surprised by what happens."

"Six—love was a big surprise, all right," Matthew said.

They were sitting in the club's coffee shop, a screened-in area adjacent to the swimming pool. This was Saturday morning, the pool was full of squealing kids. Most of the men hadn't yet come in from their early-morning doubles games, the shop was full of women waiting to play. On Saturdays and Sundays, men were given preference for morning court time. Unless a woman could prove she was a *working* woman. Nine to five. Like Patricia Demming. Don't you ever sleep?

Matthew, and at least a dozen other men he could name, had voted against the proposed rule, but the majority had prevailed. His former wife, Susan, nonetheless decided that Calusa

Bath and Racquet was an overtly sexist club and switched her membership to the Sabal Key Club, even though it meant a fifteen-minute-longer drive from the house he once had shared with her. Her protest seemed mild; there were some women in Calusa who would tear out your throat if you so much as opened a door for them.

When Matthew was a little boy, his mother had taught him to open doors for women. Ladies, she'd called them. Another taboo, he guessed, the word *ladies*. She'd said it was good manners to open a door for a lady. She said gentlemen opened doors for ladies. Nowadays only sexist pigs opened doors for women. When was the second stage going to *get* here, Betty?

Everywhere around him and Kit, there was female conversation, bright and lively at this hour of the morning, punctuated with laughter. He realized with a start that half the young mothers sitting here, chatting and laughing over their coffee cups, could beat him one-to-one on a tennis court. Or was *this* a sexist observation, too? The hell with it, he thought; it's too damn dangerous to live in these trigger-happy times.

"If you plan only for the moment," Kit was saying, "you'll . . ."

"Who says I plan at *all*?" Matthew said.

"Well, you've got to have *some* kind of plan," Kit said, surprised.

"Not very often."

"At *least* in that split second before you hit the ball."

"Well, yes."

"You've got some idea of where you're trying to place it, haven't you?"

"Yes. Not that it always goes there."

"I understand that. But what I'm saying is you've got to think of the game as a logical succession of shots. If you hit the ball to a specific place, there should be only one possible shot I can make to return it, and you should know where that place

has to be, and you should be waiting there for the ball. And because I'm where I am, then your plan should include where you've got to return it so I can't get to it, do you follow me?"

"Yes. But I have enough trouble just getting the ball back. Without having to worry two shots ahead."

"That's exactly my point. You're having trouble getting it back because I *do* have a plan. I hit the ball here, you have to return it here," he said, using the tabletop as a court, moving the tip of his index finger back and forth across it. "You don't have a choice. You either return the ball the only way it *can* be returned, or you'll miss it entirely. So it comes back here," he said, using his finger again, "and I'm waiting for it, so I hit it *here*, where you can't possibly get to it. But let's say you *do* manage to get all the way cross-court in time," he said, moving his finger swiftly to the other side of the table, "and you reach the ball, you actually get your racket on it. The only place you can *possibly* hit it — because the ball is here on your backhand — is down the line. And I'm waiting for it because I *know* that's your only possible shot. So I drill it to the other side of the court, and the point is mine."

"You make it sound easy," Matthew said.

"It *is* easy, if you have a plan," Kit said. "It's like chess, in a way. The best player is the one who can think the most moves ahead. Tennis is less predictable, of course, the moves aren't *fixed* in tennis . . . well, maybe that's the wrong comparison, chess. Tennis is more like a battle. You don't just return fire haphazardly unless you suddenly find yourself in deep shit, excuse me. But if this is a planned maneuver, if for example you *know* where the enemy is out there, and you *know* approximately how many of them there are, then you can situate your platoon so that *this* specific fire forces *this* specific response," again moving his finger across the table, "while you're all the while moving your people to *another* position," the finger moving again, "so they can lob in a mortar from the left, or rush the flank from the right, or whatever. It's all a matter of calculating

what choices, if any, the enemy has for his response, and then being ready for those choices so you can step in and cream him. A plan," Kit said. "Simple."

"Sure," Matthew said.

"I mean it. Figure out a plan for next Saturday, okay? Work it out on paper, if you have to. Your shot, and where you think it'll land on my side of the net, and what my possible responses might be, and where you'd have to be standing to be ready for my return, and where you'll put the next shot to take advantage of my position on the court, and so on. Figure a plan for maybe five or six shots ahead, okay, and we'll try it next week."

"Okay," Matthew said dubiously.

"It'll work, wait and see," Kit said, and smiled and looked at his watch. "I have to go," he said. "Next Saturday at eight, okay?"

"See you," Matthew said.

The call came at a little before ten that morning, while he was in the shower. He climbed out of the tub, wrapped a towel around his waist, went running into the study, and picked up the receiver.

"Hello?" he said.

"Matthew?"

"Yes?"

"Patricia Demming," she said.

"Naturally," he said. "I'm dripping wet."

"Sorry, is this a bad time, have you seen the papers this morning?"

"Yes."

"What'd you think?"

He hesitated. She was the enemy, and this morning Kit had taught him a few things about dealing effectively with the enemy, either on a tennis court or a battlefield. Moreover,

when the lady who was trying to cook your client called at ten in the morning wanting to know what you'd thought about the murder of her investigator . . .

"What'd *you* think?" he asked.

Lob a mortar from the left, he thought. Then hit the ball to her backhand and when she returned it down the line, smash it cross-court to where she wasn't.

"I'd like to talk to you," she said, surprising him completely. "Can you meet me at my office in an hour or so?"

"All right."

"Thanks, Matthew," she said, and hung up.

Matthew wondered what her game plan was.

On the baseball field adjoining the renovated motel that now served as the State Attorney's office complex, some kids were playing pickup ball. Their voices carried on the stillness of the Saturday morning air, floating out over the ballpark fence and drifting in over the motel courtyard. In the tick of an instant, the voices carried Matthew back to Chicago. The house the family had lived in, the school he'd gone to, the park he and his sister had played in as children, all appeared in his mind like browning snapshots in an old album. He had not spoken to his sister in more than a month now. He realized all at once how much he missed her. The voices from the ballpark soared up over the fence. Summer voices. Baseball voices. He sighed as if burdened and walked quickly toward Patricia's unit.

It was still relatively cool for this time of day, but the air conditioning was on in her office. She was dressed casually: jeans, sandals, a white T-shirt, her long blond hair pulled back into a ponytail. This was her day off, the State Attorney's offices were officially closed for the weekend. Except for the two of them, the place was empty. It felt strange being here without typewriters clacking and phones ringing, people running around with papers in blue legal binders.

"I'd have asked you to my house," she said, "but I'm being painted."

"407 Ocean," he said. "Fatback Key."

"Good memory," she said.

"It's a shorter ride here."

"Whisper's much closer, that's true."

"But Fatback's much nicer."

"Well, I'm not so sure."

"Wilder, anyway."

"Still a bit wilder, yes," she admitted. "More Florida."

A common expression down here. *More Florida*. Meaning as yet unspoiled. Florida as it used to be. People down here were always sighing for the Florida that used to be. Hoping to find it somewhere. But it wasn't here anymore. Not even in the Everglades. Maybe no place in America was "here" anymore.

"I need your help," she said.

He raised his eyebrows.

"This isn't a trick, Matthew."

He waited.

"I've never been as confused about a case in my life," she said.

He kept waiting.

"If I've already got the real killer in jail," she said, "then he's a very stupid man. But if the real killer is still out there, *he's* very stupid, too."

"He's out there, I'm sure of that," Matthew said.

"Then why is he still killing people? We've already *charged* someone, why doesn't he just leave well enough alone?"

"Nobody says a killer has to be a nuclear physicist."

"Granted. My point is . . ."

"I understand your point."

"If he's *already* home free . . ."

"He may not think so."

"But why would he play against such odds?"

"Maybe he's worried."

"About what? A witness who didn't even see the right license plate?"

"But maybe Trinh was close enough. Maybe the killer was worried about that."

"This is all arguendo, you realize."

"I realize."

"Because I'm not admitting there *is* a killer out there."

"Right, we're just exploring the possibility."

"And I'll be getting to *your* man in a minute."

"I figured."

"But let's say, arguendo, that we've made a mistake, okay? We've got the wrong man. Arguendo."

"Arguendo."

"And let's say, I'll even give you this, let's say he *was* worried about Trinh having seen that license-plate number, and he went out to kill him. Witnesses are killed all the time, you know . . ."

"Yes."

". . . so it's not an unlikely scenario. But if he thought we were in possession of the *right* number, why didn't he just get the hell out of town before we pounced on him? Why kill Trinh? That doesn't make sense, does it?"

"No, it doesn't."

"And why go after Bannion next? An investigator for the S.A.'s office? That doesn't make sense, either. The man would have to be crazy."

"Maybe he is."

"So I can't find any *reasons* out there, Matthew. It all seems too . . . *suicidal*. We've already got a man in jail for the crimes, why cast doubt on the case? Which brings me to Leeds."

"Leeds is in jail, you just said so. He's not out on the streets murder —"

"His wife isn't in jail, Matthew. And his brother-in-law isn't in jail, either. Who happens to have a record, did you know that?"

"Yes, I know it."

"Nice family."

"They're not related by blood, if that's what you're suggesting."

"Cheap shot, forget it. What I *am* suggesting . . ."

"Don't say it, Patricia."

"Hear me out, we're exploring."

"All right, explore. Cautiously."

"Let's say Leeds *is* guilty of the crimes as charged. Let's say, further . . ."

"Maybe we ought to quit right there."

"We are *not* in a fucking courtroom, Matthew!"

He looked at her.

"Okay?" she said.

"Okay," he said.

"Good. Let's say Leeds realizes he hasn't got a chance of beating the rap . . . no reflection on your ability . . ."

"Thanks."

". . . but he's seen what we've got, and he's read the writing on the wall, and he knows the next stop is the electric chair. Okay," she said, and nodded, and began nibbling her lip. She was reaching for ideas, he realized, searching her mind, her brow furrowed, actually trying to dope this thing out. He suddenly trusted her. To a degree.

"Let's say his wife is still furious about the bum verdict the jury brought in. By the way, Matthew, we tried our best on that one. She was raped, no question about it. And we indicted the right people for the crime. It was just her tough luck — *and* ours — to come up against a bleeding-heart jury."

Matthew nodded. "Let me hear the rest," he said.

"The rest is the brother-in-law. Weaver. Who's done hard time and who knows a trick or two about hurting people. He's never gone the distance, true, but that's an easy step to take, isn't it? If you've already *tried* to kill someone, then *actually* killing someone is a breeze."

"Maybe."

"Trust me on that."

"Okay."

"So Leeds has an angry wife and a violent brother-in-law. And if he can get them to . . ."

"You're saying . . ."

"I'm saying he could have engineered those murders from his jail cell."

"But he didn't."

"How do you know?"

"I know."

"Have you asked him?"

"No."

"Then you don't know for sure."

"He's innocent of the *first* murders. Why would he . . . ?"

"Because the state doesn't *believe* he's innocent, Matthew, the state has him behind bars, the state's going to try him for three counts of murder!"

"The state's wrong."

"Yes, Matthew, the state's wrong, I'm wrong, you're the only one who's right. But you're not listening."

"Oh, I'm listening, all right."

"Isn't it at least *conceivable?*"

"No, damn it!"

"Then convince me."

"One," Matthew said, "there's no love lost between Leeds and his brother-in-law. The very *notion* of Weaver doing a favor for him is ridiculous. No less a favor like murdering two people."

"How about the wife?"

"She weighs what? A hundred and twenty pounds, max? Can you imagine her and Bannion . . . ?"

"Okay," Patricia said.

"Which is the second thing. I guess you noticed that Bannion wasn't killed with a knife."

"Sarcasm doesn't become you, Counselor."

"If your theory's going to hold . . ."

"Yes, yes, I see where you're going. In fact, it's a good point."

"Thank you."

"In fact . . . maybe *more* than just good."

She was nibbling her lip again. He had to remember this habit for when the case eventually came to trial, *if* it ever came to trial. Whenever she started nibbling her lip, she was searching for something. And when she found it . . .

"Bannion had to've surprised him," she said.

Her eyes met Matthew's.

"The killer," she said.

Their eyes held. Blue locked into brown.

"Because otherwise . . . ," she said.

"He'd have used a knife," Matthew said.

Charlie Stubbs was working on a boat engine when Warren got to the marina at a little before noon that day.

"Just about to take my lunch break," he said. "You'da missed me again."

The parts of the engine were scattered all about him on the concrete floor of the tin-roofed shed adjacent to the office. Rods, pistons, valves, roller tappets, rocker arms, camshaft, crank — Warren wondered how he'd ever put all those pieces together again. He himself had never been good at assembling jigsaw puzzles.

"Had to go to a funeral up in Brandentown yesterday," Stubbs said. "Which is why I wasn't here when you stopped by."

"Your son told me," Warren said.

"All that rain yesterday, perfect day for a funeral, wasn't it?"

"If you've got to have one, I suppose you ought to have rain to go with it," Warren said.

"Seems like more and more of my friends are having them all the time," Stubbs said. "With or without rain. Seems like the current thing to do, have yourself a little funeral."

He was wiping his grease-stained hands on what looked like a pair of torn lady's bloomers. Not panties. Bloomers. Very *large* bloomers. Warren had never met Stubbs's wife, but if the bloomers were any indication . . .

"Man who got buried yesterday moved down here to Florida 'cause he was afraid he'd catch pneumonia and die up there in Cleveland, easy to get a bronchial disease where the climate's so harsh. Either that, or he'd slip on the ice and land on his spine, be an invalid for life, something like that. He was scared to death of all the terrible things can happen to you up north. Get mugged by a street gang, something like that. Get shot by accident in a dope war, something like that. It's terrible, the things that can happen to you up north. But you know how he died down here?"

Warren shook his head.

"He drowned," Stubbs said.

He tossed the soiled bloomers into a gasoline drum, said, "Guess this engine'll keep for a while," and walked Warren down toward the docks. "There's Mr. Leeds's boat right there," he said. "*Felicity*. Slip number twelve. Ain't been a soul on her since that night he took her out."

"You're still pretty sure it was him, huh?" Warren said.

"Well, no, I'm not at *all* sure anymore," Stubbs said. "Not after Mr. Hope played that tape for me. Because it sure as hell wasn't that voice I heard on the telephone. So I got to figuring maybe it wasn't Mr. Leeds going out on the boat neither. Sure looked like him, though. I got to tell you, it's puzzling."

"Maybe this'll help," Warren said, and took a tiny tape cassette out of his pocket and held it up between his thumb and forefinger.

"Not another one," Stubbs said.

"If it's no trouble," Warren said, and took a microcassette

recorder from his other pocket. He was wearing a floppy sports jacket made out of handkerchief-weight Irish linen, guaranteed to wrinkle under even the best of conditions. The jacket was pink. His *Miami Vice* look. It had wide lapels and deep pockets. He had ordered it from a store in New York, and it had just arrived yesterday. He could not wait for Fiona to see it. The recorder was a Realistic Micro-27, small enough to fit in the palm of his hand, capable of playing tapes recorded on his answering machine. He opened the load panel and snapped in the tape.

"Few key words I want you to listen for," he said. "*Little moonlight spin*, and *alarmed*, and *thirty*. All those words were used by the man who called you, do you remember?"

"Sort of," Stubbs said.

"Well, what he said was, 'I just wanted to tell you I'll be taking the boat out again for a little moonlight spin, around ten, ten-thirty, and I don't want you to be alarmed if you hear me out there on the dock.' Do you remember that?"

"I guess," Stubbs said.

"What you're going to hear won't be that whole thing," Warren said, "so just listen for the key words, all right? *Little moonlight spin, alarmed*, and *thirty*. This'll be a bit more difficult than what Mr. Hope played for you."

"Sounds that way," Stubbs said, and looked at the recorder suspiciously.

"But if you want to hear anything again, I can stop the tape whenever you say. Let me know when you're ready, okay?"

"I'm ready now," Stubbs said.

Warren hit the PLAY button.

The telephone conversation with Ned Weaver had been a stop-and-go, fits-and-starts, tooth-pulling battle to get him to say some of the words the caller had used on the night of the murders. Warren wasn't too sure about the word *thirty*, but he was hoping that at least the words *alarmed* and *little moonlight spin* were distinctive enough to allow for positive identification.

Weaver did not say the words *little moonlight spin* until thirty-two seconds of tape had elapsed.

"Play that back," Stubbs said.

Warren rewound the tape and then played the conversation again:

Mr. Weaver, had you ever known Mr. Leeds to take his boat out for a little moonlight spin?

A what?

A little moonlight spin.

Sure. All the time.

You understand what I mean, don't you?

Sure. A little moonlight spin.

Warren hit the STOP button.

"Recognize the voice?" he asked.

"I can't say for sure. Let me hear some more."

Warren started the tape again. It was not until twenty-seven seconds later that Weaver said the word *alarmed*.

Stubbs squinted at the tape recorder.

Six seconds later, Weaver said the word again.

"Play that section back for me," Stubbs said.

Warren played it back:

But when there wasn't a moon, if he took the boat out for a little moonlight spin when there wasn't a moon — would that have alarmed you?

Alarmed me?

Yes. Would that have alarmed you?

Nope.

How come? You know what I'm saying, don't you?

Sure. Would I be alarmed.

Yes. Him being out in the dark and all.

Man knows how to —

Warren stopped the tape.

"What do you think?" he asked.

"That's not the man who called," Stubbs said.

"Are you sure?"

"Positive. The man who called had a funny way of saying that word. *Alarmed*. I didn't think of it at the time, maybe because he told me he was Mr. Leeds, but listening to that tape . . . this man just doesn't say that word the same way. *Alarmed*. I can't do it the way the man on the phone did, but . . ."

"Well, was it some kind of *accent*? Is that what you're saying?"

"No, no."

"Like a Spanish accent?"

"No."

"Or an English accent?"

"No, nothing like . . ."

"French?"

"No, nothing foreign at all. I wish I could do it for you, but I'm no good at that sort of thing. It just sounded . . . different. The way he said that word. *Alarmed*."

"Not the way this man on the tape said it, huh?"

"No, not at all like that."

Wonderful, Warren thought.

"He sounded like somebody famous," Stubbs said. "I wish I could remember who."

"Yours is the rental car, right, sir?" the valet said.

"Yes," Matthew said.

The kid's a mind reader, he thought. There was nothing on the Ford to identify it as a rental, not a bumper sticker, not a windshield decal, not anything.

"They all know it's a rental," he said to Mai Chim. "It's the mystery of the ages."

"Maybe there's something on the keys," she said.

"Must be."

But the man at the body shop this past Monday hadn't *seen* the keys.

Who's driving the rental?

Was what the man had said.

Could you please move it? I gotta get a car out.

Mai Chim was wearing a short beige skirt and a cream-colored, long-sleeved silk blouse buttoned up the front, the top two buttons undone to show a pearl necklace. High-heeled shoes, long legs bare; this was summertime in old Calusa and the formality of pantyhose or stockings seemed foolish in such withering heat. She had been chatty and relaxed all through dinner, perhaps because she'd drunk two tropical-looking, fruity confections laced liberally with rum, and had also shared with Matthew a bottle of Pinot Grigio. Dreamily, she looked out over the water now, her arm looped through his, her head on his shoulder, watching the lights of the boats cruising past on Calusa Bay.

The valet pulled the rented Ford up, hopped out, ran around to the passenger side, and opened the door for her.

"Thank you," she said, and got into the car. Her skirt rode up onto her thighs. She made no motion to lower it.

Matthew gave the valet a dollar and came around to the driver's side.

"Thank you, sir," the valet said, and turned to a grey-haired man coming out of the restaurant. "Yours is the Lincoln, right, sir?" he said, doing his mind-reader act again.

Matthew closed the car door and immediately snapped on the overhead light. Reaching down for the keys, he looked at the plastic tag attached to them. Sure enough, the name of the rental company was on it. Which still didn't explain the man at the body shop.

Who's driving the rental?

"I hate mysteries," he said to Mai Chim, and turned off the light.

"*I* hate *raccoons*," she said mysteriously.

He wondered if she was slightly drunk.

"We didn't have raccoons in Vietnam. We had a lot of animals, but not raccoons."

Matthew drove the car around the circle in front of the restaurant entrance and then headed out toward the main road. One of the valets had switched the radio to another station. He hated when they did that. It conjured images of strangers sitting in his car listening to the radio and wearing out the battery while he was having dinner. He hit the button for the jazz station he normally listened to, the *only* jazz station in Calusa.

"Do you like jazz?" he asked.

"What's jazz?" she said.

"What we're listening to," he said.

She listened.

Gerry Mulligan.

"Yes," she said, and nodded somewhat vaguely. "In Vietnam, there was only rock," she said. "The streets of Saigon were full of rock music. I hate rock," she said. "I hate raccoons, too. Raccoons look like big rats, don't you think?"

"Only down here," he said. "Up north they look cute and furry."

"Perhaps I should move up north," she said.

The word *perhaps* came out somewhat slurred.

"Lots of good cities up north," he said.

She nodded again and then fell silent, as if seriously considering the move. "My father hated soldiers," she said abruptly. The word *soldiers* also seemed a little thick. "Which meant he hated *all* men," she said. "Because in Vietnam, that's all there *was*. Soldiers. *Our* soldiers, *their* soldiers, *your* soldiers." Having a lot of trouble with that word *soldiers*. "My father wouldn't let a soldier come near me. He once got into a fight with an American corporal who smiled at me. That's all he did was smile. My father actually hit the man. My *father*, can you imagine? This skinny little man, hitting this big, husky soldier. The soldier laughed."

Soldier again. Tough word to wrap her tongue around.

"Could we go to my apartment, please?" she asked.

They drove in silence.

The sound of Mulligan's saxophone flooded the automobile. Matthew was thinking he'd love to know how to play saxophone like that.

"I was afraid of them," Mai Chim said. "Soldiers. My father taught me to fear them. He said they would rape me. They raped many Vietnamese girls, the soldiers. I was afraid they would rape me, too."

Everything that goes around comes around, he thought.

Vietnamese girls being raped by American soldiers.

An American woman being raped by three Vietnamese men.

"But I'm not afraid of you," she said.

"Good," he said.

But he was thinking, *Not* so good. He was thinking she'd had too much to drink, and if what she'd told him earlier was true, he didn't want to be the one who made love to her for the first time, not while she was drunk or close to it. Oscar Peterson's piano burst into the rented Ford like a mortar explosion. He thought suddenly of Chicago and the backseat of his father's steamy Oldsmobile where a sixteen-year-old girl named Joy Patterson lay back with her eyes closed and her breath heavy with the smell of booze, and her legs spread, either really drunk or feigning drunkenness while he explored the ribbed tops of her nylon stockings and the soft white thighs above them, and drew back his trembling hand when at last it touched the silken secret patch of her undefended panties. Pulled it back with the certain knowledge that if Joy was drunk, then this was rape.

If he made love to Mai Chim tonight, it would be rape.

Everything that goes around comes around.

They had reached the condo she lived in on Sabal Key. Zoning restrictions out here, since changed, had kept the condos at a maximum five-story height. You could actually see the ocean beyond them. He pulled into a space marked VISITORS and turned off the ignition and the lights.

"Will you come up for a night hat?" she asked.

This was not inebriation, this was merely an unfamiliarity with the language. *And where there is no common language*, she'd said, *there is suspicion. And mistakes. Many mistakes. On both sides.* He wondered if he was about to make a mistake now. But he thought of something else she'd said, the last time he'd seen her, *Is that why you want to go to bed with me? Because I'm Asian?* And he wondered about that, too, while the question hung between them in the silence of the rented car, *Will you come up for a night hat?*, and he thought, No, Mai Chim, I don't think I'll come up for a night hat, not tonight while you're feeling all that booze and maybe not *any* night because yes, I think maybe that's why I *do* want to go to bed with you, only because you're Asian and I've never been to bed with an Asian. And that's no reason to go to bed with *anyone*, not if I plan to look at myself in the mirror tomorrow morning.

"I have an early day tomorrow," he said. "Can I take a rain check?"

A puzzled look crossed her face. She was unfamiliar with the expression.

"Rain check," he said, and smiled. "That means some other time."

She kept looking into his face.

"I'll walk you up," he said gently.

He came around to the other side of the car, opened the door for her, and then offered her his hand. She came out of the car unsteadily, looking a trifle disoriented and somewhat surprised to find herself home already. He put his arm around her to support her. She leaned into him.

"Thank you," she whispered.

At the front door, she searched in her handbag for a key, inserted it in the lock, turned to him, looked up into his face again, and said, "Will there really be some other time, Matthew?"

"I hope so," he said.

And wondered if he meant it.

*

Warren's car was sitting at the curb outside his house. Warren was sitting behind the wheel, asleep. The window on the driver's side was down. Matthew reached in and gently touched his shoulder. Warren jumped up with a start, his hand going under his jacket to a shoulder holster. A very large pistol suddenly appeared in his hand.

"Hey!" Matthew shouted, and backed off.

"Sorry, you scared me."

"*I* scared *you*, huh?"

Warren holstered the pistol and got out of the car. They went up the front walk together. Matthew unlocked the door and snapped on the lights.

"Something to drink?" he asked.

"A little scotch, please, no ice," Warren said. "Can I use your phone a minute?"

"Sure. On the wall there."

Matthew looked at the clock. A quarter past ten. He wondered if he should call Mai Chim, apologize or something. But for what? At the kitchen counter, Warren was already dialing. Matthew went to the dropleaf bar, lowered the front panel, and poured some Black Label into a low glass. He wondered if he felt like a martini. He wondered if he'd done the right thing tonight. Warren was talking to someone named Fiona. Matthew wondered if she was black. Fiona? Could be Irish. Fiona was an Irish name, wasn't it? He wondered if Warren was sleeping with her. If she was Irish, if she was white, was Warren sleeping with her only *because* she was white? He wondered. Back in Chicago . . .

Back in Chicago, in his high-school English class, there'd been a gloriously beautiful black girl named Ophelia Blair. And he'd taken her to the movies one night, and for ice-cream sodas later, and then he'd led her into his father's multipurpose Oldsmobile, and he'd driven her to a deserted stretch of road

near the football field and plied her with kisses, his hand fumbling under her skirt, pleading with her to let him "do it" because he'd never in his life "done it" with a black girl.

Never mind that at the age of seventeen he'd never done it with a *white* girl, either. His supreme argument was that she was black and he was white and oh what a glorious adventure awaited them if only she'd allow him, a latter-day Stanley exploring Africa, to lower her panties and spread her lovely legs. It never occurred to him that he was reducing her to anonymity, denying her very Ophelia-ness, equating with any *other* black girl in the world, expressing desire for her only because she was black and not merely *herself*, whoever that might have been, the person he had not taken the slightest amount of trouble to know. He was baffled when she pulled down her skirt and tucked her breasts back into her brassiere and buttoned her blouse, and asked him very softly to take her home, please. He asked her out a dozen times after that, and she always refused politely.

Chicago.

A long time ago.

He had not made that same mistake tonight.

He had not denied Mai Chim her selfness.

But he wondered if she realized this.

"Whenever I'm done here, Fiona," Warren said into the phone.

Fiona.

White? Black? Vietnamese?

Ophelia Blair had been very black, a truly beautiful girl. He wondered where she was now, what she was doing. He suspected she had grown up to be an extravagantly beautiful woman. He imagined her living in a luxurious home on Lake Shore Drive. She would be hostessing a formal dinner party, the men in tuxedos, the women in long, shimmering gowns. Ophelia Blair. Who, once upon a time, he'd hurt severely.

He turned his back toward the kitchen counter, where

Warren was still on the telephone, and began mixing himself a martini. Had he similarly and stupidly and for exactly the opposite reason hurt Mai Chim tonight? Had he made yet *another* damn mistake? In trying to do the right thing, had he done the absolutely *wrong* thing? He dropped an olive into the glass. And another one.

"Warren," he said, "are you almost finished there?"

"Right this second," Warren said, and then, into the phone, "See you later," and hung up.

"There's one call I have to make," Matthew said, and carried his martini to the telephone in the study. He took a sip of the drink, pulled the phone to him, and dialed Mai Chim's number. She answered on the fourth ring.

"Hello?" she said.

"Mai Chim?"

"Yes?"

"It's Matthew."

"Oh, hello, Matthew."

"Are you all right?"

"Yes," she said. "But drunk."

"Well, maybe a little tipsy."

"What's that? Tipsy?"

"Drunk," he said.

They both laughed.

And suddenly the laughter stopped. And there was silence on the line.

"Thank you for not hurting me," she said.

He wondered if she knew what she was saying. Wondered if the English word *hurt* meant to her what it meant to him. Because he felt he *had* hurt her. Stupidly and foolishly hurt her.

And where there is no common language, there is suspicion. And mistakes. Many mistakes. On both sides.

"Matthew, did someone pay the check?" she asked.

"Yes," he said. "You did."

"Oh, thank *God*, I couldn't remember. I thought, oh boy, he's my guest and I let him pay for it."

Oh boy. So alien on her tongue. So completely charming.

"I drank too much," she said. "I'm not used to drinking so much."

"Please don't worry about it," he said.

"I was so afraid, you see."

He said nothing.

"It was that I thought . . . if I drink a little, I won't be so afraid. Of soldiers," she said.

Soldiers. No thickness of the tongue this time. No slurring. Soldiers.

"Men," she said softly, and fell silent.

They were both silent.

"We'll try again," he said at last.

"Yes, some other time," she said.

"When we *really* know each other better," he said.

"Will we ever know each other better?" she asked.

"I hope so," he said, and this time he meant it. "I don't want this to be . . ."

"Yes, just white and Asian," she said, and he wondered if they didn't *already* know each other much better than they suspected.

"I'll call you soon," he said.

"You must come for your raincoat," she said.

"Rain *check*," he said, and smiled.

"Yes, rain check," she said.

"Sleep well," he said.

"I still dream of helicopters," she said.

There was a click on the line.

He picked up the martini glass and went out into the kitchen. Warren was still at the kitchen counter. The glass of scotch was now in his right hand.

"Learning your p's and q's?" he asked.

"What?" Matthew said.

Warren indicated the slip of paper tacked to the small cork bulletin board near the phone:

a ă â b c d đ e ê g h i k l m n o ô σ p q r s t u ư v x y

"Oh," Matthew said. "That's the Vietnamese alphabet."

"It's missing a lot of letters, did you notice that?"

"No, I didn't."

"That's why I'm a detective and you're not. There's no F, J, or W. No Z, either. But there are three A's, two D's and E's, three O's, two U's, and a partridge in a pear tree. What do you call these funny little marks?"

"Diacritical."

"That serious, huh?" Warren said, and raised his glass in a toast. "We struck out, Matthew," he said, and drank. "Ahhhh," he said, "delicious. Weaver isn't the man who made that phone call."

"Cheers," Matthew said sourly, and raised his own glass in a toast. He drank, looked into the glass appreciatively, and then said, "Who's Fiona?"

"Fiona Gill," Warren said. "Lady who works in the Tax Collector's office. She's the one who told me we had a bad make on that license plate."

"White? Black?"

"Black. Why?"

"Just wondered."

"You seeing a black lady?" Warren asked.

"No, no."

"Sounds like it."

"No."

But close, Matthew thought.

In American movies, Asian women were permissible substitutes for black women. The white hero was allowed to have a meaningful love affair with an Asian woman, but never with a black woman. This was how courageous American film produc-

ers broke the taboo. It was okay for the hero to kiss an Asian woman but if he kissed a black woman, watch it, mister. As for a black man kissing a white woman, that was science fiction. Matthew wondered what it would be like to kiss Mai Chim. Maybe he could get some brave Hollywood movie producer to film their first kiss. Tastefully, of course.

"Want to share the joke?" Warren said, and Matthew realized he was smiling.

"I'm just a little tired," he said. "What else did Stubbs tell you?"

"Only that the man on the phone sounded famous."

"Famous?"

"Famous. When he said the word *alarmed*."

"How do famous people say *alarmed*?" Matthew asked.

"You got me, pal," Warren said, and sighed heavily. "I'd better be on my way, Fiona's expecting me." He hesitated, and then said, "Are you sure you don't want to talk about anything?"

"No, thanks a lot."

"If you change your mind, here's where I'll be," Warren said, and wrote a number onto the pad under the phone. He drained the glass, shook hands with Matthew, and went out. Matthew could hear him starting the Buick outside. In a little while, the sound of its engine faded on the night. Now there was only the hum of the air conditioner. He carried his glass to the counter, sat on one of the stools, and looked at the number Warren had written for him:

381-3645

The 381 prefix told him that Fiona lived on the mainland. He tore the page from the pad and tacked it to the bulletin board, just under the alphabet Mai Chim had Xeroxed for him. When he was in college at Northwestern, a friend of his began dating a Chinese girl whose father ran a restaurant on La Salle.

The guy's name was Nathan Feinstein, the girl's name was Melissa Chong. Nathan and Melissa shared what Nathan called an Eemie-Wess relationship, which was shorter and easier to say than an East-Meets-West relationship, a tongue-twister on *anybody's* lips.

Matthew picked up the pencil alongside the pad and wrote:

EEMIE-WESS

He looked at the hyphenated word. It conjured a multimillion-dollar film starring Le Mai Chim and Matthew Hope — not necessarily in that order. The first scene would open with a shot of a green Oldsmobile Cutlass Supreme parked under a pepper tree outside Little Asia in lovely downtown Calusa. A couple would be necking on the front seat. They would be our hero and heroine, Leslie Storm and Lotus Blossom Wong, as their names were in the picture. The camera would cut away from a close shot of their torridly joined lips to an antiseptic close shot of an orange-and-white Florida license plate over the rear bumper. The numbers and letters on that plate would read 2AB 39C.

On the pad, Matthew wrote:

2 AB 39 C

He looked at what he'd written. And then he wrote it again:

2 AB 39 C

And again and again and again and again . . .

2 AB 39 C
2 AB 39 C
2 AB 39 C
2 AB 39 C

And kept writing it over and over again, faster and faster and faster until the last several times he wrote it . . .

2 AB 39C

2 AB 39C

. . . the numeral 2 resembled . . .

There's no F, J, or W. No Z, either.

His eyes darted to the alphabet pinned to the board.

a ă â b c d đ e ê g h i k l m n o ô σ p q r s t u ư v x y

No Z in it. But a 2 in the language, for sure, *Oh, yes, our numbers are Arabic.* No Z, but a 2! And if you were seeing a Z through a screen door at night, and you didn't know what the hell a Z looked like in the first place, then you could easily mistake it for a 2! Ike and Mike, they look alike, a Z and a 2! Trinh had seen ZAB 39C, but his eye and his brain had automatically translated it into something familiar, 2AB 39C.

Matthew yanked the receiver from its cradle and dialed the number Warren had left him. It rang once, twice . . .

"Hello?"

"Miss Gill?"

"Yes?"

"This is Matthew Hope . . ."

"Yes, Mr. Hope."

"I'm sorry to be calling at this hour . . ."

"Don't be silly."

"Is Warren there yet?"

"No, he isn't."

"I wonder if you'd ask him to call when he . . . as a matter of fact, maybe you can help me."

"Happy to."

"Are there any license plates in Florida that begin with the letter Z?"

"Oh, yes," Fiona said, "Y and Z both. Those are the letters we set aside for rental cars."

"*Rental* cars?"

A rental car, he thought. A goddamn *rental* car! No *wonder* the killer had to . . .

"Hertz, Avis, Dollar, what-have-you," Fiona said. "The plates on all those cars begin with either a Y or a Z. Check it out."

"I will," he said. "Thank you very much, Miss Gill, I really appreciate this."

"Not at all," she said. "Did you still want Warren to call you?"

"Not unless he wants to."

"I'll tell him. Good night," she said.

"Good night," he said, and put the receiver back on the cradle.

A rental car, he thought. *That's* how those mind readers knew what I was driving, they looked at the license plate. He pulled the telephone directory to him, opened it to the yellow pages, and was running his finger down the page with the listings for Automobile Renting & Leasing when the phone rang. He picked up the receiver.

"Warren?" he said.

"Mr. Hope?" a man's voice said.

"Yes, who's this, please?"

"Charlie Stubbs. I'm sorry to be bothering you at home, but I tried to reach that other feller and there's no answer there. I remember now who that voice sounded like. Remember I said it sounded like somebody famous? Or did he tell you?"

"Yes, he told me."

"Well, I remember who it was."

"Who was it, Mr. Stubbs?"

"John F. Kennedy," Stubbs said.

12

He lived in one of those little shacks up on stilts that lined the beach just north of Whisper Key Village. At this time of year, and especially at this time of night, there was a ghostly silence shrouding the strip of wooden structures standing in a row on the edge of the sea. During high season, there would be music into the empty hours of the night, laughter, the sounds of young people flexing their muscles and their hormones. Tonight, all was still. The shacks stood on their stilts like tall wading birds, silhouetted against the shoreline sky. It was almost midnight, but a light was burning in the second-story apartment. Matthew climbed the steps and knocked.

"Who is it?"

The distinctive voice, plainly evident when you were listening for it. The John F. Kennedy voice.

"Me," he said. "Matthew Hope."

"Just a minute, please."

Puzzlement in that voice now; it was almost midnight.

The door opened.

He was wearing only tennis shorts. Barechested, barefooted. Forty-one years old, but still looking like a boy, the way many athletes that age looked, the well-defined muscles on his arms, legs, and chest, the tousled blond hair, the welcoming grin. Your average, garden-variety All-American Boy. Who had only done murder five times over.

"Hello, Kit," Matthew said. "Sorry to be stopping by so late."

"No, that's okay," he said. "Come on in."

Matthew stepped into the apartment. A studio with a tiny kitchen area and a closet space defined by a rod with a hanging curtain on it. Double bed against the windows on the ocean side. Framed photographs on the walls. Most of them of Christopher Howell in action on a tennis court. One of them of Christopher Howell in an army uniform, posing with half a dozen other American soldiers, all of them grinning into the camera, all of them wearing combat helmets and bandoliers, some of them holding assault weapons. In the corner, several tennis rackets stood on end against the wall. There was a thrift-shop easy chair slip-covered in a paisley pattern. A telephone on a nightstand beside the bed. A lamp on the nightstand. The lamp was on. There was no air conditioning, the windows were wide open. Outside, the ocean rushed in against the sand.

"I think I've worked out a game plan," Matthew said.

Howell blinked.

"Would you like to hear it?"

"Well . . ."

This is *midnight*, his face said.

"Sure," he said.

"Did you know," Matthew said, "that in the state of Florida, all rental-car license plates begin with either a Y or a Z?"

Howell looked at him.

"No, I didn't know that," he said.

"A little-known fact," Matthew said, and smiled. "But true."

"I see," Howell said.

"Did you further know that rental-car companies keep records on all the cars they rent? Names of renters, addresses, and so on."

"Uh . . . excuse me, Mr. Hope," Howell said, "but it *is* late, and . . ."

"Later than you think," Matthew said.

Outside, an incoming wave broke with a thunderous crash. There was the whispering sound of the ocean retreating. And then silence again.

"I made some phone calls before coming here," Matthew said. "To all the rental-car companies in town. Well, not all of them, I struck pay dirt on the sixth call."

"Mr. Hope, I'm sorry, really . . ."

Blue eyes wide with innocence. Puzzled boyish look on his face.

". . . but I just don't know what you're talking about."

"I think you know what I'm talking about, Kit."

"No, really, I . . ."

"I'm talking about the car you rented."

"Car?"

The way he said that single word. The regional dialect. Caah. Paak the caah in Haavaad Yaad. The same way he must have said *alarmed* when he was talking on the phone to Stubbs. Alaaamed.

"The one you rented on August thirteenth," Matthew said. "An Oldsmobile Cutlass Supreme with the license plate ZAB 39 . . ."

The racket was in Howell's hand before Matthew could complete the sentence. His right hand. Shake hands with the racket. The racket firm in his grip. He had a powerful forehand and a devastating backhand, and moreover he was ambidex-

trous. Matthew suddenly knew which blunt instrument had crushed Frank Bannion's skull.

"So let me hear your game plan," Howell said, and swung the racket at Matthew's head.

Matthew had no game plan.

The racket came at him edgewise. Howell wasn't trying to hit a ball, he wasn't concerned about meeting a ball solidly on the strings, never mind a sweet spot, the sweet spot was Matthew's head. Howell was concerned only with inflicting damage. The aluminum frame of the racket, for all its lightness, was thick enough and dense enough and strong enough to knock plaster out of the wall. Which is exactly what it did in the next second because Matthew did the only thing he could do, he sidestepped and ducked. The plaster flew out in a large solid chunk, exposing naked lath and what looked like chicken wire behind it. Howell danced away, positioning himself for his next shot.

"Guess which hand?" he said, and grinned, and tossed the racket into his left hand and then immediately tossed it back to the right. He was bouncing on his bare feet. Priming himself for the big match. Matthew did not want his skull to become the U.S. Open.

If your opponent is armed, and you're not . . .

Bloom's voice. In the gym this past Tuesday. Teaching him the tricks of the trade. Teaching him a game plan.

Don't try to disarm him. You'll be dead before you figure out how.

Howell was bouncing. Circling. Tossing the racket back and forth between his hands. Guess which hand? Where will it be coming from? The right or the left?

Forget the weapon.

But the next one was going to be an ace.

The next one was going to crush Matthew's skull.

Go for the man.

Howell was pulling the racket back for the shot. It was going to be a left-handed shot, and it was going to be a back-

hand shot. Matthew had seen that backhand in action. Its force could tear off his head. Arm crossing Howell's chest now, racket coming back, mouth set in a tight line, eyes blazing, arm coiled like a spring, in a moment he would unleash the shot, the arm would unfold, the edge of the racket . . .

Matthew hit him while the racket was still back.

Threw his shoulder into Howell while his weight was still on the back foot. Surprised, Howell staggered for an instant, trying to keep his balance, the racket still back, the weight on that right foot, the proper form for the shot, his full body weight working against him now, fighting against gravity and losing as he went crashing to the floor. He landed solidly on his right hip and was rolling over when Matthew stomped on his groin. He did not *kick* him in the groin, he *stomped* him. He did not use the point of his shoe, he used the heel. Stomped his balls flat into the carpet, the way Bloom had taught him.

Breathing hard, Matthew went to the telephone.

Howell was still writhing on the floor.

It was a little after two in the morning when he got to the farm on Timucuan Point Road. Not a light showing in any of the buildings. Not in the main house, not in the guest cottage at the far end of the road, where Ned Weaver lived. Matthew rang the doorbell. He kept ringing it. A light went on at the other end of the house. The bedroom. He kept ringing the doorbell.

"Who is it?"

Jessica's voice. Just inside the door.

"Matthew Hope."

"What?"

"Please open the door."

"What? *What?*"

Incredulously. This was two o'clock in the morning.

"Please open the door, Mrs. Leeds."

Silence.

Then: "Just a minute."

He waited. It took almost five minutes for her to open the door. She had undoubtedly gone back to the bedroom to put on the robe she now wore over her nightgown. Green nylon. Over white nylon. Barefooted. The way Howell had been barefooted when he'd opened the door to *his* place.

"Do you know what time it is?" she asked.

"Yes, I do," Matthew said. "May I come in?"

"Why?"

"Because the police have just arrested Christopher Howell and charged him with five counts of homicide. There are some questions I'd like to ask you, Mrs. Leeds."

"What questions?" she said.

"We both want your husband cleared," he said. "I just want to make sure Howell doesn't try to implicate him."

He was lying.

"Howell?" she said. "*Kit*, do you mean? The tennis pro at the club?"

She was lying, too.

"May I come in, please?" he said.

"Yes, certainly. Forgive me, I . . . I was asleep . . . all that ringing . . . I didn't mean to be rude. *Kit*, did you say? What does *he* have to do with any of this?"

From the switch panel just outside the entrance to the living room, she turned on the lights and then led him in. She sat on the leather sofa. He sat in a leather easy chair opposite her. There was a large green pillow behind her, the color of her eyes, the color of her robe. He remembered that the lady favored green.

"I just drove out from the police station," he said. "They're trying to locate Skye Bannister so he'll be there for the formal Q and A. He's down in Sanibel for the weekend, they're not sure where."

"Skye . . . ?"

"Bannister. The State Attorney. His office is going to have a lot of explaining to do."

"I still don't understand . . ."

"Howell confessed to the murders."

"Kit?"

"Yes."

"Amazing."

"Isn't it?"

"Such a quiet, unassuming person," she said.

"Yes."

"Why would he have . . . are you saying he killed *all* of them?"

"Yes."

"He's admitted that?"

"Yes."

"Amazing," she said again.

The room went silent. The house was still. She sat in the center of the sofa, looking at him, her hands clasped in her lap. He sat opposite her, watching her.

"And you think he may try to implicate Stephen?" she said.

"Yes."

Lying again.

"How?"

"He might claim Stephen put him up to it."

"*Has* he done that?"

"No. Not yet."

"Well . . . what *has* he said?"

"I told you. He's confessed to killing the three men who raped you . . ."

"Yes, I understand that part of it."

"*And* the old man who saw the license plate on the rented car . . ."

"One of the Vietnamese witnesses."

"Yes. And also the investigator who learned what the number on that plate really was. He killed all five of them. He's already made a statement to that effect."

"I see. I'm sorry, but I'm not familiar with . . . which investigator do you mean?"

"You didn't see this morning's newspaper?"

"No, I'm sorry."

"This was an investigator from the State Attorney's office. A man named Frank Bannion."

"And he learned . . . what was it he'd learned?"

"He figured out what the license plate was."

"I see."

"Which led him to Howell."

"I see."

"The same way it led *me* to Howell."

"I see," she said, and hesitated. "Did . . . ?"

And hesitated again. Wondering quite how to put this.

"Did Kit say . . . *why* he'd committed these murders?"

"Yes," he said.

"Why?" she said.

"For you," he said.

"For me?"

She seemed almost amused.

"For *me*? I hardly *know* the man!"

"Mrs. Leeds . . ."

"That's perfectly ridiculous," she said. "For *me*? Is the man crazy?"

"Mrs. Leeds, outside of the . . ."

"He said he did it for *me*?"

". . . various lawyers and law-enforcement people working on this case . . ."

"I can't believe he . . ."

". . . only two other people knew that license-plate number."

She looked at him.

"The number Trinh thought he saw."

She kept looking at him.

"You and your husband," Matthew said.

"No," she said.

"Yes," Matthew said. "I told your husband, and he told you."

"I don't remember hearing . . ."

"You and I talked about it later, Mrs. Leeds. You knew the number, and you . . ."

"I did *not!*"

". . . gave it to Howell."

"You're mistaken. I don't even *know* the man, except as . . ."

"He's admitted it."

She looked at him again.

"He said you gave it to him."

She kept looking at him.

"He said he killed Trinh *because* of that number."

And suddenly she was crying.

Tonight, she cannot get enough of him.

This is four days before Christmas, the twenty-first day of December, a Thursday. In the motel room, she is insatiable. She knows she will not be seeing him over the holidays; she and her husband are going up to New York on the twenty-sixth and will not return until the second of January. And so tonight's lovemaking must hold her until then, a junkie's last desperate fix before an anticipated shortage of supply, she cannot get enough of him.

She is dressed provocatively for him. She always dresses provocatively for him. Black bikini panties, lace-edged. A black garter belt. Black, seamed nylon stockings. No brassiere. Black, high-heeled patent-leather pumps. He tells her she looks like a hooker in the Combat Zone. That's an area in Boston, he explains. Where all the hookers parade. She asks if he's ever been to bed with a hooker. Only in Nam, he says. He tells her he

killed seven people in Nam. This excites her. The idea that he has killed people. Her husband has killed people, too, in the same war, in the same place. But when Kit describes cutting off cocks, it excites her.

She has been seeing him for almost a year now, ever since he took the job at the club. A sun god. Walking out onto the court, his head bent, blond hair glowing, looking up suddenly, blue eyes flashing, Good morning, Mrs. Leeds, I'm Christopher Howell. They call me Kit.

Well, hello, Kit, she thinks.

Aren't you lovely, Kit.

Are you ready for your lesson? he asks.

Oh yes, she thinks, I am ready for my lesson, Kit.

He has been giving her lessons for almost a year now, on and off the court. She cannot imagine what her life was like before he entered it. He is the same age as her husband, but by comparison Stephen seems far older. Stephen and his boat. Always the damn boat. *Felicity*. She hates the name of the boat. He comes in off the boat tasting of salt. Kisses her tasting of salt. She hates his kisses, they make her want to wash out her mouth. Stephen is a big man going to fat. Kit is the same age, they both fought in the same war, but Kit is lean and hard and savage, and she cannot get enough of him.

They talk a lot about her leaving Stephen. Divorcing him. But Florida's courts aren't quite as liberal with alimony as they are elsewhere in the United States. Most judges down here will grant alimony for a so-called period of adjustment and then you're on your own, sink or swim. She is trying to figure out some way to get him to put the farm in her name. She has told him that if something happened to him, God forbid, the estate taxes would murder her, they'd be giving the government enough money to invade Grenada all over again. Over and over again, she hits on the Grenada theme. He'd hated Reagan when he was president, hated the invasion of Grenada, the bombing of Libya, a man who'd killed people himself, it was strange. Try

to get the farm in her name. The farm was the fortune. Get him to put it in her name and then kiss him off, spend the rest of her life lying in the sun with Kit, making love to Kit. They talk about that tonight, too. They always talk about that. In each other's arms, they talk about her leaving Stephen once the farm is in her name.

Their watches are on the dresser, lying side by side, hers tiny and gold with a slender black strap, his massive and steely, with digital readouts and stubby little studs.

Their watches toss seconds into the room.

Minutes.

More minutes.

On the bed across the room, they are making love again, lost in their need for each other, savoring these last passionate moments before their long separation, she cannot get enough of him. And at last they lie back on the pillows, her head close to his, his arm lying across her breasts, spent, content, silent. A fire engine races past on U.S. 41, its siren howling.

Fire someplace, she says.

Mmmm, he says.

They listen to the sound of the siren fading, and then it is gone, and the room is silent again save for the ticking of her watch on the dresser. She wonders aloud what time it is, and gets out of bed naked, and walks flatfooted across the room and picks up the watch and —

Jesus!

It's a quarter past eleven!

This is when the nightmare begins.

Not later.

Now.

This instant.

It will take at least fifteen minutes to get back to the mall. This will put her in the Maserati at eleven-thirty, an hour and a half later than she'd planned. It'll take another half hour to get back to the farm, she won't be home till midnight! Never mind

him putting the farm in her name, he'll kick her out of the house if she walks in there at midnight! He'll throw her out on the street! He'll file for divorce tomorrow morning! How could they have *been* so stupid, wasn't *somebody* watching the time? She is saying all this to Kit as she dresses, hastily putting on the garter belt and then the seamed nylon stockings, and fastening the stockings to the garters, He'll kill me, she says, and stepping into the black lace-edged bikini panties, I can't *believe* we let this happen, and then putting on the short black skirt and the sleeveless white silk blouse, and buttoning the little pearl buttons up the front, What can I *tell* him, she says, what can I possibly *say* to him?

The mall has been closed for an hour and a half by the time they reach the parking lot. There is an hour and a half she must account for. The movie has already let out, even the restaurant is closed, its neon sign dark, its front plate-glass windows black. The parking lot is empty, everything is dark, everything is still, save for a single light hanging over the rear door of the restaurant and a light shining through a narrow window beside the door. Kit drives her directly to where she's parked the car. She does not even kiss him as she gets out. She is thinking ahead. She is still wondering what she can possibly tell her husband. She is thinking there is no possible way to explain a time lapse of an hour and a half, it's all over, finished and done, he'll kill her. Swiftly, she unlocks the door to the Maserati.

She has parked it behind the restaurant, which is shaped like a pagoda, and which in fact is *named* The Pagoda. The car is an expensive one, and this is four days before Christmas. With all the traffic in the mall's lot a dented fender is a distinct possibility, but this was not her prime concern when she chose this deserted spot; she is a married woman having an affair, and moving from car to car is the most dangerous time. So she has parked it far from where — if she'd been back here on time — there would have been other cars, parked it instead here behind The Pagoda, alongside a low fence beyond which is unde

veloped scrub land. She climbs in behind the wheel, locks the door, and starts the engine.

The dashboard clock reads twenty minutes to twelve.

The sound of the engine tells Kit that everything's okay, but she flashes her headlights anyway, signaling, and he flashes his own headlights in farewell and begins backing his car away from the fence. She puts the gearshift lever in reverse. Kit makes a wide turn and then begins driving toward the exit. It is best not to follow him too closely, the night has eyes. She waits until in her rearview mirror she sees him turning out of the lot. Then she steps on the accelerator, and begins backing her own car away from the fence, and realizes almost at once that she has a flat tire.

The nightmare is about to escalate.

She knows how to change a flat tire, she has changed many of them in her lifetime, she is not one of these helpless little women who eat bonbons on a chaise longue while reading romance novels. She takes the jack out of the trunk, lifts out the spare, lays it flat on the ground behind the rear bumper, and then kneels beside the right rear tire to loosen the lug nuts on the wheel. She has removed one of them and placed it in the inverted hubcap, when . . .

The first thing she hears is the rear door of the restaurant opening.

And then voices.

Foreign voices.

Well, a Chinese restaurant, she figures they're Chinese voices.

And then three men come out of the restaurant, through the back door, talking and laughing, and she recognizes them as the men who'd been out back here smoking earlier tonight when she'd parked the car, eight o'clock tonight when she'd parked the car, three hours and forty minutes ago when she'd parked the car. Three young men out back smoking. "Good evening, boys," she'd said cheerfully — well, perhaps a bit flir-

tatiously, too; she was a woman on her way to meet her lover, and a woman with a lover thinks the whole *world* is dying to fuck her. "Good evening, boys." Three hours and forty minutes ago. A nightmare ago.

One of them reaches in to snap off the inside lights. There is only the light over the door now. Another one pulls the door shut. The sound of the spring bolt clicking into place is like a rifle shot on the night. The three are still talking among themselves, their backs are to her, they haven't yet seen her. One of them laughs softly. And then they turn from the door, and . . . and . . . they . . . they . . .

"They were starting to move away from the restaurant," she said, "when they saw me. And they . . . stopped and . . . and . . . one of them . . . the leader, Ho . . . smiled at me and . . . and said in his singsong English, 'Oh, good even-ing, boys,' imitating me, *mocking* me! And then they . . ."

She fell silent.

She took a tissue from a box on the coffee table, dabbed at her eyes and her cheeks.

Matthew waited.

"You know the rest," she said, "I told you the rest. I had to lie about the time, but the rest was all true."

"So you risked a conviction . . ."

"Yes."

". . . to protect your lie."

"To protect my *life!*"

"You let three rapists go free . . ."

"They were my alibi."

"Your *what?*"

"Stephen believed it, that's all that mattered. He believed I left the mall at ten and was raped fifteen minutes later. He believed it."

"The jury didn't."

"That was a chance I had to take. Otherwise, I'd have lost everything."

"You've still lost everything."

"No, I don't think so," she said. "Stephen will still believe me."

"The State Attorney won't. Kit told the police you planned it together."

"Oh? Planned *what* together?"

There was a faint smile on her face now. He had seen this smile before. On the faces of people who had decided to bluff it through because there was nothing worse that could possibly happen. Kit Howell had told them everything; Jessica Leeds would tell them nothing.

"They have his sworn statement," Matthew said.

"He's lying. Besides, he's a tennis bum."

"Whatever he is, he signed . . ."

"Tell me," Jessica said. "If an infatuated tennis bum goes out on his own to redeem the honor of a farmer's wife . . . how is the lady to blame?"

"Where's the lady?" Matthew asked, and walked out.

The Q and A took place in Captain Rushville Decker's office in the Public Safety Building at 6:25 A.M. that Sunday morning, August 26. Present were the captain himself, in cleanly pressed blues and looking wide awake at this early hour; Christopher Howell in jeans and a blue T-shirt; Skye Bannister, who'd finally been located at his sister's house in Sanibel, and who looked tall and blond and suntanned and elegant in a dark-blue tropical suit and silk rep tie; Patricia Demming, who was dressed now in a grey pin-striped business suit and low heels, looking extremely beautiful but also very grave; Matthew Hope, who had not slept at all the night before and who needed a shave and who was still wearing the clothes he'd lived in all day yesterday; and a uniformed police stenographer, who was operating the recording machine and taking backup shorthand notes and looking essentially bored. Bannister read Howell his

rights, confirmed that he understood them, further confirmed that he did not, repeat *not*, wish a lawyer present, and then began the questioning:

Q: Can you tell me your full name, please?

A: Christopher Leslie Howell.

Q: Where do you live, Mr. Howell?

A: At 2115 Ocean Drive, Whisper Key.

Q: Any apartment number?

A: 2A.

Q: Mr. Howell, earlier today you made a voluntary statement to a Detective Howard Saphier of the Calusa Police Department, is that true?

A: That's true.

Q: I show you this, and ask if it is a true representation of the statement you made?

A: It is.

Q: Is this your signature at the bottom of the statement?

A: It is.

Q: And is the date alongside your signature the correct date?

A: It is.

Q: Mr. Howell, with your permission, I'd like to go over some of the things you told Detective Saphier. To make sure we've got them right.

A: Sure.

Q: You told Detective Saphier, did you not, that on the night of August thirteenth, you drove a rented automobile to so-called Little Asia and ambushed and murdered three Vietnamese men named . . . Pat, have you got those names, please?

A: (*from Ms. Demming*) Yes, Mr. Bannister, right here.

Q: Let's see now . . . that would be . . . Ho Dao Bat . . . and Ngo Long Khai . . . I'm not sure I'm pronouncing these

correctly . . . and Dang Van Con? Are those the men you say you murdered?

A: Not in that order.

Q: Pardon?

A: Ho was last.

Q: Mr. Howell, perhaps it would be helpful to go over the events of that night chronologically. I'm still talking about August thirteenth, the night these three men were murdered.

A: Where do you want me to start?

Q: You told Detective Saphier that you called the Riverview Marina . . .

A: Yes.

Q: And identified yourself as Stephen Leeds . . .

A: Yes.

Q: And spoke to a man named Charles Stubbs . . .

A: Yes.

Q: At approximately nine o'clock that night.

A: Yes. To tell him I'd be taking the boat out.

Q: Where'd you make this call from?

A: My apartment.

Q: What'd you do then?

A: I waited for Jessie's call.

Q: By Jessie, do you mean Jessica Leeds?

A: Yes.

Q: What was the nature of her call?

A: She told me it was okay to come on over.

Q: Come on over where?

A: The farm.

Q: Do you mean the Leeds farm?

A: Yes.

Q: What did you do after you received her call?

A: I drove out there.

Q: Why did you go there?

A: To pick up some things.

Q: What things?

A: Jessie's car, for one. The Maserati.

Q: What else did you pick up?

A: Her husband's jacket and hat.

Q: Stephen Leeds?

A: Yes.

Q: Anything else?

A: The boat keys. And his wallet.

Q: Whose wallet?

A: Her husband's.

Q: Did you go *into* the Leeds house to pick up all these items?

A: Not the car. The car was parked outside.

Q: Why are you smiling, Mr. Howell?

A: Well, the car couldn't be in the house, could it?

Q: You find that amusing, do you?

A: Yes. That you asked if I had to go in the house for the car.

Q: How about the other items? The jacket and hat, the wallet, the . . .

A: Yes.

Q: You went into the house to gather those, did you?

A: Yes.

Q: Where were Mr. and Mrs. Leeds while you were doing all this?

A: Jessie was helping me. Her husband was asleep in the bedroom.

Q: Asleep all the while you were in the house?

A: Asleep till sometime the next morning.

Q: Mr. Howell, did you tell Detective Saphier that you knew Mr. Leeds would be asleep because his wife had administered sleeping pills to him?

A: Two pills. In his drink. They were having an after-

dinner drink when the movie started. She called me the minute he went off.

Q: Would you know what kind of pills these were? The *name* of the drug?

A: They were prescription pills. That's all I know about them.

Q: Which movie are you referring to?

A: A rented movie. They were watching it after dinner.

Q: So Mr. Leeds was asleep when you got there . . .

A: Yes.

Q: What time was that?

A: About ten o'clock.

Q: Was he asleep when you left the farm?

A: Yes.

Q: How did you leave the farm?

A: In Jessie's car.

Q: The Maserati.

A: Yes.

Q: You left your car there?

A: In the garage.

Q: What time was it when you left the farm?

A: About ten after ten.

Q: Where did you go then?

A: To the Riverview Marina. On Willowbee Creek.

Q: Why did you go there?

A: To take out the boat. I was wearing his jacket and hat . . .

Q: Mr. Leeds's jacket and hat?

A: Yes. I was hoping whoever saw me taking the boat out would think it was him. That was the plan. To have people see me and think it was him. Because I'd called ahead, you see. We're about the same size, you see. He's a bit heavier, but basically we're the same size.

Q: When you say 'That was the plan' . . . whose plan do you mean?

A: Jessie's. And mine. Our plan.

Q: To be mistaken for Stephen Leeds?

A: Yes. That was the whole idea. That was why I went to all the trouble of calling the marina and telling them I'd be taking the boat out, and then wearing his clothes, you know, and dropping his wallet where it was sure to be found. That was all part of the plan.

Q: When did you concoct this plan?

A: Monday morning.

Q: Monday morning? The day of the *murders*?

A: Yeah. That's my day off. Monday.

Q: Why are you grinning now, Mr. Howell?

A: I just think it was a good plan to have thought up on the spur of the moment like that.

Q: You're saying that you sat down with Mrs. Leeds on Monday morning . . .

A: We were in bed, actually.

Q: I see.

A: Mondays were when we usually got together.

Q: I see. And you figured out . . .

A: Yeah, all of it. The whole plan. Two birds with one stone.

Q: What do you mean by that?

A: Get the gooks who raped her, and get rid of her husband at the same time.

Q: So you drove to the marina in Mrs. Leeds's car . . .

A: Yeah, that was part of it, too. To make sure somebody saw the car.

Q: Wearing Mr. Leeds's jacket and hat . . .

A: Yeah.

Q: And you took his boat out . . .

A: *Felicity*, yeah. I had the keys, you see.

Q: And went *where* with it? Where did you take the boat, Mr. Howell?

A: To Kickers. That's a place just south on the Intercoastal. Just past marker 63, near the south bridge to Whisper. Willowbee is just off 72, it's a quick run down, especially at night when there's no traffic on the water. Kickers is where we dropped the rental car that afternoon.

Q: We?

A: Me and Jessie. I rented the car and drove it to Kickers, and then she drove me back to my place.

Q: Why did you leave a rented car at Kickers . . . is that the correct name? Kickers?

A: Kickers, yeah. To pick up when I got off the boat. Because we didn't want the Maserati to be seen where those gooks lived. Little Asia.

Q: Is that where you drove in the rented car?

A: Little Asia, yeah.

Q: And what did you do there?

A: I took care of the gooks.

Q: By the gooks, do you mean the men we mentioned earlier? Pat, would you read those names again, please?

A: (*from Ms. Demming*) Ho Dao Bat, Ngo Long Khai, and Dang Van Con.

A: (*from Mr. Howell*) Yeah, the three gooks.

Q: What do you mean when you say you took care of them?

A: I stabbed them. And blinded them. And cut off their cocks. Excuse me, miss.

Q: And then what?

A: I dropped the wallet on the floor.

Q: Mr. Leeds's wallet?

A: Yes.

Q: And then?

A: I drove back to Kickers and left the rental car in the parking lot there, and got back on the boat, and took it back to Willowbee. Then I drove the Maserati out to the farm and went back home in my own car. And that was that.

Q: Why are you grinning again, Mr. Howell?

A: Because it worked out so neat. It *would've* worked out anyway, if that old gook hadn't've seen me getting in the Olds and driving off. He got the plate wrong, but he wasn't off by much, and I figured it'd come back to him sooner or later. So I had to go after him, too. Actually, Jessie and I discussed that, and we figured he had to go. Had to be killed. So I did it.

Q: You seem not to have any remorse about killing these people.

A: Well . . . they were gooks. You know.

Q: By gooks, do you mean Vietnamese?

A: Gooks. Yes.

Q: Is that an expression you learned in Vietnam?

A: Yes. Well, sure.

Q: During the war?

A: Yes.

Q: You served in Vietnam during the war?

A: I was in the Army, yes.

Q: Did you see any combat?

A: I did.

Q: How long were you over there?

A: I got there in time for the Tet Offensive.

Q: I see.

A: Something wrong with that?

Q: No, no.

A: Nothing wrong with a man serving his country.

Q: I was simply wondering . . . you haven't expressed any remorse for killing Mr. Bannion, either. Now, certainly, *he* wasn't what you'd term . . .

A: That was different.

Q: Different how?

A: He was *there!* The man shows up on my fucking . . . excuse me, miss, I'm sorry. He shows up on my doorstep, flashes his badge, tells me it's all over, he knows I'm the one who rented that fucking car, excuse me. What was I supposed to do? Let him take me in? Blow the whole thing? We were home free, don't you see? The gooks were dead and Jessie's husband was in jail for the murders. She'd get the farm, she'd get everything. It was a terrific plan, I mean it. Sure, a few things went wrong, but that doesn't mean it wasn't a good plan. It should've worked. I'd have bet my life on that plan.

Q: You did.

A: What?

Q: Mr. Howell, is there anything you'd like to add to what you've just told us?

A: No, nothing.

Q: Any corrections you'd like to make?

A: No.

Q: No additions or corrections?

A: No.

Q: That's it, then. Thank you.

The stenographer snapped off the tape recorder. Captain Decker pressed a button on his desk and a uniformed cop came into the room. He merely nodded to the cop. The cop went over to Howell and said, "Let's go, mister." Howell got up from where he was sitting, and then, to no one in particular, said, "It *was* a good plan," and went out with the cop.

"You'd better send someone to pick up the woman," Bannister said.

"Right away," Decker said, and went to his phone.

Bannister turned to Matthew, a penitent look on his face; he was going to make a good politician.

"What can I say?" he asked, his arms outstretched, his hands palms up, the fingers widespread.

"You can say you're dropping all charges against my client," Matthew said.

"Well, of *course* we are. We'll start the formal machinery at once, won't we, Pat?"

"Yes, sir," Patricia said.

"Appreciate your getting down here so early," he said, and put his arm around her and gave her shoulder a brief comradely squeeze. "Matthew," he said, extending his hand, "you're a good lawyer and a good man. I've always known that."

"Thanks," Matthew said drily, and shook hands with him.

"Let me know if there's any problem, Rush."

"Will do."

"Talk to you tomorrow, Pat," he said, and walked out.

Patricia glared at his retreating back.

"I'll walk you down," she said to Matthew.

The sun had been up for almost half an hour.

Everything outside was wet with early-morning dew.

Everything smelled so sweet and clean and fresh.

Everything looked so very Florida.

"Want to have breakfast with me?" Patricia asked.

He looked at her.

"My painters are gone," she said. "I'll open some champagne. Celebrate your victory."

He looked at her a moment longer.

Then he said, "Thanks, but I'm exhausted. Some other time, okay?"

"Sure," she said. "See ya."

He watched her as she walked toward the parking lot behind the building. Confident swing to her hips, long stride, blond hair reflecting sunlight . . . *Will there really be some other time, Matthew?*

Will we ever know each other better?

There was a pay phone on the corner.

He dialed Mai Chim's number from memory. She answered on the fifth ring.

"Hello?" she said.

The singsong voice, fuzzy with sleep now.

"Want to have breakfast with me?" he asked.

511

PRAISE FOR ED McBAIN
AND
THREE BLIND MICE

★ ★ ★

"Ed McBain is a master. He is a superior stylist, a spinner of artfully designed and sometimes macabre plots."
—*Newsweek*

*

"Amazing . . .McBain's telegraphic style gives his story a hard, reportorial surface. Characters are caught in a few memorable strokes; things happen economically. What is surprising in such terse circumstances is how much you have felt, or have been led to understand that the characters were feeling."
—*Los Angeles Times*

*

"The best crime writer in the business."
—*Houston Post*

*

"It is hard to think of anyone better at what he does. In fact, it's impossible."
—*Robert B. Parker*

*

"Ed McBain is, by far, the best at what he does. Case closed."
—*People*

*

more . . .